THE
EXPERIMENT

Rebecca Raine

For my Mum,
because she'll get a
kick out of this one.

All life is an experiment.

The more experiments you make the better.

Ralph Waldo Emerson

THE INTRODUCTION

PATRICK

The guy's lips look soft and kissable, I have to give him that. And he's pretty, you know, for a guy. I'd probably think him a right catch, if I were into guys. But I've known for a long time now that I'm not—at least, not really.

"Well?" The soft lips purse expectantly. "Are you going to kiss me or not?"

"I'm getting to it." I clear my throat, hoping he won't notice me rubbing sweaty palms on my denim-clad thighs. "What's your name again?"

"Toni," he repeats, tone laced with exasperation. "With an I."

A muffled snort sounds, and I turn to glare at the man sitting beside me. "You know, mate, this would be a hell of a lot easier if you'd quit laughing."

Logan Delaney lowers the hand that was curled in front of his mouth to reveal a shameless grin. "You're right. It's just, the look on your face." He cracks up again, almost upsetting his bar stool. "You look like you're about to shit a brick."

"You would too, if you were being forced to kiss a woman."

"Nah," he scoffs. "Kissing a woman would be easy. I'd just close my eyes and think of Henry Cavill."

3

"Oh, Henry." Toni with an I gives a dramatic sigh, one hand fluttering at the base of his slender throat. "He can go super on this man any time he wants. You know what I'm saying?"

"You're preaching to the choir, man." Logan's grin widens, and he catches the tip of his tongue between his teeth. He only does that when he's trying not to laugh. Restraint he hasn't bothered using on my behalf.

"I don't mean to intrude on your gay bonding moment, but we have a kiss to get through."

Returning his attention to me, Toni holds up his frothy green cocktail. "Yeah, and you might want to get a move on because, if you don't, I'm going to need a refill." He wraps his lips around the end of the straw and the dregs disappear with a loud slurp.

I fight the urge to shake my head. It's a good thing Logan doesn't drink cocktails, or I don't think we'd be friends. Watching him suck face with whatever random guy catches his eye I can handle. But that frothy shit with the girly straw? That's a deal breaker for me.

"You know, Patrick, you don't have to do this." Logan's brow wrinkles with false concern. "We wouldn't even be here if it wasn't for your obsession with weird experiments."

"Self-experimentation is not weird, it's the fastest and most reliable route to self-awareness." We've rehashed this conversation a hundred times. He's yet to be convinced. "You should try it sometime. You could discover for yourself what a smug bastard you are."

He chuckles, his hand clamping down on my shoulder. "I'm just saying, I never should have let you turn one stupid debate into an even stupider bet. Granted, you did set the terms, and then lost. But, hey, there's no shame in being a loser."

I shrug him off. "You're a shit pool player and you were three beers ahead of me. I never should have lost that bet."

What made me choose these particular terms in the first place I don't know. The last place I wanted to end up tonight—or any night—was in a gay bar kissing some random. It's not like watching Logan force himself to experiment with kissing a woman would have been *that* entertaining. But once the words were out of my mouth there was no going back, and though I'd done my best to win the game, I'd fumbled the final shot, sinking the white ball on the black. An instant loss.

"If nothing else," Logan adds, "this little experiment will teach you not to be cocky at the pool table. There's some genuine self-knowledge right there." He gestures to Toni, who's waiting impatiently before me. "It's time, Patrick. Pucker up or admit defeat."

Narrowing my gaze, I rise from my bar stool. "I will not accept defeat—not tonight." I step closer to Toni, who remains seated but straightens at my approach. His head is only a few centimetres below mine, perfect for kissing. "All right, let's get this over with."

He tuts in disgust. "Wow, you really know how to make a guy feel special."

"Can you stop talking for a second?" Indignant eyebrows lift at the curtness of my order. "Please," I add through gritted teeth. He lets loose another sigh but remains blessedly silent.

I ignore the way my stomach turns as I lean forward. I can do this. If I feel the need to barf about it later, fine. But right now, I'm going to man up and kiss this dude.

"Remember, it has to be a real kiss," Logan chimes in from the sidelines. "Not some wussy close-mouthed crap. Tongue, or it didn't happen."

Lifting my hands, I place them on either side of Toni's head. His eyes widen at the sudden move, but then his chin lifts and he parts his lips in anticipation of my kiss. I try to close my eyes against the reality of the situation, but they refuse to do anything other than stare at his partially open mouth. There is no part of me that wants to stick my tongue in there.

It's a fucking kiss, Patrick. Do it already!

My muscles lock up, resisting all attempts to seal the deal. A mere few centimetres separate my lips from Toni's, but it may as well be a vast chasm for all the luck I'm having crossing it. My hands become a vice around his head, and he winces. Damn it, I'm hurting him. Letting go, I fall back onto my stool. "I can't do it."

A mixed chorus of cheers and boos surrounds us, and I look around to see money changing hands between perfect strangers. When the hell did we draw an audience?

"Screw this." Toni slams his empty glass down on the high table and launches off his stool. "There aren't enough free Grasshoppers in the world to make me put up with any more of your straight boy bullshit." With that, he flounces off into the crowd.

"Mate," Logan groans beside me. "It's a kiss. You're not gonna catch gay cooties, you know?"

"Don't give me that bullshit," I say, levelling a glare at him. "That's not the problem."

He frowns. "Then what is?"

I don't like kissing guys. Plain and simple. That particular experiment was conducted years ago, and the results were pretty damned conclusive.

It's not like I have a problem with guys kissing with each other. I'm not immune to the heat generated by some quality man-on-man action. But while the idea of kissing a guy myself has always appealed in theory, the reality of it makes me queasy. That means I'm straight. It doesn't make me a homophobe. Still, if I try to explain it out loud, what with the nausea and all, I'm going to end up insulting one of my closest friends.

"He was too much of a pretty boy," I say when Logan continues to stare at me, waiting for a response. "Did you see how smooth his cheeks were? It would have felt too similar to kissing a woman."

Logan laughs out loud. "That's why I chose him for you. Figured you'd be more comfortable with someone like Toni. He's the single most delicious gay morsel ever to adorn the planet. I'm surprised there aren't more straight guys vying to take an experimental bite." I gape at him and he shrugs. "As it turns out, not so much."

Turning to face the crowd, he leans his elbows back on the table. "Toni's not your type. Fair enough. He's not my type either." He glances at me sideways. "Do you even have a type when it comes to guys?"

A flash of dark hair and strong forearms sparks in the back of my mind. Shuddering, I push the memory away and stand up with a new sense of determination. It's time to take this bet seriously. I've never been a welsher and I'm not about to start now. Besides, there has to be at least one man in this bar I can kiss without my stomach rebelling. "Let's go find out."

LOGAN

After trailing Patrick for one full circuit of the club, I give up and head for the bar. By the time I find him again he's standing at a tall table on the side of the dance floor, his gaze scanning the crowd.

I place a beer in front of him. "Figured you could use one of these. To cry into over your failure."

"Don't count me out yet," he insists, though he takes a long swallow of the amber liquid. "The night is young and we're still here. Mark my words, I'll be tickling man tonsils before we're done."

With a solemn nod, I pat him on the back. "Sure, you will, mate."

The nearby dance floor writhes with male bodies in various states of undress and I rest my elbows on top of the table, content to enjoy the view. Patrick is similarly occupied, though he looks about as relaxed as a cornered cat.

I try not to laugh as I watch him out of the corner of my eye. His behaviour comes as no surprise to me. I knew before we even walked into this bar, he wouldn't be able to honour our bet. I've seen a guy try to come on to Patrick once before. He backed up so fast it's a wonder he didn't warp the timeline. There's no way he'll be able to bring himself to kiss a man with his own two lips. But it's damned funny watching him try.

"I've been thinking," he says, leaning closer so I can hear him over the music. "If I were going to be attracted to a guy, it would be someone bigger and more burly, like me. Not some stick figure who could break if I squeeze too hard." He nods, agreeing with his own assessment of the situation. "I mean, if I'm gonna kiss a dude, I should *know* I'm kissing a dude, even if my eyes are closed."

"That's a well-developed opinion you've got there, Patrick," I point out. "I'm thinking tonight isn't the first time you've put thought into this."

His gaze slides away from mine as he shrugs. It's a long moment before he replies. "Don't get all excited, you can't go around being friends with gay men and not have it cross your mind." He gestures to me with one hand. "Haven't you ever wondered what kind of woman you'd be attracted to if you were straight?"

I take a swig of my beer and smirk at him, loving that my answer will screw with his logic. "Can't say I have."

Clearing his throat, he responds, "I guess I must be more confident in my sexuality than you are."

My head falls back as I crack up laughing. "Why? Because you're so self-aware?"

"You can laugh all you want," he tells me, "but I've put a lot of time and effort into finding the answers to questions most people struggle with their whole lives. I know who I am and I'm not afraid to show it."

"Which means you can sit around pondering which guys you'd be attracted to *if* you were gay, all without ever having to question your straightness?"

"Exactly," he confirms with a smug grin. "What you see is what you get and what you get happens to be straight. That's not going to change."

I swallow the urge to argue, along with another mouthful of beer. "If you say so."

Most of the time I'd be happy to agree with Patrick. He comes across as a breeder, complete with the involuntary flinch at the touch of an amorous gay hand. But every now and then something he does or says makes my gaydar zing. Like the time I made out with a guy right beside him at a party. The man didn't even bother getting up off the other end of the couch. In fact, I'll swear I caught him watching, when he thought I was too distracted to notice.

I'm never too distracted to notice Patrick.

Whatever. It doesn't actually matter which way his soul swings, Patrick Seymour is in a monogamous relationship with his straightness, and that means he's off limits. If I thought otherwise, I would have fucked him myself the day we met. It's probably a good thing that didn't happen. I'm not a fuck and befriend kind of guy—and Patrick is a good friend to have.

We fall into a comfortable silence for a few minutes before I gesture to a tall, muscular guy who's standing nearby. "What about him?" He's been eyeballing Patrick since I came back from the bar. My presence is probably the only thing stopping him from coming over. I snort as I realise I'm actively cock-blocking my straight friend. Life never ceases to surprise me.

Patrick looks him over. "He's bald," he says flatly. "Bald guys are out."

"Okay." I continue to evaluate the pickings. It's Saturday night, so there are plenty of hot guys to go around. If I were here alone, I wouldn't have any problem finding someone to kiss. In fact... "Him." I place a hand on Patrick's shoulder and lean in so he can follow my line of sight when I point. "That guy. He's plenty hairy."

"The douche-bun with the beard?" He pauses to consider the suggestion. "What's it like kissing a guy with a beard?"

"Prickly."

"I don't know, that could be overkill." He's frowning when he turns to inspect my face. "You're scruffy, let me feel yours." Not bothering to wait for permission, he reaches out to run a hand over my jaw. "This might not feel *too* bad," he mutters with a grimace, as if he's grading a slightly rancid side of beef. "But I think a full-on beard would be too scratchy."

Staring into his blue eyes, I swallow hard. "Are you done touching me?"

The motion of his hand stills. Breathing out a laugh, he pinches my cheek like I'm all of ten years old, before letting go. "I'm done."

I drag my gaze away from his, ignoring the snug fit of my pants. "Hairy, but not too hairy. Attractive, but not a pretty boy. Any other stipulations you want to add?"

Patrick gives me a blank look I take to mean *not yet, but probably.*

"All right then." Desperate to put an end to what was supposed to be a lark but is fast becoming a chore, I pick the first half-decent guy I see. "Blue shirt, by the bar."

His eyes narrow as he spots the target. "Too short."

"Patrick, mate." I groan, burying my face in my hands. "You are picky as all fuck. Are you this hard to please when it comes to women?" I've only ever seen him with his last girlfriend, Robyn. Since their break-up some months ago, he hasn't gone to much effort to find a replacement.

"Absolutely," he confirms with a nod. "One of the benefits of self-awareness is that I already know the kind of woman I'm compatible with, so I don't waste time going after anyone who isn't going to be a good fit. There'd be no point."

"I can think of a point," I mutter under my breath. If I only went to bed with guys I thought were a good fit for my personality, I'd never get freaking laid.

"I'll find her when the time is right," he adds, ignoring my comment, "or she'll find me. We'll be like two little puzzle pieces clicking into place."

It sounds like nonsense to me, but he seems confident in his delusion. "While you're waiting, I'm pretty sure there are any number of guys here who would be happy to click into your place." I bite back a laugh at the appalled look on his face. "If you ever manage to choose one, that is."

Rolling his eyes, he turns back to the crowd. "I can do this," he mutters, more to himself than me. "I just need to find someone I can kiss without—" He cuts off suddenly, his gaze darting to mine. "Without losing my nerve."

Yeah, right. That's so what he was going to say. The original ending of that sentence did not have anything to do with him blowing chunks all over the club floor at the taste of gay tongue. Unbelievable.

"I give up," I announce, lifting my hands in a show of defeat. "It was a stupid bet anyway. Let's forget about it and head over to Mitchie's Cafe for a feed." All this indirect rejection has me craving a big bowl of hot chips with gravy.

"No. I refuse to give up," he insists. "I came here to kiss a man and I'm not leaving until I do."

Dropping my head back, I swear at the ceiling. "Fine, but you'll have to find him yourself. I'm done."

"I will." He tugs at his bottom lip with two fingers as he leans on the table, eyes intent. "I just need someone more like…" The words trail off uncertainly. "Someone like…" His head swivels and those blue eyes widen as they lock with mine. "You."

My eyebrows make a leap for the ceiling. "What?"

"I could kiss you." His whole body turns towards me, catching up with the insanity of his brain. "Why not? You're hot. Guys fall all over you, and if I had a guy-type it would totally be you—obviously."

"Obviously?" I repeat. "How is that obvious?"

He tuts. "We don't hang out all the time because you rub me the wrong way."

I haven't rubbed him in any way—right or wrong. Still, the words make my stomach drop, in direct counterpoint to my cock.

"I don't kiss straight guys," I tell him. "You're more trouble than your tight little virgin arses are worth." I've already learned that lesson, and I don't need a repeat.

"I'm not some random straight guy. We've been friends forever."

"It's been a year, Patrick."

"Yeah, but it feels like forever." He licks his lips. "I would feel comfortable doing this with you."

My jaw drops. "It's nice to know the thought of kissing me makes you feel so... comfortable." I make sure to emphasise the last word, exposing it as the flaming insult it is. "It's still not happening."

"But—"

"Nope." I hold up a hand to cut him off.

Releasing a breath, he slumps forward over the table. "Fine. Don't kiss me."

The silence isn't comfortable this time. Actually, it's really fucking awkward.

"I'm gonna go get us another drink," Patrick announces, straightening from his lean. "Then, I'll kiss the hell out of the first guy who says yes, and we can call it a night."

He doesn't look at me as he walks away. I sure do look at him though. From the top of his brunette head all the way down to his well-formed arse. It's not a temptation I give in to often. I wouldn't be doing it now if he hadn't opened his bloody mouth.

The second he suggested the stupid bet I should have known it would end badly. I didn't even bother trying to win the game of pool. Kissing a woman would have been no big deal. I've done it before, back when I was a kid and I wasn't ready for the world to know my interests lay elsewhere. At least me losing the bet wouldn't have ended in all this drama.

Gazing out at the sea of men, I wonder who Patrick will end up kissing. Probably some arsehole who'll try to grope him or get his grind on before the kiss is done. The idea doesn't sit well. If anybody is going to grope my friend, it bloody well should be me.

"Fuck it," I mutter before taking off after him. If he kisses some wanker before I get my hands on him, I'm gonna be pissed.

PATRICK

I'm still waiting for the bartender to reach me when Logan appears at my side, all deep frown and intent stare. "All right, I'll do it."

My shoulders drop and I release a pent-up breath. Thank God for that. I didn't have a clue what to do next. Even so, when I turn to look at him, I can't help but tease. "You'll do what now?"

"I'll let you kiss me," he grits out, before pushing at the centre of my chest with an emphatic finger. "On one condition."

"What's that?"

"Don't go all fucking weird on me afterward. I don't want to have to put up with any bullshit."

The demand seems warranted considering my behaviour with Toni, not to mention the upheaval that continues to knot up the area around my stomach. I hold up a couple of fingers scout-style. "I solemnly swear not to turn into a raging arsehole." *And to hide my reaction if kissing you makes me want to gag.*

A bartender approaches. "What can I get you?"

"Two vodka shots," Logan answers before I have a chance to open my mouth. When they arrive, I beat him to handing over the money. Huffing, he passes me one of the shot glasses. "For courage."

Nodding, I tilt my head back and allow the harsh liquid to slide down my throat. Logan does the same. He watches me as we slam our empty glasses down on the bar. He's waiting for me to make the first move.

My gaze lowers to his mouth and I wait for the same rebellion that overwhelmed me when I tried to kiss Toni. Thankfully, it doesn't come. This I can do.

I'm still deciding how to make my approach when an elbow jabs into my side. I jerk away, glaring at the blond who pushes between us to get to the bar. It seems we're taking up valuable real estate.

"Come with me," Logan says as he takes my hand and pulls me after him through the crowd. Allowing him to lead the way, I stare at our joined hands. His palm is warm against mine; the hold of his long fingers is firm and steady. After we break free of the crush of bar-bound bodies, I realise he's released my hand. I'm the only one holding on now. With a silent intake of breath, I let go.

We exit the club's interior through a side door. The second-storey balcony overlooking the main road is almost as crowded as the inside of the club, but we manage to make our way to the far side. Logan turns to stand with his back against the railing. A mild early-Autumn breeze stirs the dark hair on his forehead as I stop in front of him.

This is it. I'm supposed to kiss him now.

A fresh riot starts up in my stomach. This time it spreads to my limbs, up through my chest and into the back of my throat. It's different from before though.

The thought of kissing Toni made me sick to my stomach. With Logan it's more like having a severe case of butterflies. That's not so bad. But then, we haven't gotten to the kissing part yet. There's still time for shit to go south in a big way.

"This is awkward," I admit, shifting from one foot to the other. "I'm not sure how to start."

The corners of his mouth twist upward at my total ineptitude. "Approach me the same way you would a woman," he suggests. "You must have some moves you use to make ladies swoon. Use them on me." He doesn't move a muscle as he speaks. He just stands there, his hands clasped around the top of the railing as he waits for me to get my shit together.

"Will you swoon for me, Logan?" I tease, wanting to keep the tone light. This man has become one of the best friends I have over the past year. I respect him. I care about him. Most importantly, I don't ever want him to know how distasteful kissing him will be for me.

"It's unlikely, but it gives you a place to start." His lips curve into a sultry grin. I've seen him use that smile on more than one man. It works every time. The skin on the back of my neck begins to prickle and I clear my throat. Maybe it's even working this time.

"All right, let's start there," I murmur. "First, I'd move in close. Enjoying the anticipation, but not rushing into it." Logan's gaze roves over my face as I move closer, but otherwise he remains motionless. "I'd put one hand on her hip."

I reach out, surprised by my lack of hesitation. The thin cotton of Logan's trousers, sitting flat against the jut of his hipbone, does nothing to shield my hand from the heat of his body. My thumb slips under his shirt to brush against bare skin. The muscles there twitch and I suck in a deep breath, but I don't withdraw. It's okay. This is okay.

"Next, I'd cup her face." My other hand lifts to curve around his cheek, feeling his scruff for the second time tonight. It's rough against my palm, reminding me this is no woman I'm about to kiss. Logan is all man.

I want to hit pause. Right here. In the instant when I almost believe I want this. When I still feel the beating of a thousand tiny wings against my rib cage and I can pretend nothing will go wrong.

"Then what?" he murmurs, so quiet I almost don't hear him.

"This," I breathe, right before pressing my mouth against his. He hesitates before kissing me back, but then our lips are moving against each other, brushing back and forth, experimenting.

My stomach pitches. I feel queasy. Except it's a good kind of queasy, and my fingers curl into him, holding on instead of pushing away.

It's not long before he retreats, breaking the contact between us. "There." His voice is little more than a growl, reverberating low in his throat. So fucking sexy. "The requirements of the bet have been met."

"But..." Further words fail to come, and I fall silent. But what? But it still feels good? But I'm not done yet?

Logan licks his lips, bringing to mind his own words from earlier in the evening. They provide the perfect excuse. "Tongue, or it didn't happen."

I kiss him again—harder this time. I try not to think. Maybe, if I don't think about what I'm doing, the repulsion won't kick in and I can have more. Go further. My tongue runs over the seam of his lips, seeking a way in. With a low groan, he gives me what I want.

His tongue goes to war with mine. His hands land on my waist, dragging me closer. I flinch. I can't help it. But when he starts to pull away, I follow him, and our bodies meet as I push him back against the railing.

We feast on each other's mouths for long minutes before I'm forced to grapple with a solitary conclusion. That reaction I've been expecting, the one I've been waiting for? It isn't going to come.

I don't understand. This isn't the way this goes. I'm straight. I hate this. I think I want it but hate it when I get it. That's the way it's always been. Because for all the times I've been turned on by the thought of men—by the sight and smell and sound of men—I don't like to be touched by them. I don't like the way they make me feel.

"You're hard," Logan rasps between kisses.

I look down, though I can't see anything in the total absence of space between us. A slight tilt of my pelvis brings my hard length in contact with his through our clothing. We both gasp. Cool air rushes into my lungs. "So are you."

21

His chuckle is husky with arousal. "I'm making out with a hot guy. It happens."

"Right. That must be it." That's not it—not for me. Logan is hot, by anyone's standards, but the hotness of the guy has never made a difference before.

"Are you freaking out?" he asks, one eyebrow lifting.

Shaking my head, I pretend my pounding heart knows the difference between lust and panic, even if my head is unsure. "What's a little wood between friends?"

A second eyebrow joins the first. "Who are you calling little?" Gripping on to my arse, he hauls me closer and rubs himself against me. Oh hell, he's definitely not little.

My eyes slide closed on a groan as I fall on his mouth, sucking on his tongue and clutching at him in places that five minutes ago we both would have sworn were off limits. The heat of his body does things to parts of me that have never welcomed a man's touch and my senses go freaking wild for him.

Finally, he lifts his hands to cup my face, tearing his lips from mine. "Patrick, what the fuck is happening here?"

I pull back, looking into his hazel depths. The confusion there is nothing compared to the maelstrom twisting inside me. "I don't know," I whisper, taking a shaky breath. "This isn't... I'm not..."

I'm not bisexual. I'm not. There was a time when I thought maybe I could be, but it's been years since I faced those questions, since I subjected my answers to experimentation. The result could not be denied. A result that has proved reliable on the few occasions it's been retested. An occasional fascination with the idea of being with men doesn't mean anything if I can't do anything about it. For all practical purposes, I'm a straight man and sexual orientation can't be changed— not by willpower or prayer or discipline. And not by a single kiss. It's fact, not opinion. I can provide the research to back it up.

"You're okay." Logan wraps an arm around my shoulders and draws me into a hug. "I've got you." The sense of comfort I know he's aiming for is complicated by the matching erections still pressed together between us. Every subtle movement makes me shiver as arousal streaks through my body. It makes no sense.

Burying my face in the crook of his neck, I take a breath. The rich, masculine scent of him finds its way deep into my lungs, obliterating all remaining thoughts of my identity crisis. "Since when do you smell so good?" I open my mouth and latch on to his neck, groaning as the taste of salt and man coats my tongue. Logan bites out a curse, his head tilting to give me better access. I suck harder, moaning my appreciation.

"Fuck a duck, you're kissing him?" The high-pitched shout manages to penetrate my lust, probably because it's right beside my ear. When I lift my head, Toni with an I glares at me in righteous fury. "If you wanted to hook-up with your 'friend'," he uses actual air quotes, "you should have manned up and said so. There was no need to toy with other people's emotions."

23

It takes a moment for me to stop wallowing in everything Logan long enough to figure out what Toni's talking about. When his words finally register, I make a sound of disbelief. "You were in it for the free drink."

"So?" he screeches. "You refused to kiss me, even after buying said drink. Do you think that didn't hurt? Am I made of stone?"

Holy hell. Now I'm glad I didn't kiss him. I may not have escaped if I'd gone that far. Still, the lift of his chin makes me uncomfortable. The way I backed out at the last second was kind of douchey of me.

Straightening, I disentangle myself from Logan's body and turn to face Toni. "You're right," I tell him, giving him my full attention. "I'm sure you're a great guy and any man would be lucky to have you, with your pretty eyes and those dimples." They might not be visible now he's frowning, but I saw them earlier. I know they're in there.

"Most men find my dimples adorable."

"They are adorable," I agree, though they do nothing for me personally. "I'm sorry it didn't work out between us, but as it turns out," I tip my head in Logan's direction, refusing to look at him in case I laugh and end up back in Toni's shit tin, "he's more my type."

With a dramatic sigh, Toni crosses his arms over his chest. "I can't say I blame you. He does have something of a roguish quality to him." He sneaks a glance at Logan before heaving a sigh. "All right, I give you my blessing."

Logan snickers. We both ignore him.

"Just don't mess with him," Toni demands, lowering his voice to a mere whisper. "Gay hearts break hard. Even if we don't always show it."

I nod with appropriate sincerity. "Thanks for the tip."

After he struts away, I wait a full five seconds before turning to Logan. He's practically doubled over with laughter. "One night at this and you're already causing damage," he gasps. "Heaven forbid you should announce you're queer. The gay community might not survive."

"Ha bloody ha," I say flatly. "You're hilarious." Crossing my arms, I lean a hip against the railing beside him, unsure how to proceed considering how much time we spent sucking face. "I don't know about you, but I could do with that feed now."

Logan turns his head to look at me, his gaze dragging from my mouth up to my eyes. He gives a sharp nod. "I could eat. Mitchie's?"

"Done."

As I follow Logan towards the exit, my gaze drags over the long lines of his body. The way he walks. The curves of his arse. I've never done this before, never watched him so closely—at least not consciously. I'm sure as hell conscious of it now.

We emerge from the crowded confines of the club and turn in the direction of our favourite late-night cafe, letting go of the night's events. But I already know, without a doubt, the questions posed by the really freaking hot make out session we shared will be harder to leave behind.

LOGAN

S tanding in my designated position at the university library's service area, I watch the multitude of students who come and go through the automatic glass doors at the main entrance. Not a single person has approached me for assistance in the past half hour, unless you count the woman who asked about the location of the toilets. The way I see it, if the same information can be gleaned from reading the map on the wall three metres to my left, it doesn't count.

With a quiet sigh, I check my watch. It's a few minutes after eleven. Two more hours and I'll be able to break for lunch.

A glimpse of brown hair catches my attention and my gaze snaps to the left. When I finally locate the owner, who is a stranger, my shoulders slump, right before I'm hit with a sharp pang of self-disgust. What is wrong with me? Patrick is *not* going to randomly show up at the library. His office is way over on the other side of campus and, even when he does drop in to say hello, it's never at this time of day.

Reminding myself of these facts does nothing to stop me being all jumpy. I'm like a kitten who's had its first taste of catnip. I can't think of anything but getting another hit.

It doesn't help that this little patch of carpet is where Patrick and I first met. I'd been working at the library for about six months or so, having taken the job as a temporary gig. It both supplemented the income I was getting from web development work, and provided a handy way to avoid the encroaching walls of my apartment.

Patrick was already well into his PhD in Developmental Psychology, but had been having trouble locating a newly arrived textbook on the shelves. He could have accessed it through the online system, but insisted he preferred reading physical books. They're more flippable, he'd told me, as if the superiority of paper was obvious. I'd barely managed to refrain from rolling my eyes at that one.

It took some time, but I managed to use my ninja librarian skills to track down the book. When I delivered it to his office the next day during my lunch break, he'd been so grateful he offered to buy me a coffee. We got to chatting and have been friends ever since.

At first, I thought he was flirting and we were heading for something more—then he introduced me to his girlfriend. I took the information in stride and, from that instant, firmly ignored any stray thoughts about what his skin might feel like.

After the events of this past Saturday night, I don't have to wonder anymore. Touching him is like running my fingertips across live wires. It sets my whole body to thrumming and is likely to end in one hell of a painful shock if I keep at it.

Not that I have anything to worry about in that regard. I'll never have another opportunity to take the risk. There is no doubt in my mind, Patrick is as straight as he ever was—or at least as straight as he wants to be. Making out with me might have been fun and all, but there is no way he's spent the last four days questioning everything he's ever known about his sexuality just because I gave him a boner.

Fuck.

I really, really, truly need to stop thinking about Patrick—and his boner.

"Are you planning to do any actual work today?" The deceptively sweet voice comes from behind me and I turn around. Naomi glares up at me, hands on hips and eyes flashing. I would never tell her this, because she'd skin me alive if I did, but it would be easier to take her seriously if her hair wasn't green. "Or are you going to stand there in a puddle of drool all day?"

Dragging my thoughts away from Patrick, who frankly is worthy of a little drool, I shrug. "I am working." I'm present in the service area. I'm wearing my work shirt, with the university library's logo emblazoned on the front, just as she is. "It's not my fault no one needs my help."

She makes a rude sound. "Logan, a student from engineering waved a hand in front of your face to try and get your attention. You didn't even react. Your body may be here, but there ain't nobody home, honey." Her eyes narrow. "Are you hungover? Because I'm hungover, and yet I'm managing to pay attention to the world around me. What's your excuse?"

"All right, I'm distracted. I can't help it." Glancing around, I check for any incoming students, but no one is heading our way. "I did something stupid last weekend." And I'll be damned if I can hold it in any longer.

The disgruntled grimace falls away, replaced by guarded interest. "The fun kind of stupid?" she asks. "Or *the cops are looking for you* stupid?"

I can't hold back my grin as I recall the shocked expression on Patrick's face when he realised he liked kissing me. "Definitely the fun kind of stupid."

With a delighted gasp, Naomi abandons all traces of irritation. "Tell me everything."

I hesitate. While I'm dying to spill the beans to someone, Naomi and Patrick are friends too, having met through me. I don't want to give him away. No one wants their closet door opened from the outside. "Let's just say, I got a taste of someone I shouldn't have, and I think it's going to take a while to get the flavour out of my mouth."

"Damn." Naomi's eyes roll back in her head. "I want that kind of stupid. I haven't had a forbidden love in ages."

My jaw drops. "No one said anything about love." I'm hot for Patrick, there's no doubt about it, but I'm not *that* stupid. "It was more like… a moment that got out of control." A moment I haven't been able to stop thinking about for the past four goddamned days.

"Who was it?" Naomi asks.

"Just a friend." The words spill out in a rush, which sounds suspicious, so I add a dismissive shake of my head. "No one you know."

"You are such a bad liar," she says with a laugh. "If I don't know them, why are you being so cagey about it?" A speculative gleam appears in her brown eyes, right before she gives a loud gasp. Grabbing my arm, she bounces lightly on the balls of her feet. "Oh my god, you screwed Patrick Seymour!"

"What? No!" I glance around to see a couple of nearby students glare at us before returning to their own, much quieter, conversation. "There was only kissing," I whisper. But then a quiet, undignified mewl manages to escape. "Long, thorough, boner-inducing kissing." I wince as I realise I did nothing to deny the identity of the person involved. "And what makes you think it was Patrick?"

Naomi snorts. "You only have one 'friend'," she says, and why do people keep using air quotes when they say that word, "you avoid looking at for more than five seconds at a time."

I knew that, but I didn't realise anyone else had noticed. Has Patrick noticed? He's never hinted at the fact.

"And he was into it?" Naomi asks with a grin.

There's not much point in denying it now. "Yeah, but it didn't mean anything. We were being stupid. He lost a bet, it happened. But that's the end of it. Patrick is straight." *Ish.*

"That's what all the boys say. It's what all the girls say, too," she adds, "right before they start worshiping my boobs." She winks at me and I shake my head in amusement. "How did you leave things? Did he lose his shit?"

"No, nothing like that." We'd managed to put the whole experience aside for the hour or so we spent hanging out at the cafe. We talked about work mostly. He caught me up on how his thesis is going. I filled him in on some training I'm doing for the library. We had plenty of topics to discuss without hitting on any dangerous ground—like that time, earlier in the evening, when I ground my erection against him while joking about my generous size.

There was one moment, though, when all our efforts towards seeming normal threatened to evaporate. It happened in the early hours of Sunday morning, when I pulled up outside his apartment building after driving him home. Maybe it was the way he paused after taking off his seatbelt. The way his gaze flickered to my mouth. Or maybe it was nothing more than my craving for more of what he could offer. But, for a few, lust-infused seconds, I thought for sure he was going to kiss me again. My hands tightened around the steering wheel and I held my breath as I waited to see what would happen next.

In the end, he shook his head with a short laugh. "'Night, mate," he said, opening the car door. "I'll see you next week."

"Yep," I'd croaked, ignoring the twinge in my gut. "See you then."

I drove home, managing to make it up to my apartment without incident—walking with an erection is no picnic—and headed straight for the shower. The second I finished stripping and stepped under the hot spray of water, I soaped up my hands and dived headlong into a fast and furious masturbation session that ended in minutes with Patrick's kiss held fast in my mind. It had been a long time since I'd come that hard from nothing more than a kiss, let alone the memory of one.

By the time I collapsed into bed, I was exhausted and fell into a dreamless sleep, only to wake up the next morning with a fresh hard-on and Patrick's name on my lips. Wrapping a hand tight around my aching flesh, I'd vowed it would be the last time I allowed thoughts of Patrick to bring me to orgasm.

Turns out, I lied. Total shocker.

Bringing my attention back to Naomi's expectant face, I say, "We went out for food afterward. Then I dropped him off at his place on the way home. I haven't spoken to him since, but we've texted, same as usual. It's all good. No weirdness."

Naomi tilts her head to one side, looking thoughtful. "Are you sure? No weirdness at all?"

I shrug. "None. Why?"

"I don't know. A straight guy kisses one of his best friends, and he doesn't feel even a little bit weirded out by it? The absence of weird sounds weird to me."

When she puts it like that... Patrick should have been at least a little freaked out. Not by the kiss itself maybe, but by the way he reacted to it. "Shit. Maybe it is weird."

"You think?"

A couple of students approach with confused expressions and we know we're about to be interrupted. "Let's reconvene in the stacks," Naomi says with a conspiratorial whisper. "Five minutes."

I nod before we get back to work.

It takes us longer than expected to escape the service area, but eventually we manage to disappear upstairs to a mostly deserted corner of the library. We find a nice heavy library cart and begin sorting the books for reshelving.

"Here's what you should do," Naomi announces, "invite Patrick to hang out on Friday night, but include other people so it doesn't look like you're asking him on a date. You can bring me; Patrick can bring his PhD friends." She slides another book into place. "It's a bunch of people going out for a couple of drinks. Playing pool and having a good time."

That's her big idea? "We already do that every other weekend."

"That's the point," she says. "He'll think nothing of it. Then, when he's had a couple and he's nice and relaxed," she looks up at me with a predatory smile, "you lure him into a dark corner and slip him some tongue."

"Goddamn it, Na, I'm not doing that!" Grabbing the handle on the end of the freshly sorted cart, I push it towards the shelves. "Messing around with straight friends does not end well. Trust me on this."

I wait for the faint throb of pain to come at the stark reminder of Ben, my ex-boyfriend, or ex-friend—I'm not even sure how to classify him anymore. It's been a while since I thought about him but, even so, I'm surprised when there's no pain. It's more of a numbness now. An absence of pain. I can be grateful for that, at least. It's only taken nearly two years.

I'm not about to celebrate my freedom from heartbreak by falling for yet another friend.

"Patrick and I are friends, and I'd like to keep it that way," I tell Naomi. "Yes, we kissed. Yes, it was hot. But now, I just want to get past it, you know? Go back to the way things were before this happened." Before I knew kissing me could make Patrick so fucking hard and hot and... stop already!

"Fair enough." Naomi shrugs as she inspects the spine of another book before easing it into a tight spot on the shelf. "Even if your goal is to get things back to normal, I still think going out with friends is your best bet. Which means following my original plan, but without the tongue." There's a weighty pause. "I know I'm free Friday night. Do you think Patrick and his friends will be?"

I stop with a book still in hand to stare at Naomi. "This isn't about me and Patrick at all, is it?" I don't want to accuse her, but she's so fucking guilty. "This is about you wanting to see Stacey again."

"Hey, I'm trying to help you out here," Naomi insists. "Seeing Stacey is nothing more than a side-benefit."

"Yeah, right." Na's had a crush on Patrick's friend for ages. I should have known. She was pushing this little plan of hers way too hard. "So, best case scenario, you get laid and I'm left with a case of blue balls. Fantastic. Thanks, Na."

"Look, you said you and Patrick haven't spoken since *the incident*," she gives extra emphasis to those last words, as if we committed a crime or something. "You guys have been joined at the hip since you met. So, don't tell me it's not unusual for you to go so long without speaking."

"It is unusual, but—"

"Which means you need to get your friendship back on track as soon as possible, or you can kiss it goodbye." She snorts. "No pun intended."

"Don't you think putting us back into the exact situation that got us into this mess in the first place is a bad idea?"

"No, it's perfect," she insists. "Patrick can see nothing has changed between you."

Except everything has changed. I managed to get through a full year as Patrick's friend without actively lusting after him. I was into him, yes, but I had that shit under control. Now my feelings have slipped their leash, I have no idea how to rein them back in—if it's even possible.

I let out a sigh of frustration. "You're only saying this because you want me to agree to your plan."

"That might be part of it, but I still think it will work." She sidles up to me. "Please, Logan. You're my friend too, you know. I need your support in my time of need."

"You're asking me to support your sex life now. You realise that, right?"

"I do." She gives a solemn nod. "And my loins are on standby to applaud you."

Rolling my eyes, I heave a sigh. "All right, I'll do it."

With a quiet squeal, she bounces on her feet. "Thank you. Thank you. Thank you."

I chuckle at her obvious excitement. "You know me," I say, hoping I can pull this off. "Anything for a friend."

A couple of hours later, I grab a book I've been meaning to return to Patrick and leave the library for my lunch break. Scoffing my sandwich as I cross the lawn, I head straight for the psychology building, knowing exactly where Patrick will be.

He's been preparing for today's seminar for weeks. He, and the other PhD students involved in his study, are presenting some preliminary findings from their research. It's an open seminar, anyone can attend, and I intended to go when he told me about it. Patrick hates public speaking and I wanted to be there for moral support.

As the week wore on, I'd started to reconsider attending. Seeing him again could be awkward, depending on his reaction to what happened between us. The last thing I want to do is add to the pressure of an already stressful situation. But after talking to Naomi, I've decided going to the seminar, as I normally would, is the best option.

I need to act normal. As if the kiss never happened. As if nothing has changed. It's the only way Patrick and I will get through this with our friendship intact.

THE RESEARCH QUESTION

PATRICK

T he seminar is due to start in a couple of minutes and I'm still making last minute changes to my speech. After the ridiculous number of hours I've already spent working on it, it should be perfect. Instead, it's only getting more convoluted.

"Will you stop that?" Stacey hisses from beside me. "You're making me nervous."

Capping my pen, I drop it into my bag. "Okay, I'm done." Gathering the pages together, I check to make sure they're still in the correct order. I only printed them this morning, but already they're worn around the edges.

"It's fifteen minutes, Patrick. And you're first. You'll be done before you know it."

"I know," I croak as our supervisor, Professor Mitchell, takes his place behind the lectern.

"Then quit bouncing your leg," Ian complains from my other side, "you're shaking the whole damned row."

My leg goes still. I didn't even know it was moving. With a sigh, I turn in my chair and scan the partially filled lecture theatre. No joy. Pulling my phone from my pocket, I check for new messages. Nothing.

Logan's not coming.

Last week he said he wouldn't miss it for the world. I watched him check the details in his calendar myself.

But that was before I kissed him, and kissed him, and then kissed him some more.

The why of it has plagued me ever since. Out of all the men in the club, why did I choose to kiss Logan? More importantly, why did I kiss him *like that*? It may have started out as a way to satisfy a bet, but by the time we were interrupted, there was something else entirely going on.

Then there was that weird moment, as Logan dropped me off, when I found myself fighting the urge to kiss him goodnight before getting out of his car. As if we were on a date or something. Talk about the cherry on top of a whole night of mind-fuck cake.

We haven't spoken since—we've barely even texted. And now this. Logan has never bailed on a commitment to me before. He's never so much as cancelled a lunch date—damn it, there's that word again.

Is he regretting letting me kiss him? Given how carried away I got, I can hardly blame him if he's concerned about my follow-up behaviour. Maybe he's worried I want to do it again. Is he avoiding me? Crap. Have I messed us up completely?

"Thank you all for coming to hear about our research project, *Inside and Out*," Prof Mitchell begins, smiling at our small audience. "The broad aim of the project is to develop a web-based platform to support the mental health of adolescents around Australia, through a combination of education, and practical tools and exercises. Each of the PhD students you'll hear from today has been instrumental in getting the project off the ground, developing their own program for inclusion in the larger project and then evaluating the effectiveness of their program. I know the students are looking forward to sharing their research findings to date."

My sweaty hands and knotted stomach say otherwise. For someone who prides himself on his self-confidence, speaking in front of an audience still manages to send my nervous system into a meltdown. I blame eighth grade English. Being forced to read your own poetry in front of a bunch of bored thirteen-year-olds should be illegal. But Prof Mitchell is a fan of these seminars so, when he says jump, we grit our teeth and start bouncing.

"Our first presenter today is Patrick Seymour." My head snaps up. It's time. "Patrick is specialising in the area of identity formation in adolescence. Please welcome him."

There's a faint smattering of applause as I stand and make my way to the lectern. It takes two tries to get my PowerPoint presentation to show up on the screen overhead. When it finally appears, I look out at the audience. Stacey gives me a thumbs up. Gripping on to the sides of the lectern, I begin my speech.

"Know thyself." My voice rasps and I clear my throat. "These are the words given to us by the ancient Greeks, and we still attempt to live that same advice today. We use modern terms, such as being yourself, keeping it real, or living your truth. But in essence, each of these phrases is used to describe the same phenomenon: authenticity."

I glance around the room. Apart from my two fellow PhD students, there are about two dozen undergrads, most of them first-years. They stare at me with earnest expressions and pens at the ready, eager to absorb any scraps of knowledge I might manage to impart. The handful of academics are less attentive, but more likely to tug on any loose threads in my argument.

"Humans long to be authentic," I continue, clicking the button that advances my presentation to the next slide. "That is, we want our external actions to match our internal identity. But in order to achieve a high level of authenticity we must first have a clear understanding of that identity. We need to know who we are."

A door opens at the back of the lecture theatre and I look up to see Logan poke his head into the room. His searching gaze finds mine and he gives a quick up-nod of acknowledgment, his smile tight.

Breath rushes into my lungs and my spine straightens. Maybe I haven't totally screwed us up.

He pulls the door closed behind him and slides into a vacant seat at the back of the room, taking care not to make any noise as he brings up the swivel desk and places the book he's carrying on top. If he's trying not to disturb me, he's too late. I'm disturbed—on a whole host of welcome and unwelcome levels.

A polite cough from Prof Mitchell snaps me back to the present. A present where I'm still staring at Logan and the audience is getting restless, heads turning to see what's caught my attention.

"As I was saying," I rush on, shuffling my notes in front of me. "The researcher Erik Erikson proposed that identity formation, this process of discovering who we are, is the key developmental task of adolescence. It's during this time we begin to ask the big questions. What do I believe? How do I fit into society? What's my purpose for being here? It's through finding answers to these questions that we begin to feel comfortable, even cosy, inside our own skin." I'm warming up now. The words come easier and the trembling in my limbs has subsided. Raising the remote over my head, I click the button and switch to the next slide.

"The aim of my research is to provide adolescents with a framework that allows them to explore these issues in a way that gives them both control over, and responsibility for, the formation of their personal identity. This is done by reframing the process in terms of scientific research." Another click, next slide.

The foundational belief of my program appears on the screen. "Every adolescent is a scientist conducting the most important research of their life." I pause for a moment, allowing my audience to take in this earth-shattering paradigm shift. A couple of the students nod. One of the professors yawns. I'm used to the lukewarm response, but it does nothing to dampen my own enthusiasm. "This reframing allows adolescents to see their behaviour as a form of experimentation, with each experiment bringing them closer to resolving the one question that haunts us all, until we arrive at a satisfactory answer: Who am I?"

My chest swells with emotion, as it always does when I talk about my research. This isn't simply a degree for me, it's my life's purpose: to develop the most effective large-scale strategies for supporting adolescents as they get a handle on their identity, so they can live authentic lives surrounded by people who love them for who they are. Not who they think they should be, or who others want them to be, but their authentic selves.

These kinds of experiments saved my sanity when I suffered through my own adolescence. Now, it's my mission to ensure other young people have the opportunity to use the strategies I used on myself—and to prove their efficacy.

My gaze darts back to Logan, who's listening intently. He gives me a reassuring smile and my pulse trips over itself. That's new.

Forcing my attention back to my speech, I move on to a quick overview of my program. How it was developed and implemented, and the outcomes I've measured so far.

"Does anyone have any questions?" I ask as I near the end of my allotted time. Professor Walker, one of the Counselling Psychology lecturers, lifts his hand. My stomach sinks. Of all the academics in the room, he's the one most likely to tear me a new one.

"You appear to be making the assumption adolescence is the only important time in the formation of identity," he says with a telltale hint of condescension. "What about the rest of the life-span? People change over the course of their lives, as do their identities."

"Yes," I say, nodding in agreement, "we do continue to mature and develop our sense of identity as we age. However, my research is aimed at supporting the development of the core foundations of self, the parts that don't tend to change, such as sexual orientation, or introversion versus extroversion. The parts that have Lady Gaga proclaiming, 'Baby, I was born this way'." Quiet laughter ripples through the room. Prof Walker doesn't join in. "If adolescents can successfully uncover these core parts of themselves, they'll have a solid foundation for the transition to adulthood and the next stage of development: intimacy and deep, connected relationships with others. Mixing the two stages can be problematic." Watching the disintegration of my parents' marriage during my own adolescence taught me that lesson the hard way. Love and personal growth don't mix. "How can we expect anyone to love us for who we really are, if we ourselves don't know who that is?"

Prof Walker opens his mouth to speak again, but his response is forestalled by another voice, coming from the back of the room.

"What if they get it wrong?" Logan asks. He's leaning forward in his chair, a deep frown drawing his brows together. Does he disagree with my argument? We've never gotten into the nitty-gritty of my research theory before, but he knows the sort of program I've developed, and he's always been supportive. "What if a kid believes they've figured out who they are, but they make a mistake? Are they supposed to go through their whole life believing something about themselves that isn't true because of one experiment they did as a teenager?"

"Not one experiment," I point out. "Numerous experiments. A result is only reliable if it can be repeated. If we get the same result over and over, a genuine result that feels right to the person experiencing it, how can it be wrong?"

There's a brief silence while Logan considers his response. "What if later experiences present contradictory evidence? Something that flies in the face of those initial experiments?"

Clearing my throat, I try to answer as if I'm not completely aware he's talking about the life experience that included me sticking my tongue down his throat. "Fundamental changes in identity can happen, but they're rare. It usually takes an experience of seismic proportions to cause any sort of substantial shift."

A smirk appears on Logan's face, causing a subtle rush of blood to my groin. "Seismic experiences can and do happen," he says, oblivious to the fact I'm now hiding a semi behind the lectern while a room full of people stare at me. "What then?"

I've been asking myself the same question for the last four days. My past has taught me to expect one reaction to kissing a man, but my reaction to kissing Logan was the polar opposite. I have no idea how to integrate the new information. I was sixteen when I came to the conclusion I was straight. It felt genuine at the time. Totally authentic. To be drawn into questioning my sexual orientation all over again, in my mid-twenties, feels like a giant leap backward in my development. Still, I can hardly encourage adolescents to be courageous and take control of this process if I'm unwilling to do the same myself. At least there would be upsides to reopening my investigations—not the least of which would include a more thorough exploration of Logan's mouth.

Gripping the sides of the lectern once more, I meet the intensity of his gaze head on. "I suppose such an experience would pose a new and interesting research question, thus indicating the need for further experimentation." The widening of Logan's eyes has a smile tugging at the corners of my lips. "Why not be excited?"

Prof Mitchell starts to clap loudly as he rushes towards the lectern. "Please join me in thanking Patrick for his presentation on identity formation in adolescence."

Heads swivel back and forth between me and Logan as the audience applauds. I barely notice. My fascination with whatever the hell's going on between me and Logan has me caught somewhere between lust and hysteria. The question now is, has our kiss altered how he feels about me?

LOGAN

I shouldn't have said anything. I absolutely should not have said anything.

My index finger beats a tattoo against my thigh as I wait for the seminar to come to a slow and excruciating end. Patrick looks tense as he sits in his chair at the front of the room. Every now and then, he rubs a hand across the back of his neck, as if my gaze makes his skin twitch. Whether that's a good or a bad thing is yet to be seen.

I'm such an idiot. He's going to think I want more of what happened between us last Saturday night. Which I do, technically, but it's not like I'm planning to act on those desires. I doubt he is either, despite his talk of further experimentation. It was tough talk. He responded to the challenge implied by my questions, that's all. He doesn't actually want to make out with me again.

Cursing under my breath, I grab the book off the swivel desk and use it to cover my groin. It doesn't matter what my dick wants, my head is keenly aware getting involved with a friend, especially a sexually ambivalent friend, is trouble waiting to happen. I need to follow through with the plan and get our friendship back on its platonic track—as soon as possible.

Near the end of the hour, Prof Mitchell finally concludes the seminar with a few words of thanks. As the audience prepares to leave, I see several of the undergrads sneak glances in my direction before whispering among themselves. Patrick runs tutorials for most of these kids and now I'm sparking rumours about his love life. That's fantastic. Well done, me.

Taking the book, I duck out of the lecture building through a side door and find a place to wait.

A few minutes later, Patrick exits with Stacey and Ian. Catching sight of me, he slows to a halt. The others keep walking and he calls a quick goodbye before heading my way. He stops more than a metre in front of me, a tentative smile on his face as we stare at each other.

"Thanks for coming," he says, finally.

I wince. "Maybe it would have been better if I'd stayed away. At least I would have kept my mouth shut."

"You were fine. Your questions stopped Prof Walker from getting any more in. He's way better at tearing people apart."

Shaking my head, I take a step towards him. "I wasn't trying to tear you apart, Patrick."

"I know," he says, raising a hand. "I didn't mean it like that."

Another awkward silence lengthens, until a steady stream of students begins to swarm around us, all of them heading into the building through the nearby door.

"Walk back to the library with me?" I suggest. "My lunch break is nearly over."

Patrick nods and we start strolling in that direction.

"I was thinking," I say as we make our way across the lawn, "we should get together Friday night."

His steps falter and he glances at me sideways. "Really?" Again with the tentative. "You'd want that?"

My look is pointed. "Mate, I'm not asking you out on a date."

Surprise widens his eyes and then he gives a stilted laugh. "No, I know. I didn't mean... a date." He sighs, shaking his head. "Sorry. I guess I'm a little on edge after..." he waves a hand in the space between us, "you know."

I give a mental snort. That's what I figured. If he can't even talk about it, there's no way he wants a repeat. *Why not be excited, my arse.*

"Look, forget whatever we said back there." I gesture to the lecture building now in the distance behind us. "We were both talking bullshit. It didn't mean anything."

Patrick's gaze drops to the grass beneath us and I can't tell if he's relieved or... oh crap, he's not disappointed, is he? No, no, no, we are not going there. "All I want, is to put this whole thing behind us and get back to normal. Okay?"

There's a slight hesitation, but then he nods. "Of course."

"Good." I exhale, smiling. "I figure, the best way to do that is to go out for a couple of drinks, invite some friends, play pool, hang out. Same old, same old."

"Sounds good." His nodding is more enthusiastic now, but he hasn't stopped staring at the ground. "I don't regret what we did, though," he says suddenly. "Just so you know."

"Hey." I stop walking, putting a hand on his arm to bring him to a halt beside me. "I don't regret it, either. Not for a second. Although, I'll admit it took me by surprise."

His gaze finally lifts to mine and he grins. "It did?"

"Maybe I wasn't as surprised as you," I tease, and I'm grateful when he laughs. I've always loved his laugh. "But it was unexpected, yeah. It's taken me a few days to process it." Granted, those days involved minimal thought and a lot of jerking off.

"Me, too." The deepening of his voice makes me wonder if his method of processing has been as hands-on as mine. "I guess that explains the radio silence between us." He starts walking towards the library again and I fall into step beside him.

"We've been texting," I point out. "It hasn't been totally silent."

"It may as well have been." Reaching into his back pocket, Patrick holds up his mobile phone. "Do you know how many times we've texted since we last saw each other?"

"A dozen maybe?" I've been playing it cool this week. I didn't want to go all text-crazy on him.

"It was six," he announces. "And how many times did we text each other during the same time frame last week?"

"I have no idea," I say, throwing my hands in the air. "It's not like I keep count."

"Well, I counted, and it was 73. We sent 73 texts in more than a dozen separate conversations."

I should have expected this. Overthinking shit is Patrick's personal trademark. "We've both been busy this week. You've had your seminar to prepare for and I've had..." a lot of jerking off to do. "Besides, last week we watched that movie on Netflix together." Technically, we were both in our own apartments, but we watched it at the same time and texted each other through the whole thing. Mainly to bag the bad acting.

At this point, I can all but hear the collective unconscious of the entire world snorting at me in amusement. But the entire world can fuck off. It's not weird for two guys to chat while watching a movie together—apart.

It's not *that* weird.

"You counted our texts?" Yeah, I had to circle back around to that eventually.

"That's not the point," he insists. "The point is, that kiss changed things between us, which is my fault because I'm the one who chose you to kiss, but..." His words seem to disappear on him and it's weird to see him so unsure of himself. "I need to know we're not going to implode because of it."

So do I, which is the point of this conversation. Still, I can't help but tease him a little. "What if I promise to text you more? Will that satisfy your needy little boy heart?"

He rolls his eyes, smirking at me. "Don't be a bitch, Logan. You know what I mean."

"Yeah, I get it." We stop at the entrance to the library, turning to face each other once more. "Look, we made out. It was hot. But it doesn't have to be all dramatic and meaningful. I won't let it mess with my head, if you don't let it mess with yours."

He nods. "Sounds fair."

"Which means we're still friends, right?"

"Yes, friends," he agrees with a tight smile. "That's what we are."

"Good. So, let's act like friends. Let's go out and have some fun. Before you know it, everything will go back to the way it was." I can pretend, at least.

"I suppose so." He sounds almost as convinced as I do. "Just promise me one thing."

I cock my head to the side. "What's that?"

"No more bets," he insists, and the teasing glint in his eyes makes me laugh out loud.

Goddamn, he's gorgeous. But then, he's always been gorgeous. I've done my best not to notice, and I'm certainly not allowed to notice now. But it's hard to ignore the obvious.

Allowing a slow smile to curve my lips, I nod. "No bets."

I expect him to say goodbye then, but instead he gestures downward, in the direction of my groin. "Is that for me?"

My dick gives an enthusiastic throb of excitement. *Fuck, yes. If you want it, it's all yours.*

"The book, Logan," he drawls in a knowing way that has nothing to do with friendship and everything to do with the *fuck me now* look I no doubt have plastered all over my face. "It's mine, right?"

I stare down at the paperback I'm still carrying. "Yes," I blurt out. "It's yours. I finished it. It was good." I really need to shut up now.

He snorts a laugh. "I thought you might enjoy it."

I hold out the book. He takes it. Our fingers don't brush. We don't stare into each other's eyes for long moments of subliminal communication. The transfer takes all of two seconds and there is nothing sexual about it at all. Because this isn't some forbidden romance where we're being forced to deny our feelings for each other. If Patrick wanted me, he'd say so. That's the kind of man he is. But he doesn't want me—not like that. And I can't allow myself to want him.

"See you on Friday, then." His voice has dropped half an octave. It's adopted a husky quality.

I don't notice, because it doesn't matter. The memory of our kiss will soon fade, taking any residual attraction he may or may not be feeling with it. Then all this madness will be over, but I'll still get to be Patrick's friend. It's the best possible outcome here, and I have to be okay with it.

"See you Friday," I say with a nod.

Watching him walk away, I sigh heavily before reaching down to pull my phone from my pocket. I tap away on the screen, sending him a series of text messages.

Here's.

A few more.

Texts.

For your.

Total.

He's halfway across the lawn when he glances down at his phone. Without looking back, he lifts one hand to give me the finger. Laughing, I turn to head through the main doors of the library. Despite the vague hollowness in my chest, I feel more relaxed than I have in days.

Patrick and I are going to be okay. If I have to bury my feelings for him to make that happen, so be it.

PATRICK

E verything he does is hot. The way his hand slides along the length of the pool cue makes my dick twitch in envy. His throat works as he tips his head back to take a sip of his beer and I want to lick his neck. He laughs at some joke Stacey makes before taking her shot, and the sound sends tiny bolts of lightning pinging through me. Fucking hell. I've always known Logan is an attractive man. I may even have caught myself staring a time or ten. But has he always been this damned sexy?

Ian drops into a seat beside me. Plonking his beer on the table, he rips open a bag of corn chips and pops one into his mouth. "What's up, buttercup?" he says as he settles back in his chair.

Dragging my gaze away from Logan, I give him a questioning look. "Nothing. Why?"

"You've been acting weird all night." He turns the bag my way in silent offering, but I shake my head. Shrugging, he tosses the packet on the table. "What's going on? Did you and Logan come to blows or something?"

Hearing the words Logan and blow in the same sentence brings to mind the slew of lewd images I've been living with for the past week. I choke on a mouthful of beer, spitting it all over the table.

"Dude!" Ian pushes his chair back from the table, lifting his bag of chips out of the spreading wetness. "That was so not cool."

"Sorry. It went down the wrong way." I grab a couple of paper napkins to wipe up the mess. When I'm done, I toss them into a nearby bin before sitting back down. "Logan and I are fine. Nothing's going on."

"Then quit staring at him, mate, you're giving me the creeps."

"Who's giving you the creeps?" Naomi returns from the bar with two drinks in hand.

"Patrick," Ian tells her as she joins us. "He's only got eyes for Logan tonight. I'm wondering why."

"I did notice that." Naomi rests her chin in the palm of her upraised hand. "Do tell, Patrick. Why the sudden fascination?"

My eyes narrow as I take in her teasing smile. Does she know? If she knows, it means Logan told her. Which means he felt the need to talk about it. Which means... I have no idea what it means.

"There's no fascination and I'm not staring."

Ian snorts his disbelief. "Is this about the stupid bet you lost last week? The one where you're supposed to kiss a dude. Because you have to follow through." A devious grin sneaks onto his face as he demolishes another corn chip. "A bet is a bet, man. You can't back out now."

"No need to back out," I reply. "It's already done."

"No shit. Really?" At my nod, Ian barks out a laugh. "When?"

"The very next night." Glancing over at the pool table, I see Logan and Stacey shaking hands over their finished game as they head back to our table. I need to end this conversation now. Things are awkward enough between us already. "Logan took me to a club in Fortitude Valley. I picked a guy, laid one on him, and we left. End of story."

I manage to finish as Stacey sits down beside Naomi, leaving Logan to squeeze into the last vacant chair at the small table—right beside me. Maybe I should go and get a drink from the bar. Not because I'm avoiding Logan, but because sitting beside him might result in actual electricity arcing between us. This whole *going back to the way things were* idea is proving harder than I thought it would be.

Naomi slides the extra drink she bought in front of Stacey. "The bartenders are swamped, so I grabbed you another vodka and orange while I was up there."

With a shy smile, Stacey lifts the glass off the table and takes a small sip. "Thanks, Na."

Naomi's face lights up at the use of her nickname. As far as I know, Stacey's never called her that before. "You're welcome," she murmurs, reaching up to tuck her hair behind one ear.

Holding back an amused snort, I glance at Logan. He's grinning from ear to ear. On the other side of me, Ian is on the verge of drooling, all thoughts of last week's bet vanquished by the sight of two beautiful women flirting with each other. With any luck, our previous conversation is already dead.

"What were you guys talking about?" Stacey asks.

I slump in my chair. So close.

Naomi, on the other hand, perks up as she turns her mischievous gaze back to me. "Patrick was about to tell us the tale of his gay kiss." Stacey gives her a confused frown. "Apparently, he lost a bet to Logan last week and this was the payment."

Stacey gapes at me. "You kissed a guy?"

"So he claims," Ian clarifies, "but I'm not convinced. I mean, if there were no witnesses, how do we know you actually went through with it?"

I shrug and tilt my head towards the man beside me. "Logan was there. He's my witness."

All three of them stare at Logan, waiting.

He clears his throat and then takes a hit of his beer before answering. "Can confirm, he did the deed. The bet was satisfied." He looks at me then, his lips quirking upward. "And then some."

My cheeks warm, but I lean back in my chair and smile right back at him. "No point in doing shit by halves."

Stacey lets out an excited squeak while Ian throws back his head and laughs out loud.

Naomi bites down on her bottom lip, her gaze darting between me and Logan. "How was it?" she asks me. I glance at Logan, who's now glaring at Naomi, but all her focus is trained on me. "Did you like it?"

Damn. She's not going to let this go. I let out a long-suffering sigh. What the hell? I am who I am, and I've got nothing to hide. "All right, I'll tell you." Picking up my drink, I drain the last of it before putting the bottle back on the table. "The truth is..."

I allow my pause to hang there for a while. Logan is practically vibrating beside me. The others are leaning forward in their chairs. Once the tension reaches an appropriately heightened pitch, I lift my arms out wide and grin like a maniac. "It was freaking awesome."

A chorus of cheers erupt around the table. "Seriously," I continue. "This dude was lava hot. I'm talking gorgeous, with a hard body and a day's growth of beard and a kiss that hit me like a freaking truck."

Logan turns beet red. Closing his eyes, he lowers his face into his hands. Thankfully, everyone else is too busy talking to notice.

"It was good then," Ian manages to say over the others.

With a low chuckle, I nod. "Yeah, it was good."

"What does this mean?" Stacey asks, excitedly. "Do you want to do it again? Are you gay now?"

"No, I'm not gay." I shake my head at her. "You remember the part where I dated Robyn for nearly two years, right?" Granted, we broke up because, even after all that time, I still couldn't say I was in love with her. We ticked all the boxes in terms of compatibility, and we got along well enough, but that was it. The flare of desire that brought us together had long since faded by the time we entered our second year. She seemed as relieved as I was when I ended it.

"Maybe you're bisexual," Naomi suggests teasingly. Her gaze flickers to Logan and back, and I know she's messing with us. She expects me to go the route of vehement denial.

Instead, I relax back in my chair with a non-committal shrug. "Maybe I am."

Every visible part of her body yanks upward at my response. Eyebrows, shoulders, spine, it all goes up. "Really?" she whispers. "You think it's a possibility?"

I think I wouldn't be back here asking this question again if it wasn't. At the same time, my favourable reaction to Logan's kiss doesn't negate my previous attempts to settle the matter, which were nothing short of abysmal. "I honestly have no idea," I tell her. "But..." If I was looking for a way to let Logan know about my newly formulated plan, this is as good a time as any. "I do know I can't draw any reliable conclusions based on one kiss."

Logan barks out a laugh beside me.

I turn to look at him. "What's so funny?"

"It was more than one kiss." He sits back in his chair, arms crossed over his chest. "Just saying, I'm pretty sure the bloke got more than he bargained for. What with you sucking on his tongue and all."

Heads swivel in my peripheral vision as meaningful glances pass between our friends.

"He tasted like vodka. I happen to like vodka." I huff out a vaguely indignant breath. "Besides, I didn't hear him complaining."

"Logan has a point, though." Ian strokes his fingers across his chin in a show of false contemplation. "In my experience, as a straight man who is, you know, actually straight, I don't go around sucking on guy tongue, no matter what it tastes like." He gives a slow, exaggerated nod. "I agree with Logan, the bi thing is more than a possibility."

"Hold up." Logan sits up with an impatient groan. "I never said that. I only said it was more than one kiss." He turns to look me dead in the eye. "Patrick, mate, you may not be quite as far up the straight end of the spectrum as you thought, but there's no need to get all existential about it. One boner does not automatically make you queer."

Stacey gasps, slapping a hand over her mouth. "You got a boner from the kiss?"

"Hang on a minute." Ian points an accusing finger at Logan. "How do *you* know he had a boner?"

Logan's mouth drops open. I can all but see his brain stalling as he searches for a reasonable explanation.

I have an explanation, and I don't see much point in keeping it a secret. "I couldn't exactly hide it from him," I blurt out. "Who else do you think I was kissing?"

Chaos ensues. Naomi whoops in delight, clapping her hands together. Stacey's jaw hits the floor and Ian laughs his damned head off again.

I sneak a glance at Logan, who's watching me closely. "I can't believe you did that," he mutters, but I can hear the amusement underlying his words.

"Do you mind?" I ask, belatedly. Logan may be out, but that doesn't mean it's okay for me to kiss and tell.

"Of course I don't mind." Turning his body towards me, he leans closer and puts a hand on the back of my chair. "With all those compliments you were tossing around about my fine form? At least now I get to lay claim to them."

We're in each other's personal space again, straining the spatial boundaries of friendship, even if we aren't breaking them. The way his presence curves around me, it feels like he's laying claim to more than my bold words—or wants to. My heart thuds heavily in my chest at the thought. What would it feel like to be claimed by a man like Logan? Would I like that, too?

"That thing we noticed earlier makes a lot more sense now." Ian's quiet words draw our attention. He's talking to Naomi, who nods in agreement.

"What are you talking about?" Logan asks him.

I glare at Ian, my eyes promising death if he reveals my earlier ogling. Not *every* secret needs to be shared.

Glancing my way, he clears his throat. "It's nothing. Some earlier behavioural observations have now been put into context. That's all."

With narrowed eyes, Logan removes his hand from my chair, muttering something under his breath about psychologists being nosy buggers.

"What happens now?" Stacey asks, gesturing between me and Logan. "Are you two going to—"

"No." Logan jumps in, with an emphatic shake of his head. "It was a onetime thing. We're friends, nothing more." His gaze swings to me. "Right, Patrick?"

I sit frozen as tiny slivers of hurt cut into me. I get Logan isn't interested in me that way. He made his feelings perfectly clear when we talked after my seminar. But does he have to be quite so forceful about it? Would it really be so bad for us indulge in the odd repeat performance? It was only kissing... and touching... and him being hard and me wanting to grind myself against—

"Patrick!" Logan is frowning and the whole table is staring at me, still waiting for me to confirm our friendship status.

"Right," I blurt out, forcing a laugh. "Nothing is going on. One-time only." I meet Logan's gaze, repeating his words from a couple of days ago. "We're not going to let it mess with our heads." Much.

His smile seems more genuine than mine, and I detect the release of a held breath in the movement of his chest. "Exactly."

"What about the part where you might be bisexual?" Stacey asks, interrupting our moment. "Because, you know, that's a big deal." She uses her straw to stab at the ice in the bottom of her glass as she speaks, a slight quiver in her voice. "You can try to ignore those feelings, but they never really go away."

A quiet gasp comes from Naomi's direction. We all pretend not to notice.

"You're right," I tell her with a nod. "And this is a question I need answered, sooner rather than later." I sit up straight in my chair, ready to make my announcement. "Which is why I've decided to conduct an experiment."

"Oh, crap," Ian moans. "I knew we'd end up here again." He grabs another handful of corn chips. "You know you're kind of predictable, right?" he adds, before stuffing them in his mouth.

I roll my eyes. "That's the whole point of self-awareness, being able to predict how I'll react to stuff." I gesture to Logan. "What happened with you was *not* what I predicted—at all."

His eyes flash and he grins. "Glad to know I can shock you."

"Yeah, well, I don't like being shocked. At least, not like that," I add as I turn my attention back to the others. "I need to know if I'm bisexual, once and for all. If I am, I want to know how far that goes." I avoid even glancing at Logan as I speak. After his earlier words, I don't want him to think I'm trying to include him in my plans. While he would be the ideal partner for the experiment—he *is* the only man I've ever kissed that made me want more—he's made it clear he doesn't want to go there again. I have to respect his wishes.

Taking a deep breath, I slap a broadside of bravado into my voice and force a smile. "All I need to do now, is find a man who wants to do the experiment with me."

PARTICIPANTS AND
METHODOLOGY

LOGAN

Hell no! The words erupt in my mind the instant Patrick states his intention. No fucking way is he going to go out and choose some random stranger to take home, just so he can decide whether or not he's into guys. The idea is ludicrous!

Apparently, I'm the only one who thinks so. Stacey is already suggesting a friend she knows who would definitely be up for it, while Ian high fives Patrick's above and beyond attitude. Only Naomi is silent. But instead of dismissing the idea, she's glaring at me and nodding her head in Patrick's direction as if to say, 'What are you waiting for?'

And that's another hell no. I'm not getting dragged any deeper into Patrick's sexual confusion. The first time was bad enough—in that it was really freaking good, and that's bad. I'm not about to get caught up in his boundless curiosity, only to be tossed aside when the novelty wears off. I've both been there and done that. It's not worth the heartache, no matter how hungry I am for another taste of him.

"Do you think this is actually grounds for an entire experiment?" I offer, managing to catch Patrick's attention. "I mean, come on, you got a little excited. The expert touch of my lips is bound to confuse anyone," I add with an air of narcissistic confidence.

"That's no reason to start running around looking for fuck buddies."

"Whoa, slow down." Patrick holds his hands up in a defensive gesture. "I only said I want to see how far this all goes before I hit my limit. I probably won't end up going much further than what we've already done." His voice drops as he mutters to himself, "I've never gotten that far before."

Before? Has he run this sort of experiment in the past? The thought doesn't exactly shock me, but it does make me wonder. I remember the way he acted that night, the look on his face before he kissed me the first time. He fully expected kissing a man—any man—to make him sick to his stomach. What happened the first time to turn him off guys so badly?

Patrick's thirst for knowledge about people, including himself, has always been intense. It makes him a great developmental psychologist, but maybe there was a time when he pushed himself too hard in his quest for answers. If so, it sounds like he's about to make the same mistake all over again.

Leaning one elbow on the table, I move in closer to him. "Patrick, mate, if you want to explore your attraction to guys then why don't you start by opening yourself up to meeting one." The thought of seeing him with another man makes me want to poke my own eyes out, but it's not like I have the right to stop it, and it has to be better than his current plan. "That's the way it's supposed to work. You ask someone out, get to know them. Let it happen naturally."

He throws an odd expression my way. "I'm not looking for a relationship, Logan. I'm looking for the answer to a specific question. Am I bisexual or not? Once I have enough data to draw a reliable conclusion, the experiment will end."

I quirk an eyebrow at him. "Then what?"

"I go on with my life, but as a more authentic version of me. Which means when I *do* meet someone I want to have a relationship with, I'll be confident I'm presenting myself as I really am." I continue to stare at him, dumbfounded, and he throws his hands in the air. "If a woman is getting into a relationship with a bisexual man, don't you think it's important for her to know upfront? It could be a deal breaker for some women."

My stomach sinks lower with each and every word. Patrick hasn't even begun to wrap his mind around what being bisexual could mean for his life. I need to steer clear of this whole situation.

"What would you have me do, Logan?" he hisses, his body tensing under my scrutiny. "Ignore what happened and hope it goes away? That's not me. I need to sort it out now, or it will come back to bite me on the arse later. I am not about to let that happen."

I want to growl at him in frustration, but somehow, I don't think that will strengthen my case. I need to find another tactic. "Well then, I guess there's nothing left to do but drink to your success." I give him a slap on the shoulder. "Come on, my shout."

Patrick releases a breath. "Thank you."

We make our way to the bar and grab a couple of rum and cokes. Instead of returning to our friends, I lead him to a bar table in a quieter area of the room. Pushing aside a collection of recently emptied glasses, we put our drinks on the table.

"Let's talk logistics for a minute." If I can make him see how difficult it will be to pull this off, maybe I can get him to back down. Except, I've yet to see Patrick back down on anything. He's got the whole *dog with a bone* routine down pat. "How are you planning to find a man to do this experiment with?"

A flicker of uncertainty crosses his face. Finally. I was beginning to think the man had balls of titanium. "I haven't gotten that far yet, but... I could do it with Stacey's friend," he suggests. "I've met him. He's nice."

"But are you attracted to him?"

"Not exactly, but—"

"There's no point in doing it with someone you aren't attracted to," I scoff. "I think you know that already." His gaze snaps to mine, but he says nothing. "What other ideas do you have?"

He shrugs. "I could go back to the club you took me to. Maybe I'll meet someone there."

My jaw threatens to drop, but I manage to keep it shut tight. "Patrick," I begin, struggling to keep my voice calm, "please tell me you aren't going to walk around a gay club propositioning guys with a scientific experiment into your own questionable sexuality."

He stares at me in surprise. "Well, I wouldn't put it like that, I do know how to be subtle!" There's some more staring, then he sighs. "It does sound way worse than it is, doesn't it?"

His crestfallen expression tugs at my conscience. I'm not actually against him getting his gay on, despite my initial resistance to the idea. And if he decides he wants to do it with someone who isn't me, I can find a way to handle that, too—but not like this.

"The problem is, the kind of man you need for something like this isn't going to want a bar of your experiment. Most will probably be offended by the idea of it. But the kind of men you will attract?" I shudder at the thought. "It could end badly. I don't want to see you get hurt."

"I'm not some lightweight, Logan," he scoffs, gesturing to his own muscular body. I try not to inspect it too closely. "I can take care of myself."

"There are a lot of different ways to get hurt." If he does this, he'll be putting himself in an emotionally vulnerable position. I don't want him to get hurt while doing it because the guy he's with turns out to be a dickhead who's only in it for the easy lay. But how do I say all that to Patrick without looking like some kind of mother hen? Or like I'm jealous—which is probably closer to the truth.

"What would you suggest?" he asks with an exasperated sigh.

I try to think of a solution. One that will provide him with the freedom to experiment he wants, but without the potentially disastrous pitfalls. Only one solution comes to mind, because there's only one man I trust to do this right.

My mouth opens and I spit the words out, not allowing myself time to think them through. "You can do your experiment with me."

We both go still, staring at each other. Unmoving. Unspeaking.

This is such a bad idea. I swore to myself I would never again allow a man to use me to try homosexuality on for size. Patrick's being upfront about it, at least, but that won't make it any less painful when it ends. And it *will* end. Patrick's spent his whole adult life lusting after women. He's not about to switch teams permanently— certainly not for me.

But I'm not seeing any other feasible solution to his problem and at least I already know my heart can heal from this particular kind of pain. If I'm careful to keep this restricted to the physical plane, rather than getting emotionally involved, maybe neither of us have to get hurt. Either way, keeping Patrick safe is worth the risk.

My heart pounds, as I wait for him to respond to my offer. The part of me that's sure he'll say yes is already weak with relief that he won't go out looking for anyone else. I don't want other men touching Patrick. If he's only ever going to do this experiment with one man, I want that man to be me.

"I thought you wanted to go back to the way things were." His gaze is wary, and he has yet to move a muscle. "We're friends, nothing more. That's what you said."

"Yes, and it's still true," I assure him. "I do want to go back to being friends. But we can do it after the experiment."

His breath has quickened and, when he speaks again, his voice is rough. "Are you sure you want to do this?"

"It's the best viable solution," I tell him, as if coating my possessiveness with a thick layer of pragmatism will make it less obvious. "Don't forget, it was *my* kiss that breathed life into your queerness." My body reacts to the idea of doing it again... and again... and again. However many times he needs to be satisfied. I make a show of licking my lips, enjoying the way he watches with rapt attention. "How much do you want to bet I can get more than a boner out of you?"

With a start, his eyes narrow and he points a finger at me. "No more bets."

Laughing out loud, I nod. "That's right. How could I forget?"

He runs a hand over the back of his neck as he looks around the bar, before returning his gaze to me. "I'll admit, when I decided to do this, my first instinct was to come to you." He gestures at me with an impatient hand. "You're the only guy I've ever enjoyed kissing and it totally blew my mind. Why do you think I'm doing this in the first place?" he growls, his frustration coming through. "It's not just because of what happened when we kissed. It's the fact I can't stop thinking about it."

He's not the only one. I've rubbed my cock raw in remembrance. The urge to shove him back against the nearby wall washes over me. I want to give him something new to think about. Ignoring the impulse, I swallow hard and speak in a low voice. "When you're thinking about it, are these analytical thoughts about what it all means? Or are they wanking thoughts?"

He glances away, trying to appear nonchalant. "Both."

My muscles tighten at the thought of him with his hand wrapped around his throbbing dick, fantasising about kissing me while he pants and moans his way to orgasm. I want to know what he looks like when he comes. What he sounds like. How he feels.

"But," he says, with emphasis, interrupting the lustfest going on in my head, "I decided against it because I know you don't want—" The words cut off abruptly and his eyes close briefly. "I don't want us to stop being friends."

"I don't want that either but, Patrick, you're playing with fire here and assuming no one will steal the matches. I'm the only one I trust to do this right."

He's still reluctant. I can feel the force of his doubts. But he hasn't said no.

"Patrick, listen to me." I slide a hand around the back of his neck, urging him to meet my gaze. "You need someone you can trust to stop when you say stop, no matter what's happening when you say it. Someone who won't get pissed at you and accuse you of being a tease when you leave them with blue balls." Releasing him, I grin. "Besides, you tried looking for someone else to kiss. It didn't work. You chose me and now you're stuck with me for the duration."

He huffs out an indignant sound. "I could find someone else to kiss," he blusters, "if I looked really hard... for about ten years."

I laugh out loud, knowing I almost have him convinced. "Yeah, but even if you did, it wouldn't matter."

"Why is that?" He leans closer, as if he's looking forward to my response.

In that instant, I realise how badly I want this—him. I want to tug on every thread of his sexuality, freeing each strand for thorough inspection. I want to tie him in knots, before making him unravel for me. And I want him to know, every second along the way, I'm the one who is doing this to him. That I'm the only man to ever make him feel this way.

Licking my lips, I take a step closer and bring my face in next to his. "Because even if you did hit your limit with someone else, you'd always wonder how much further I could have taken you." I lower my head, so he can feel my breath against his neck as I go in for the kill. "Patrick, my friend, I'm going to drag your arse so far down my end of the spectrum, you'll have to claw your way straight."

When I pull back, his eyes are closed, and his lips have parted. Is he already anticipating the taste of me? I hold still, waiting for him to blink his eyes open.

He stares at me in wonder, a smile curving his lips. "I have to ask this, because it's been bothering me all night. Were you always this unbelievably sexy?"

"Oh yeah," I tell him, a little smugly. "I was careful not to direct it your way before. Not to look at you too closely, not to let myself think of you that way. But that's all over and I'm telling you, right now, if you're determined to go through with this experiment, you *will* be doing it with me."

His face turns serious. It's the flinch that comes right before the fall. "Promise this won't end with you hating me."

My own smile fades, because we both know what's at stake here. It's a cost neither of us wants to pay. "I know what this is, Patrick, and I know what it isn't. So, yes, I promise." After a momentary pause, I tilt my head. "What do you say?"

He releases a slow, measured breath, and then he gives in. "I say yes. Let's do it."

PATRICK

"When do we start?" Logan asks, waggling his eyebrows at me. "Is it now? Because I've got a whole shitload of sexual tension that needs someplace to go." Snaking his hands onto my hips, he tugs me against him. "I would be tickled pick to unload it all on you."

My body goes into overdrive, excited to finally be touching him again after almost a full week of deprivation, but my head yanks on the brake. "Not tonight," I manage to say, through a groan. "We can't start tonight." My cock disagrees, only too happy to be nestled against his—and getting happier by the second. Swearing under my breath, I put a hand on his shoulder while I peel my lower half away from his. "Let's um... let's sit for a minute." With any luck, putting a table between us will prevent me from embarrassing myself in a room full of people.

Taking our drinks, we manage to find a small table in a corner of the room. I glance over to where our friends have now been joined by a few more people we know. Naomi's gaze meets mine and she smiles, giving me a thumbs up. I'm not sure what that's supposed to mean, but okay.

As we take a seat opposite each other, my knee brushes against Logan's under the table. The simple contact sends a fresh bolt of lust streaking straight to my groin and I jerk my leg away. When I look at Logan, he's relaxing back in his chair, with crossed arms and a satisfied smirk.

I clear my throat, attempting to get rid of any traces of arousal before I speak. "This may not be a serious experiment, but we should still do our best to stick to some kind of scientific protocol. That means engaging in a series of prearranged experimental sessions, with an increasing level of exposure to the chosen stimulus." I shift my gaze to his. "That's you."

"I am ready and willing to stimulate," he says, raising his arms. "So, what's the hold-up? Unless you're stalling."

I'm stunned by his accusation. Does he think I have cold feet? Not a single part of me has been anything other than hot since he walked into the bar. In fact, it's taking all my willpower to sit here having a sensible conversation instead of tossing the table aside and crawling into his lap. Stalling, my arse.

"Come to my place tomorrow night," I suggest. "We'll have privacy, protection from the ridiculous number of extraneous variables currently surrounding us." I gesture to the bar, including everything from the number of people to the erotic beat of the music with a single sweep of my hand. "Plus, we'll have the whole evening to…"

"Increase your level of exposure to the stimulus?" he finishes dryly.

"Exactly." I nod. "How's that for not stalling?"

Uncrossing his arms, he leans forward to rest his elbows on the edge of the table. "I already have plans tomorrow but make it Sunday night and I'm all yours."

I wait for him to elaborate, but he falls silent. Does he have a date tomorrow night? Or has he planned a hook-up? The thought of him kissing someone else has green-eyed monsters squirming in my brain. It's hardly fair. It's not like we're dating or anything, but still. He said I was stuck with him for the duration. Surely that should go both ways.

"Sunday night it is." Pushing aside any thoughts of what he might do between now and then, I pull out my phone and open a notetaking app. "In the meantime, we need to decide on our methodology, which in this case means making a list of ground rules, things we are and aren't comfortable with. So we both know what to expect." Opening a new note in the app, I type out *Experiment Ground Rules* as the title.

Logan leans across the table so he can see my screen better. "You know you think too much, right?" He glances upward through his lashes. "Do you want me to wear a lab coat? Or maybe I could hold a clipboard while we bump uglies."

"Ha bloody ha." I point a finger at him. "We don't know we'll be bumping anything yet. Stop skipping ahead." I add the numbers one to five in the body of the note. "First up, no alcohol before or during experimental sessions. That's one of the reasons tonight is out." I gesture to the drinks on the table between us.

"Alcohol lowers inhibitions, making people do things they normally wouldn't do."

"What you mean is, sometimes a little lubrication makes it easier to do what we already want to do, but are reluctant to ask for." He grins, but then narrows his gaze. "Wait a second, you aren't suggesting the booze gave you a boner last weekend, are you? Because I can guarantee, you got that from me."

"I'm only saying the alcohol may have exacerbated the issue," I insist, before adding in a low murmur, "alcohol tends to have an interesting effect on me."

"What? You mean it makes you horny?" he asks with a smirk.

Heaving a sigh, I force myself to look up at him. "In a word, yes."

"That is interesting." He eyes my half-empty glass of rum and coke. It's the third one I've had tonight. "How many drinks does it take to make you horny?"

"A few," I say with a shrug. "The more I have, the worse it gets."

"The more you have..." he begins, frowning in confusion. "I don't think I've ever seen you have more than a few."

"I try not to drink too much in public these days." The last time I let myself go was one night at a party when I sculled a couple of vodka shots with Stacey. The next thing I knew, I was staring at Logan while he made out with some guy I didn't know. The sight of his large hands cupping the guy's face while their mouths fused together was so fucking hot, I eventually had to leave the room. Escaping to the bathroom, I'd jacked out a quick but intense orgasm, shooting into a wad of toilet paper. Afterward, as I cleaned up and washed my hands, I'd reminded myself it was only the booze that had me acting so strangely. Guy-on-guy action has always gotten me hot, it was nothing new, and the alcohol made the live-action aspect of it more intense. Logan's involvement was nothing more than coincidence. Nevertheless, I try not to let myself overindulge—especially since that night. Better not to risk it.

"Are you horny now?" The deep rumble of Logan's voice catches me off guard and my gaze snaps to his. He's watching me closely, and beneath the table the outside of one of his knees is touching the inside of one of mine. I don't move away, but I also pretend not to notice.

"What does it matter?" I ask. "The experiment hasn't started yet."

"I want to know what you look like when you're horny and don't want to let on." He extends his leg, so his calf is now touching mine also. "It could be useful information, for the experiment."

Considering he was wholly against the idea all of about ten minutes ago, he seems to be warming up to it damned quick. Maybe the appeal of repeating last week's make-out session is getting to him, after all. The same way it's getting to me.

The idea of putting my hands on Logan again, maybe even without the barrier of clothing this time, has me tied in knots. I'm not stupid enough to blame that entirely on the rum I've been drinking, but the alcohol could be exaggerating the effect the man has on me. Which is why I need to be sober when we do this. So, when I get him naked, I know it's because touching him gets me hot, and not because my decision-making has been compromised. Will we even get that far before my brain rebels on me? Damn, I hope so.

"Let's move on to number two, shall we?" I suggest.

"What is number two?" As he speaks, he reaches across the table with one hand. Touching the tip of his middle finger to the back of my forearm, he trails it slowly down to my wrist. "For instance, if I was to drag you across my lap right now and grind my erection against you, would I be breaking the rules?"

"Hell, yes." My butt actually lifts from the chair as the words burst out of me. Damn it, this isn't going as planned. "I mean yes, that would be breaking the rules." Focusing on my phone, I type the second rule. "No sexual contact between experimental sessions."

Tutting, he slouches in his chair, so his knee slides another inch up the inside of my thigh. "Well, that's no fun." Above the table, his fingertip circles around to the inside of my wrist, stroking the sensitive skin. With a quiet groan, I draw my limbs back out of his reach. It doesn't help. His low chuckle still ripples over me in sensual waves.

"Logan," I say, my voice determined, if a little hoarse, "I really do want us to still be friends at the end of this. Which means keeping firm lines between the experiment and real life. If we could potentially be all over each other any time we're together, it could be difficult to keep the purpose of the experiment clear."

Logan's smile fades and then he shakes his head, as if to clear it of lust-bunnies. "You have a point." Taking a deep breath, he sits up straighter and clasps both hands under his chin. "This isn't about us being together, it's about giving you the freedom to explore a new side of yourself." He shrugs a single shoulder. "I want you to have the chance to do that, in a way where I know you'll be safe."

I'm struck once again by how amazing he is. Logan isn't only a good friend, he's a good man. A protector. I can't help but feel incredibly grateful to him for offering to do this. I don't know if I could have gone through with it with anyone else. I don't know that I'd want to.

"Why are you doing this for me?" I ask quietly, tilting my head to one side. "What do you get out of it?"

His throat moves as he swallows, and he glances away before meeting my gaze again. His hazel eyes have laughter in them now and I know, whatever he's about to say, isn't the full truth.

"Let's just say, I get to satisfy my curiosity. I mean, who doesn't want the chance to turn a straight man queer, with his full and willing participation." There's a bitter undertone to his words, and I wait to see if he'll add more, but instead he picks up his glass and drains the last of his drink.

Reaching out, he slides my phone across the table and types something into it before pushing it back to me. "That's my rule. It's non-negotiable."

I look down at the single word he's added as rule number three. "Fidelity."

"If we're doing this," he says, "we're doing it all the way. That means no dating anyone else, no hooking up, no nothing."

"Agreed," I say with a ready nod. "To do anything with anyone else would ruin the integrity of the experiment, at least for me. I promise, as long as the experiment lasts, I'm all yours."

His gaze snaps to mine. "And I'm yours."

I ignore the way those words plant themselves deep in my gut and take root. All mine—for now anyway. The idea of this man giving himself to me, even for a short time, is heady stuff.

"Does this mean you'll need to change your plans for tomorrow night?" I try to add some tease to my tone, but it falls flat.

Logan pauses before shaking his head. "No. It's not a date."

Relief floods my system, but I try to keep the signs of it to myself. I don't want him to think I'm going to start acting like some jealous boyfriend just because we'll be... doing whatever it is we end up doing.

"Also, no pushing yourself to do anything you don't want to do," he adds, moving on. "I'm not interested in being with a semi-willing partner. If you're not into something, you need to tell me so we can stop, right then and there. That includes the whole experiment," he lifts a hand to gesture between us, "if you decide this isn't for you, we end it. No harm, no foul."

"Right, exactly." I let out a short laugh, releasing the tension of the last few minutes. "The whole idea is to see how far I can go before I stop enjoying it. To push myself further would be against the point."

"Good."

Nodding, I add the fourth rule to the list. *End the experiment when it stops feeling right.*

"I can't think of anything else," I say, looking over the list. "What about you?" He shakes his head and I smile. "I guess we're done." I quickly shoot off an email to Logan, so he has a copy of the list. "We're good to go."

Smirking, Logan holds out his hand. "It's been nice doing business with you."

I stare at the offered appendage, but I don't want to settle for shaking his hand. "Don't you think, maybe..." I pause, my stomach erupting with butterflies, "we should seal the deal with a kiss?"

His eyebrows lift. "And break your precious rules? We've both been drinking, and this isn't an experimental session."

"But the experiment doesn't officially start until we seal the deal," I point out. "What if we kiss this time and nothing happens? That would render the whole thing moot."

An indignant gasp cuts the air. "Are you kidding me? We go through all this and you're not even sure you want to kiss me again? I'm offended." He's so offended he's laughing, which is fair enough considering how ridiculous I'm being.

"It's not about wanting. It's about having," I tell him, wanting him to understand. "Sometimes, you think you want something, you fantasise about it, and you think you know how you'll react to getting it, but then when you do get it… it's not anything like you thought it would be."

The laughter fades and his face creases into a concerned frown. He looks like he wants to ask me what I'm talking about and I hold my breath, hoping he doesn't.

Finally, he rises from his chair and drags it around the table, the legs scraping loudly across the wooden floor. The chair is facing me when he sits back down, spreading his knees so he can come in nice and close. "I suppose, given this is basically a sex experiment, a handshake is not going to cut it," he murmurs. "One kiss to kick us off. I'll try not to let it disappoint," he says, a teasing gleam in his eye. He leans closer and my heart rate goes through the roof. But then, as our lips are about to touch, he backs off again. "Are you sure you can handle it?" he asks. "I think we both remember how much trouble you had stopping at one, last time."

Huffing out a breath, I narrow my eyes at him. "I think I can manage to keep myself under control."

The sexy smile eases back onto his face. "We'll see."

He leans in again, slower this time. Pausing at the edge of contact, he forces me to close the gap. The kiss is light, sensual. The force of my response shoves at my insides, desperate to unleash itself, and I release a quiet whimper. The only thing holding me back is the knowledge that two nights from now this man will be all mine, to do with as I please. With a groan, I slide my tongue between his lips, chasing more of his taste. He chooses that moment to pull back a touch.

"Do you still want me, Patrick?" he growls against my lips.

"Yes." I fight the urge to claim his mouth once more, cursing the restrictions I myself put upon us. Suddenly, Sunday feels like forever away.

He backs off completely, leaving me hanging in the space between us with my mouth open.

"In that case," he says, with a leering smile, "the experiment has begun."

LOGAN

Why, oh why, didn't I cancel dinner? I know family is important and all, but seriously, I could have had Patrick Seymour squirming beneath my fingertips right this very second, and I begged off because I didn't want to miss dinner with my parents and sisters? What was I thinking?

It wasn't about the dinner, of course. If I'd told Mum something came up, she would have been okay with me missing one meal. But I didn't want to start this thing with Patrick by rearranging my life for his convenience. I did enough of that with Ben. Always making myself available for him, making sure I fit in with his plans before I made any of my own. It hadn't mattered in the end. You can't accommodate someone into wanting to be with you.

With a quick knock on the front door, I let myself into my parents' house. The smell of roast pork permeates the air and my stomach growls as I inhale. "Where's the party at?" I call out to no one in particular.

"In the kitchen." My sisters, Paula and Bernadette, yell back at the same time before dissolving into giggles. Sounds like they've been here long enough to enjoy the wine.

Heading in that direction, I'm met with a chorus of greetings. My mother pauses in the act of stirring apple sauce, tilting her head so I can drop a kiss on her cheek. "How are you, darl?"

"Excellent," I reply with a wide smile. I'll be even more excellent twenty-three and a half hours from now, when I'm due to arrive at Patrick's place. Not that I'm counting. "What can I do to help?"

Mum puts me to work slicing the roast while we all swap stories about what we've been doing over the last couple of weeks. Paula brings me a glass of wine, while laughing through the tale of a psycho budgie she treated at her vet clinic yesterday.

As I finish with the pork, Dad walks in, his arms loaded with a boxed cheesecake and two more bottles of wine. "Righto," he announces, lifting his burdens onto the counter, "you girls can quit complaining about the meagre reserves of alcohol in the house." Unscrewing the cap from one of the bottles, he hands it to Bernadette. "Never let it be said I don't provide for my family," he adds as he puts the extra bottle in the fridge. "Though the ways I'm providing get more dubious the older you get."

Words of thanks resound, glasses are refilled, and before long we're crowded around the same small dining table we've eaten at for as long as I can remember. The setting is complete with Mum's favourite white linen tablecloth and the old koala salt and pepper shakers we gave Dad as a Father's Day present back when all three of us kids were stilled aged in single digits. "These koalas are a true-blue piece of Australiana," he'd told us that morning, a proud grin stretched across his tanned face. "Totally irreplaceable." Late that night, after everyone went to bed, I'd sneaked into the pantry and scraped the *Made in China* stickers off the bottom with my thumbnail, so he'd never suspect the small figures weren't as genuine as he believed. I was twenty before it occurred to me, he'd known the truth all along.

"How's work going?" Dad asks me as we settle in to demolish the roast meal. "Are you doing more hours at the library yet?"

I shake my head, resigning myself to the same old conversation. "Still three days a week. I haven't asked for more."

"What about your web development business? Does it bring in enough extra work?"

"Yes, definitely," I tell him. "More work than I can handle sometimes." There are months when I work late into the night for weeks at a time. Then, I'll fall into bed for a few hours' sleep, only to be woken by my alarm so I can either head off to the library or go straight back to my computer. "I'd like to work less hours, but it's hard to say no to paying clients."

"Why don't you quit the library job?" Paula suggests, spooning extra apple sauce onto her pork. "You always said it was temporary. Besides, wasn't working for yourself the point of doing your IT degree in the first place?"

"Oh my god," Bernadette adds with a groan. "The number of times we were forced to listen to you go on about how you were going to design your own life and never fall for the day job routine like the rest of us plebs." She drops her head to one side, her tongue lolling out of her mouth as she makes gagging sounds.

"Yeah, yeah, I remember." Teenage me had been intensely enthusiastic about the idea of being my own boss—complete with the CEO job title and all the freedoms it implied. "I still like working for myself," I admit. "Choosing my own hours, having control over the kind of work I take on, that's all awesome. But working alone in my apartment, all day, every day. That part's not so awesome."

I started my business after moving out of the apartment I'd shared with Ben, taking on any freelance job I could get. Throwing myself into work seemed like a good idea at the time. It kept me busy enough I had little time to think about how much I missed Ben. Plus, I easily made enough money to support myself. Which wasn't a bad effort for a student who, technically, was still several months away from graduating. The downside was, I hardly ever left my apartment, except to go to the last of my classes and exams.

After graduation, it only got worse. I did nothing but eat, sleep and work. I'd pull all-nighters on a regular basis, only making it as far as the couch when I needed to sleep. Upon waking, I'd scoff down whatever food was available before starting all over again. That became my life for months. I was trapped in a prison of my own making, with no idea how to get out.

Then, one day, I went out to restock my fridge and ran into Naomi. She'd studied the same course as me and Ben, but we barely knew each other at the time. Her eyes had widened comically at the sight of me, right before she told me I looked like shit. She'd dragged me out to lunch, and we talked for hours. When she told me the library where she worked was hiring, it was like she'd brought me a lifeline.

I took it. It was the best move I ever made.

"At the library I get to be around people," I tell Dad, "and I enjoy the work." I'm lying about the second part, but I can hardly tell my father going out to work three days a week is the only thing standing between me and some sort of mental breakdown.

"Surely you'll need to choose one or the other eventually," Dad says with a concerned frown. "Do you know which direction you'd like to focus your attention on?" He's never made it a secret he'd prefer to see me making progress in some kind of singular career path. My parents are happy I'm supporting myself but, at the end of the day, they still see me as a part-timer with an insecure side hustle. It's not where they hoped I'd end up heading into my mid-twenties.

"No, I haven't decided yet." I've been using those same words for eighteen months now. They're starting to sound like stalling, even to me.

Patrick would never be so indecisive. He went from kissing a man, to launching a full experiment to investigate his own sexuality—all in the space of a week. That's the kind of man other men look for in a partner. Men with ambition, determination. Men who know what they want and go after it. Men like Patrick.

Maybe that's why I'm drawn to Patrick in the first place. Not only because I'm attracted to him physically. I admire him, the kind of man he is. His curiosity and his openness to new experiences. His willingness to constantly learn new things about himself and the world. No, my attraction to Patrick has never been purely physical. Everything about who he is draws me in.

By comparison, I'm just some wanker who can't even work up the nerve to take back control over his own career. There's not much to attract a long-term partner there. Sure, I can manage to dish out the kind of sex appeal that hooks men for a night. My looks get me through the door and my charm seals the deal. But when it comes to something deeper, and more meaningful, I've never been anyone's first choice.

After dinner, Dad and Bernadette head into the living room to watch the rugby match that's due to start at eight. They sprawl across the couches, arguing over the various players and which team will win tonight's game. I can't help but smile as I remember how many games Paula and I sat through when we were small, with a total lack of enthusiasm. Once Bernadette grew old enough to watch, she surprised us all by loving the game as much as Dad. Mum, Paula, and I had breathed a collective sigh of relief and sidestepped out of the room, never to return.

I put the kettle on while Paula hunts in the pantry for the biscuits and Mum finishes loading the dishwasher. A few minutes later, we settle in on the back patio. The sky is clear, and a smattering of stars manage to twinkle through the light pollution of the city. It's March, so the worst of the summer heat is gone, leaving a comfortable warmth in the night air.

"Maybe you should get another flatmate," Mum suggests out of the blue. Paula lives with her boyfriend, so Mum can only be talking to me.

"Why?" I ask.

She shrugs. "You were so happy when you first started sharing a place with Ben. And you said yourself, you took the job at the library because working at home was too isolating. That happened after you moved out on your own. Perhaps, if you got someone new to share with, it would help." She glances over at me with a nostalgic smile. "How is Ben these days? He was always such a nice boy."

Not too nice to fuck me over.

I grab a Tim Tam and bite off half, hoping the chocolate-coated biscuit will sweeten my mood. It's not like Ben meant to hurt me. He was doing the best he could at the time, same as me.

Paula sneaks a sympathetic look my way while Mum's attention is on me. My big sister is the only one in my family who knows the truth about what happened between me and Ben. They didn't even question it when

I told them I'd moved out of the apartment he and I shared for over a year. Ben was in love, after all. It was only natural he'd want to live with his girlfriend.

"I haven't seen him since we graduated. We're not really friends anymore."

"Nonsense," Mum scoffs. "You boys were inseparable most of your life. You should give him a call and reconnect. You don't throw a friendship like that away because you don't see each other for a year or two."

I take a sip of my tea, hoping to cover any betraying twitches in my facial expression. If Mum catches even an inkling of the pain that gutted me when Ben and I broke up, she'll be all over me like a rash—the comforting kind of rash that asks too many questions and adds looks of pity on top of the concerned ones she already throws my way.

"I don't have his number anymore." Because I deleted it. "We grew apart, Mum. It happens."

She tuts in my direction and sips her tea. "Well, you should at least think about sharing with someone new. I hate to think of you being lonely."

"I'm not lonely. Not anymore." At least I'm not lying about that. It took time, but working at the library exposed me to lots of new people. I became closer to Naomi than we ever were in uni, and then I met Patrick. Through him I became friends with Stacey and Ian. Plus, I've made other friends at the library. They're work friends rather than people I see socially, but they still count. "I have other people in my life now. I'm good."

Except I still haven't managed to put the rest of my life back together. Some part of me stopped trying after I moved out on my own. I still worked hard, but I stopped living. Taking the job at the library was like doing basic triage, it stopped my heart from bleeding out every other day, but I haven't made any real progress since then.

I've been stagnating for too long.

It's time to start living again.

DATA GATHERING

PATRICK

I frown at myself in the mirror. My hair is too neat. I shouldn't have gotten it cut. What if Logan notices? He knows I usually get a haircut before going on a date with someone new. But this isn't a date, this is a sex experiment. A sexperiment. I snort out a laugh and then groan as I smack myself in the head. What the hell am I even doing?

Forking my hands through my hair, I try to mess it up a little, make it look more relaxed. Except the damned barber cut it too short and now I'm stuck with it. There's nothing I can do.

Sweat trickles down my temple. Damn, I don't want to be all sweaty when Logan gets here, and he's due any minute. I strip off my t-shirt and grab a face washer. Wetting the small cloth, I wipe down my face before doing the same to my arms and torso. I dry off, reapply deodorant, and dab on a touch of my favourite cologne.

My stomach clenches and I wonder if I'll throw up. There! That's the feeling I expected to have when I kissed Logan for the first time. That twisting of wrongness and some sort of low-grade panic. If this feeling continues into the first kiss, I can call the whole thing off. Then, I can go back to being certain I don't like kissing men as much as I like *thinking* about kissing them, and this whole debacle can be over. Logan and I can go back to being friends and forget this ever happened.

There's a knock on the front door. My gaze snaps to the mirror. The idiot staring back at me looks like he's about to bolt through the bathroom window. Not a good idea, considering I live on the third floor.

Shutting off the bathroom light, I grab the first decent shirt I see in my closet and pull it on, doing up the buttons as I approach the door. I stop with my hand on the knob and take a single deep breath to try to slow my breathing. Panting is not a good look, at least not this early in the evening.

I open the door. Logan stands on the other side, casually sexy in a black t-shirt. His hands are tucked into the back pocket of his jeans and there's a predatory gleam in his eyes. "Hey," he says with an up-nod.

The trembling in my limbs goes nuclear. I open my mouth to speak but can't manage anything more than a croak.

Ignoring my lack of greeting, he rakes his gaze over me. "Aww, you dressed up for me," he gushes, his smile widening.

"What? No, I didn't." Looking down, I see the button-up I'm wearing. It's white with an intricate pattern of blue flowers. Classy, but casual, I often wear it—on first dates. I bite back a groan, my eyes squeezing shut.

Logan's light chuckle snaps my eyes back open. He's still standing on the far side of the doorway, because I have yet to let him in. Clearing my throat, I take a step to the side.

"Don't worry. I think it's sweet." He gives me a condescending pat on the cheek as he walks past and my face burns with embarrassment.

Closing the door, I lead him into the kitchen. "Are you hungry? I got us some dinner." A half-dozen freshly delivered Chinese takeaway containers sit in a bag on the counter.

"You didn't have to, but I can't say I'm sorry you did," he replies, rubbing his hands together. "Thanks."

"You're welcome." I take out plates and cutlery and we start dishing up the food. "I figured this would be easier if we acted like it was any other night. Takeaway. Maybe a movie. The same shit we've done heaps of times. Then we can relax, and it will be easier to…" My throat closes up and I choke on the remaining words.

"Easier for me to seduce the fuck out of you?" Logan finishes for me. His tone holds no hint of hesitation or embarrassment or anything. But then, he has no reason to hesitate. He's gay. Being a seducer of men is part of who he is. It must be nice to know for sure.

At my lack of response, he glances in my direction. I'm still frozen, staring at him with my mouth open, my stomach turning somersaults at his words. Not the throwing up kind of somersaults, though. The other kind. The electrifying kind that got me into this in the first place.

"I think it's a great idea." Logan winks, right before sliding a prawn cracker between my parted lips. "It's okay to be nervous, you know. But you don't have anything to worry about. It's just you and me. We don't even have to do anything tonight if you don't want to. There's no deadline for this. No need to rush. Okay?"

The tension in my body loosens at his words. I don't know what I thought would happen. It's not like Logan was going to come through the door and jump me like a mugger in a back alley. Someone else might have, but not Logan.

A fresh wave of gratitude rushes through me at his easy acceptance of however this plays out. "I'm glad I'm doing this with you," I tell him.

His head lifts, and there's a softness to his gaze as he swallows. "Me, too."

We return to dishing up the food and then put the leftovers in the fridge.

"What would you like to watch?" Logan asks as he leads me into the living room. He gestures at me with his fork. "Maybe we should watch a horror movie. I can wrap my arms around you when you get scared. It could be a full-on high school moment."

I laugh as we sit on the couch. "Did you ever do that to anyone in high school? Because I didn't. It's a lame move."

"All right then, pick some kind of twisted drama with lots of dark sex scenes. That should get you in the mood."

"What about your mood?" I ask, lifting an eyebrow at him.

He turns to look at me, and the predatory gleam is back full force. "Honey, I was in the mood the second you opened the door."

Multiple jolts of pleasure hit me. One for his words. Another for the heat of his gaze. The last one, which is softer and more tingly, can only be attributed to the unexpected term of affection. It's a pleasant surprise, though I know I'm supposed to be concentrating on the first two.

Without a word, I pick up the remote and turn on the television.

We settle on a dark thriller. I have no idea about the prevalence of the sex scenes, but it has some big-name actors and is supposed to be good. Making ourselves comfortable, we start eating as the opening credits play.

An hour later, we've finished dinner and dumped the empty plates in the kitchen sink. The movie is good, drawing us in, and I've managed to relax into the evening.

This is more like us. Hanging out on my couch, enjoying each other's company. Except, this time there are a few minor differences. Usually, Logan sprawls on one end of the couch with his bare feet up on the coffee table. Usually, I'm at the other end, my legs tucked up on the couch between us. There's still sprawling going on, but this time Logan is closer to the middle of the couch. He's dragged my legs over his lap and wrapped one large hand around my bare ankle. The other hand is resting on my upper thigh. It's not moving. Not stroking or caressing or edging closer to any particular erogenous zones. It's just there, on my thigh—as if it belongs there.

The touch is subtle enough not to freak me out, but different enough to make my body stir with curiosity.

It's not until Logan's gaze meets mine that I realise I've been staring at him. I don't know how long that's been going on for, but I think it's been a while. Leaning over to grab the remote, he turns the volume of the movie down until the voices are little more than a murmur in the background.

This is it. This is the part where he'll kiss me. He hasn't kissed me first before, despite all his teasing and innuendo. So far, it's always been me who's initiated the physical contact. I'm hoping that's about to change. The swooping in my stomach is nothing like nausea. It's anticipation. It's excitement.

He rises up to kneel on the couch. When he rearranges my legs, putting one on either side of his body, I let him. I want to know how he wants to do this. Putting his hands behind my knees, he pulls me further down the couch, until my head is resting on the cushioned arm. With a low hum of satisfaction, his leans over me, one hand on either side of my head, his arms straight. The outside of his thighs brush against the inside of mine as he kneels between them.

He seems so large as he holds himself above me—all big and masculine. If he lowers himself on top of me, he'll be heavy. Too heavy? I'm not sure. I'm not exactly a lightweight myself, but he has more muscle than me, and a little more height. I don't want to feel trapped.

"Are you still nervous?" His murmur is low, intimate.

"No." I don't think I'm lying, but I'm no longer sure which emotions motivate the trembling in my limbs. But I do want him to do this. For now, that's all I need to know. "I have kissed you before."

Full lips twist into a salacious grin. "I remember." He lowers his head, stopping when our faces are still several centimetres apart. "You're a good kisser."

Huffing a breath, I lift my hands and place them on the sides of his torso. His sudden intake of breath gratifies the part of me that wants him to be into this—into me. "You're a good kisser, too." My body shifts restlessly beneath him, my hips curling instinctively because, holy hell, I want him to hurry up and kiss me already.

"You think maybe that's all it was?" he asks, teasing me still. "We're both exceptional kissers and therefore it was inevitable we'd end up with matching boners to show for it?"

"I don't know." And that's the brunt of it. I honestly don't know. "Maybe it was a novelty that's worn off."

"Oh, but baby, there are so many more novelties we haven't even tried yet." His voice is ripe with the possibilities and my imagination rushes to fill in the blanks. "I want to show you what you've been missing."

My hips lift clear off the couch, seeking contact. "Yes. I want—" My throat closes and the words cut off.

What if this doesn't work? What if I get what I think I want, and then I don't want it anymore? With a stricken groan, I lower myself back to the couch. "Logan, I don't know if I can do any of those things." Shame ignites on my cheeks and I cover my closed eyes with one hand. "I'm sorry. I want to, but I've never—"

"Hey, stop right there." Logan's voice is soft, gentle. His lips nuzzle my cheek and, despite the unpleasant swirling in my gut, I turn in to his touch. "Let's back up to the kissing part," he murmurs against my skin. "I've been looking forward to kissing you again. Everything else can come later."

I swallow hard, opening my eyes. Logan is still kneeling between my thighs, his body held away from mine. Only our faces are close together as his barely-there lips make their way along my jaw. "We have to get through tonight before we can commit to a later." I hate the resignation in my tone. The expectation of failure. I didn't get this far, with this man, only to give up before we even begin. "But yes, I'd like to go ahead with the kissing part."

Logan chuckles against my neck before lifting his head. "Okay."

"Good." I smile up at him.

He licks his lips, before bringing his mouth in line with mine. "Do you trust me, Patrick?"

"I trust you." My heart hammers in my chest and I can't control my breath. "Please."

Logan's lips brush against mine and I whimper in relief. "You're safe with me," he whispers. "I promise, I won't let you fall."

LOGAN

I lower my lips to his, taking his mouth with slow, careful intent. Gentle, but without hesitation. Thorough, but without hurry.

Whatever happened to Patrick in the past, I know he's wary. If this goes badly, if he has any hint of a negative experience with me, he's going to bolt. If that happens, I have a feeling he'll never open himself to this again. I'm not anywhere near ready for him to shut me out. Not before I get my fill.

Our lips part briefly. "Good?" I murmur. His panting breath rushes across my face as he nods. His body is a live wire, shuddering beneath me. I would think it was fear if it weren't for the eagerness in his wide eyes and the way his mouth is still open in invitation. His hands are fisting my t-shirt on either side of my waist, tugging me downward, but not hard enough to actually move me. He wants this, but he's not sure what will happen when he gets it.

"Let's try something," I whisper, trying to keep my own breathing under control. "Tell me if it's too much too soon."

Another nod.

Moving slowly, I lower my full length on top of him. My hips nestle between his parted thighs, my chest touches his. I keep my elbows underneath me, so he

112

only takes part of my weight on his chest. But from our bellies down, we're flush against each other.

Patrick's eyes close and his head tilts back. A sigh escapes him as his body accepts my weight. After a short while, the shaking eases and he seems to relax.

I hold still, watching his face for any sign of reluctance. His skin is flushed, hot. The faint scent of cologne fills my nostrils and a lazy grin curves my lips. Patrick is hopeless when it comes to knowing the difference between a date and a hook-up. But it's not a problem. As long as I remember what we're doing here, we'll be fine.

Trailing kisses over the ridge at the front of Patrick's throat, I lick my way up to his ear. "You feel good," I tell him, wanting him to know how desirable he is. With any other man I might mutter words about how hard he makes me or how badly I want to fuck him, but this man… he needs to be handled with care. Again, I'm filled with relief that I'm the one holding him. The thought of anyone else touching him like this, knowing how skittish he is, fills me with a fierce sense of possessiveness. No one else, no one but me.

Patrick groans, his body restless beneath me, and I realise my hips have instinctively started to move, rocking slowly against his. The hard ridge of his arousal is evident between us and I press down harder. When he bucks against me, I moan out a curse and fall upon his mouth.

Before long, we're grinding against each other and if I don't get some skin soon, I'm going to start tearing at his clothes.

"Patrick." His eyes open when I whisper his name. They're heavy-lidded now, the earlier wideness drenched in arousal. "Can I touch you?" As I speak, I slide one hand beneath his shirt, stroking his chest before coming back down to dip my fingertips beneath the waistband of his jeans.

He stares up at me, a faint sheen of perspiration on his upper lip. "Yes." The ragged sound of his voice sends shivers down my spine.

I make quick work of removing his belt and undoing his jeans, but when I try to tug them down further, the cramped confines of the couch hit home. "Maybe we should move this to the bedroom," I suggest with a sly smile, "it will be more comfortable."

Patrick sits up suddenly, shaking his head as he backs away from me. "I don't—" His gaze darts across my body, never reaching my face. "We're only supposed to—" A harsh laugh spills and then he clears his throat. "You're skipping like five sessions."

Backing off, I turn to sit properly on the couch, my hands on my knees. "It's okay. Here is good, too." I keep my voice light, but my gut clenches at my thoughtless mistake. "You're safe with me."

He growls in frustration and moves closer, climbing onto my lap to straddle me. "I know that. I'm not afraid of you, Logan." Cupping my face, he tilts my head back and kisses me, his tongue delving deep into my mouth.

Confusion wars with lust as my hands slide up his thighs until I'm gripping on to his denim-clad arse.

When he releases me, I frown up at him. "Then what are you afraid of?"

"I don't want to stop. Which means we can't go too fast. If we do... it's like a switch gets flipped inside me, and suddenly I can't get away fast enough. I've tried to fight it and get past it. I've never managed it... until I kissed you."

I don't get it, but I suppose I don't need to—at least, not right now. "In that case, I guess you'd better kiss me again, and maybe do whatever else you feel like doing."

He smiles down at me before leaning in for another kiss. Within seconds, we're back to moving against each other. When Patrick reaches between us to undo the buttons of his shirt, I follow his lead, reaching back over my head to drag my t-shirt off. The instant hands meet skin something changes. What was tentative becomes demanding. Gentle caresses turn to clutching and raking.

"Logan," Patrick rasps against my mouth. "How are you doing this?"

I'm not entirely sure what he thinks I'm doing— other than getting off on him. My cock is like a steel rod in my jeans and every time he grinds his arse down on me it threatens to undo me.

Patrick's hands undo my jeans and then he thrusts one hand inside. His long fingers wrap around my throbbing cock and I cry out at the heat of the contact.

"I want to see you." He crawls off my lap, dropping onto his knees in front of the couch. Before I have a chance to catch my breath, he's tugging at my jeans and boxers at the same time. Dazed, I lift up so he can yank them down and off my legs. He tosses them aside before coming up onto his knees, drinking in the sight of my naked body.

My hard cock bobs gently against my stomach, jerking under the heat of his gaze. He reaches out a hand and wraps his long fingers around it. I hiss in a breath. "Fuck, yes."

A wondrous smile settles on Patrick's open mouth as he explores, stroking me at varying speeds, altering the pressure he uses, until finally he hits upon a combination that has me full-on keening.

"You like that." He sounds so proud I can't help but chuckle.

"I definitely like that." Sitting forward, I reach for him. "Now get naked and get back here so I can find out what you like."

Patrick stands, without hesitation this time, and removes the remainder of his clothes. Leaning over, I grab my jeans and retrieve a packet of lube from my wallet, tossing it onto the cushion beside me. When I'm resettled on the couch, Patrick climbs back onto my lap.

My hands wander his body, but my gaze is locked on to the thick, straight cock nestled in dark curls. My mouth waters, but I know it's too soon to get a taste of him. We need to begin at the beginning. For Patrick, the beginning involves hands more than mouths. I can work with that.

I start by trailing my fingertips up his length, smiling when he groans and bucks up into my touch. Encouraged, I circle my hand around him in an ultralight grip that barely brushes against him.

"Fuck, Logan." He's gritting his teeth, his own fingers digging into the skin of my shoulders. "Please."

Wrapping my free hand around the back of his neck, I pull his mouth to mine at the same time I grip him tight. Every one of his moans tastes like freedom. I've wanted to touch him like this for so long. Even when I didn't allow myself to think about it. Even when I pretended my longing for him was under control.

I tug him further onto my lap, so our cocks are pressed together, before reaching for the packet of lube. Tearing it open, I drizzle the cool liquid over the heat of his cock before doing the same to my own. Tossing the empty packet aside, I wrap my hand around both our straining erections and start jerking us together.

"Holy hell," Patrick shouts. His hands are wrapped around my neck and head. His forehead is pressed against mine as he jolts and shudders in my lap.

I stare at his face, taking in every expression, each defining pleasure.

Muttered curses and babbled nonsense spill from his lips between open-mouthed kisses and swipes of his tongue. "I'm gonna… Fuck, so close…"

"Yes," I hiss into his mouth, my hand moving faster. Our sweaty bodies jerk against each other as we climb to the peak. "Give it to me, Patrick." The words are an order, a command. "Give me your come."

He buries his face in my neck as he begins to shudder. I throw an arm around his back, holding him close as jets of white erupt between our heaving bodies. First his, then mine. We continue to clutch at each other as our combined pleasure spills between us, and for long moments after.

Finally, his body goes limp in my arms. I collapse back onto the couch with Patrick sprawled on top of me. My arms come around him, holding him to me as our breathing returns to normal. Turning my head, I press a light kiss to his forehead.

After a while, he stirs, lifting his torso away from mine to reveal the sticky mess between us. "Okay," he says with a quiet laugh, "that's a little gross."

I can't help but snort at the distaste on his face. "I don't know about that." I run two fingertips through our combined pleasure. Lifting one, I place it into my mouth, sucking lightly. Watching him, I offer him the other. "A little taste," I tell him. "To try it."

He hesitates, and I think he's going to refuse. Then, holding on to my gaze, he reaches out with his tongue and licks the very tip. With a quiet sigh, he takes my finger into his mouth and swirls his tongue around it, thoroughly cleaning it, before drawing back again.

"Not so bad?" I ask with a questioning look.

"Can't say the taste is overwhelming me," he declares, before leaning forward to kiss me, "but I like the way you made the offer." More kisses, and his mouth is hot and giving as it moves against mine. When our tongues meet, he makes soft sounds of appreciation.

Drawing back, he looks into my eyes and grins. "It's official, I enjoy kissing you." The way he says it... it's an announcement, a conclusion. This part of his question has been answered.

I chuckle, my hands sliding up to the top of his thighs, taking in the feel of him while I have the chance. "Maybe it was the Chinese food." I draw my brows down into a questioning frown. "Are you sure it wasn't the Honey Chicken making you horny? I know all about your sweet tooth."

"Pretty damned sure." Snorting, he climbs off my lap and heads for the hallway. "If anything about this is going to turn me off, it's not going to be your mouth."

My smile dies as I hear the bathroom tap come on. Patrick's still waiting for the moment this all goes wrong. It's not a question of if for him, but when. When will he hit his limit? When will we reach the point where my touch makes him want to pull away?

I promised him I'll be okay with it if it happens, that I won't get angry or frustrated. When I made that promise, I wasn't thinking about how much it might hurt.

Patrick returns with a couple of warm wash cloths. We clean up in silence and put our clothes back on. Sitting on the couch, I start to put on my shoes.

"You aren't going to stay to watch the end of the movie?" Patrick asks as he drops down beside me.

He runs a hand over my back, and I resist the urge to lean in to his touch. I want him touching me, but letting him do it when we aren't in *experiment mode* is bad for me.

"I can back it up to the part where we got... you know... distracted."

I finish tying my laces and glance back at him over my shoulder. His smile is wide as he relaxes back against the couch cushion, one foot propped up on the coffee table. He looks freshly satisfied and all kinds of gorgeous. That hand of his is still trailing absently across my back.

My eyes narrow and I throw a smirk at him. "You're a snuggler, aren't you?"

"Excuse me?" he cries in amused indignation.

"Admit it. You like to snuggle after sex."

He huffs out a breath, avoiding my gaze, an expression of thorough guilt on his face. "Are you saying you don't?"

The truth is, I love nothing more than a post-orgasmic snuggle. If this were real, I'd already be wrapped around him, content to watch the end of whatever movie we were pretending to watch.

But this isn't real. One of us needs to remember that and, apparently, it's going to have to be me. Because I'm the one with the hopeless crush, not him.

"I've um... I've seen it before." I didn't mention it when he suggested the movie because, let's face it, I didn't give a crap what we watched. All I cared about was getting him to relax to the point where I could seduce him without him turning tail and running the other way. "You should watch the end though; it's got a killer twist."

He puts on a fake smile. It looks nothing like the real one, but at least it matches mine. "Okay. I'll, umm... I'll walk you out."

"I guess this means the experiment will continue to session number two?" I turn to look at him when we reach the door.

Reaching for the knob, he opens the door. "Yes, definitely." His face flushes and, while I want to kiss the redness off his cheeks, I can't. The session is over, and we have to go back to friend-mode now. Goddamn, this is hard.

And kind of awkward. I didn't expect that.

"Let's have lunch together on Thursday," I suggest. "Do the friend thing. Yeah?"

He nods and I'm relieved to see the return of a genuine smile. "That would be great," he says. "Same old, same old. Right?"

"Exactly." Because that's the ultimate goal here. To go back to the way we were before. Hopefully, doing the things we usually do, as friends, will help us keep sight of that. "I'll see you then."

We stare at each other. The subtle movements of his body tell me he wants to kiss me goodnight. If he'd done that last time, when he faced the same dilemma in my car after our first kiss, I would have let him. I would have given him anything he wanted. But the rules have changed—literally. I can't allow it now.

"Goodnight, Patrick," I tell him on my way out the door.

PATRICK

I hate sitting in the backseat of my brother's car for these long drives down the coast. The tiny two-door hatchback might be an economical choice, but the extra leg room provide by a four-door would have been worth the extra dollars in my opinion.

"You'll survive, princess." Charlie laughs as he watches me fold my six-foot frame into the pint-sized space.

I glare at him. "I don't know why we can't take my car."

"Because it's *my turn*," he insists. "You've been driving us down to Dad's place for years. I'm contributing."

As much as I appreciate the sentiment, the only thing this miniature death-trap is going to contribute to is my future need of a physiotherapist.

Penny, Charlie's girlfriend, gets into the passenger seat in front of me and pulls it forward a notch. "Is that better?"

It's not, but it's nice of her to try. "Thanks, Pen."

Charlie settles himself behind the wheel. "And we're off," he announces cheerily.

We've been driving down to the Gold Coast for our monthly lunches with Dad for years—ever since I got my driver's licence. It's always been a good chance for the three of us to catch up. Plus, Dad's house is right on the beach. That's always been a pretty big draw card.

I knew Charlie was serious about Penny when he asked if we would mind her joining us one day. That happened two years ago, and she's now a regular addition to our small party.

Settling into a semi-comfortable position, I rest my head back against the seat and close my eyes. Logan came over for our third experimental session last night. It ran later than the first two, on account of my growing inability to stop kissing him once I get started. My enthusiasm, coupled with his willingness to indulge me, has left me with a serious need for sleep—and some minor beard burn.

"I managed to find a tent we can borrow for the festival next month," Charlie says to Penny a while later. "One of the guys at work is big on camping." The quiet tone tells me they think I've fallen asleep. I wish. At least a snooze would stop me feeling the growing discomfort in my cramped legs. "Two whole days of sunshine and live music. It's gonna be awesome."

"I'll say," Penny replies. "I can't wait to get out of the city for a couple of days. Will the tent be big enough to fit all four of us?"

"Should be." Charlie's voice drops to a low murmur. "I only wish I could have gotten my hands on two tents. Our friends are great, but some privacy would be nice."

Penny gives a low hum and I open my eyes a little. She's reached out a hand to stroke the back of Charlie's neck, her fingertips playing with the ends of his hair. "Don't worry. I'm sure we can sneak away during the day. At night you'll have to settle for snuggles though."

Snuggles. The word immediately brings my mind back to Logan—who is definitely not a snuggler. At least, not with me.

We've enjoyed three sessions in three weeks and every one of them has ended on a similar note—with Logan keen to find the exit. It shouldn't matter if he doesn't want to hang around once the objective of our time together has been achieved. The ground rules certainly don't cover post-sex etiquette, and it's not like we're trying to establish any sort of lasting emotional intimacy here. Even so, I can't help but think a few extra minutes to enjoy the feel of his skin while the glow fades wouldn't hurt.

The whispering in the front seat continues, punctuated by the occasional giggle from Penny, until finally I release a longsuffering groan. "Do you two mind saving the lovey-dovey nonsense for a time when I'm not already uncomfortable?"

Turning around in the seat, Penny puts a hand over her mouth as she looks at me. "Sorry."

"I'm not," Charlie says, tossing a shit-eating grin over his shoulder. "You're just jealous because you can't hold on to a girlfriend to save yourself."

I shrug. He has a point. Robyn was my longest relationship by far, at less than two years, and I've barely even dated since I broke up with her more than six months ago. It's not that I haven't been open to finding someone new. I simply haven't met anyone who seems like they'd be a good fit for me, and I don't see the point of dating a bunch of women I already know I'm unlikely to get along with long-term. But then, as it turns out, the next person I date doesn't necessarily have to be a woman.

Staring vacantly out through the front windshield, I wonder aloud, "Maybe I'll have better luck holding on to a boyfriend."

The car jerks as it speeds up suddenly. Charlie slams on the brake. We all lurch forward and Penny gives a sharp squeal. The car narrowly avoids rear-ending the truck in front of us. Behind us, a horn blares.

"Fuck!" Charlie yells once the car returns to a normal speed. There's a long moment of utter silence before Charlie clears his throat. "Excuse me, brother, could you please repeat the part about you having a boyfriend?"

"That depends," I say, still holding my crash position, "are you going to total the car if I do?"

"You don't toss shit like that out when I'm driving, you great dick." He's still yelling, though I'd lay odds it has more to do with the adrenaline surge of his near miss, than it has with my absentminded comment. "You're my brother, I'm supposed to know if you're gay!"

"I'm not gay." Running my hands over my face, I collapse back against the seat.

Penny turns around, so she can look at me. Her face glows with excitement. I have no idea why. "What are you, then? Bi? Pan? Demi?"

Rolling my eyes, I offer her my hand as if in greeting. "I'm Patrick. It's nice to meet you."

Undeterred, she skips to a new set of questions. "Who's this boyfriend? Will we like him?"

"I don't have a boyfriend. Okay?"

Charlie groans out loud. "Then why did you say you did?"

"I didn't. I only implied I could, at some point in the future, potentially decide to have a boyfriend."

Penny's eyes narrow as she continues to stare at me. She's settled in sideways in her seat now, her legs folded beneath her. All signs of an imminent interrogation. "Nobody just decides to potentially, maybe, possibly have a future-boyfriend. You have someone in mind."

"No, I don't."

"Patrick." Charlie sounds calmer now. He's using his big brother voice on me, which is entirely inappropriate considering I'm three years older than him. "What's going on?"

"I kissed a friend of mine to satisfy a bet I lost. It wasn't a big deal, except..."

A feminine gasp sounds. Penny's neck has flushed pink. She may or may not be coming in her seat at this point. "You liked it!"

Fighting a grin, I nod. "I really, really did."

"Who was it?" they ask at the same time. Always in sync, these two.

"Logan Delaney. You've met him."

Penny claps her hands with another squeal while Charlie barks out a laugh. "That's fantastic," she says, glancing at my brother. "We love Logan. Don't we, babe?"

"We do." He looks at her with an affectionate smile before glancing at me in the rear-view mirror. "So, what, are you two dating or something?"

"Not dating," I say, shaking my head. "More like... testing the waters."

Charlie's face turns sour and he groans out loud. "Patrick, please tell me this isn't another one of your stupid experiments."

My mouth opens, but it's not like I can deny it. "All right, yes. This is, literally, one of my stup— I mean, one of my experiments."

"I'm confused," Penny says, glancing back and forth between the two of us. "What experiments?"

"It's some weird idea he became completely obsessed with after Mum and Dad split, about how he can use self-experimentation to figure out all the secrets of the universe or some such rot."

Tilting her head to one side, Penny frowns. "You mean like that doctor who injected himself with syphilis to see what would happen?"

"Nothing like that," I assure her.

"Exactly like that," says Charlie at the same time. "And you know what happened to him, don't you?"

Penny snorts a laugh. "He died."

"Of fucking syphilis!" Charlie finishes.

128

Groaning loudly, I roll my eyes at him. "If I promise not to inject myself with anything, will you shut up?"

"Hey." He glares at me in the mirror before returning his attention to the road. "I was forced to share a house with you when you were deciding whether or not you liked mainstream music." He gives Penny a tortured look. "He played nothing but Taylor and Kanye for a week."

"Spoiler alert," I tell her. "I'm not a fan of either." A week was about five days too long.

"Well, I think it's admirable for a man to put so much effort into self-awareness," she announces. "Most guys don't have a clue who they are or what they want—other than boobs." She lets out a laugh. "Most men are happy with boobs."

"I'm happy with boobs," I murmur. Though I'm beginning to wonder if boobs should make me happier than they do. Because, as it turns out, Logan's penis makes me really freaking happy—like, ecstatically happy. Did boobs ever make me that happy?

"This experiment you're doing," Penny says, interrupting my thoughts. "What's going on there?"

"Again, it's not a big deal. Logan's helping me figure out if I'm bisexual." The thought of Logan's hard cock jerking in my hand as he came last night makes me want to lick my lips. "Or, I guess at this stage I'm figuring out how far down the spectrum I fit."

"But it's just sex?"

"That's the idea." I'm not sure sex with a good friend can ever be *just sex*. But we are planning to go back to being *just friends* at the end of it so… I figure it's kind of the same thing.

"Will that answer your question though?" She looks sceptical about the whole thing.

"What do you mean?"

Her gaze drifts upward and I can tell she's figuring out how to explain. "I know you and Logan are good friends," she says, "and if you guys are getting it on and you're having a good time, great. I say go for it."

"Buuut?" I let the word drag because she's barely getting started.

"But if this is about discovering who you are as a person, then fooling around with the guy you hang out at the pub with every Friday night isn't going to get you very far. You need someone you can bond with on a deeper level."

"Why? Logan and I are bonded just fine." It's not like I go around bonding with guys every day. Logan is the first new friend I've gotten close to in years. I lucked out with him.

Penny sighs in exasperation. "There's a lot more to a relationship than physical attraction, you know. There's intimacy and sharing. Being there for each other."

"I absolutely agree," Charlie pipes up. "Penny and I are connected on a deeply spiritual level. It's about way more than sex."

Penny slaps him on the arm. "Babe, please shut up. You can earn brownie points later."

"I get what you're saying," I tell her, "but I'm not looking for Logan to be my boyfriend. Neither of us wants that." Logan obviously has no interest in heading in that direction with me. For my part, my knowledge of myself is clearly still too nebulous for me to even think about getting serious with anyone. It would only end in disaster.

"So, maybe you should consider finding someone else to do this with." She throws her hands in the air. "How will you know what this new experience truly means for you, if you spend the whole time messing about in the shallow end of the pool? Take a chance, Patrick. Give yourself the opportunity to fall in love, even if it doesn't happen." The manic light in her eyes matches the giddy grin. "That's how you'll find out who you are. When you find the right person and go all in."

I don't want to go all in with anyone but Logan. He's the reason I'm asking these questions in the first place. It makes sense for me to find the answers with him.

"I'll think about it," I tell Penny. I have no intention of taking her advice, but at least my words should put an end to the conversation.

She smiles and whispers, "Good luck," before turning back to face the front of the car.

Staring out the window, I watch the scenery as I ponder the points she made. Logan and I aren't *that* close, I suppose. We've spent heaps of time hanging out together, but it's not like we sit around talking about our feelings or delving into past traumas. We're guys. We don't really do that.

But we've shared stories from our lives and supported each other at the end of a few rough days.

We may not have been there for each other on any deep and meaningful levels, but I haven't exactly suffered any great emotional upheavals in the year since we met. Neither has he—that I know of. He would tell me if he needed anything. Wouldn't he?

There's still so much I don't know about him. Stuff I've never thought to ask. I could ask though. I could reach out to him in ways I haven't before and see how he responds.

Friendships can be equally as intense as romantic relationships. It's a psychological fact. If Logan and I did develop a stronger bond, we'd be able to keep that aspect of our relationship, even after we remove the physical element.

I'm meeting Logan for lunch again on Thursday. He's been insistent on us having contact outside our weekly sessions. I think it's his way of reminding us both we have a friendship to hold on to beyond the experiment. It will be the perfect opportunity for me to test the waters of my new approach. He'll either respond in kind, or he'll back away. Either way, it will give me an indication of what kind of friendship he wants with me after the experiment is over.

LOGAN

We meet for lunch at the usual time, in the usual place. Only Patrick's greeting is different.

Before the experiment, he and I rarely touched. We did exchange the odd back-thumping hug if we hadn't seen each other for a while, but those times were few and far between. Generally, our physical contact has been limited to handshakes and the occasional whack to get each other's attention.

So, when Patrick moves in for a hug as I approach, my body instinctively locks up.

We're not supposed to have sexual contact outside experimental sessions. It's one of the ground rules I'm counting on, to keep us both in line. Maybe Patrick can still touch me without having all sorts of sexual reactions, but I can't say the same. I want him. All the time. In all the ways.

He keeps the hug short and casual, but apparently it's still enough for him to feel my resistance.

"Sorry." He avoids my gaze as he backs away, sliding his hands into his back pockets. "New habit. I'll try not to let it stick."

"It's fine." I shake my head, hoping to dismiss the sudden awkwardness between us. "I'm just hungry, I guess. Have you ordered?"

"Not yet. Figured I'd wait for you."

We join the lengthy line at the counter. This is the most popular cafe at the university, thanks to the large outdoor eating area and its lush garden boxes, so it takes a while to reach the head of the queue. We start chatting as we wait and then, after ordering, we make our way to a vacant table. By the time the food shows up, the conversation flows easily, and I laugh as Patrick tells me about his near-death experience at the hands of his brother.

"I'm surprised you told him about us," I say when he finishes his story. Except, there's no such thing as *us*. "About the experiment, I mean."

"Why wouldn't I?" He bites down on his toasted sandwich, as if telling his brother about the sex experiment he's undertaking with his friend is standard road trip conversation.

"Do you always discuss your sex life with your brother and his girlfriend?"

"I didn't discuss our sex life," he scoffs. "I only mentioned we're seeing each other, in an experimental capacity. It's not like I gave them details."

I snort. "If it was one of my sisters, the knowledge it was happening at all would already be too much information."

Patrick shrugs a shoulder. "Not saying anything would have felt like hiding, which I'm not willing to do. Besides, Charlie is family, he doesn't give a crap if I'm bi. All Penny cares about is making sure any potential future boyfriends are suitable for double dating."

Ignoring the possibility of Patrick dating men who aren't me, potentially or otherwise, I choose to focus on the part about the double dating. "I have vague memories of you doing that when you were with Robyn."

"Yeah, we did, but not often. Robyn and Penny didn't get along so well."

My eyebrows raise at his admission. Granted, I wasn't keen on Robyn either. Though, I had my own reasons for feeling that way, which had little to do with the woman herself. "Penny's so easy-going. I can't imagine anyone having trouble liking her."

"They didn't dislike each other. It was more like their personalities didn't mesh." He laughs as he puts his empty plate aside. "Penny told me a while ago she used to drink more when the four of us went out together because she found it easier to talk to Robyn if she was half-blitzed. She said me breaking up with Robyn saved her from cirrhosis."

I laugh out loud. "Sounds like Penny."

"Yeah," he agrees. "She loves you, though. So, you can imagine how excited she got when I told them it's you I'm using to explore this whole thing with."

"Stop, darling," I deadpan, "you make it sound so romantic."

He gives me an apologetic look. "You know what I mean."

"I do." There are reasons why Patrick decided to go into research, rather than focusing on a face-to-face specialty, like counselling. Foot in mouth disease is real—and he has it.

"I have to say, though," I add with a smile, so he knows I'm not offended by his poor choice of words, "being used by you is a lot of fun."

He huffs out a relieved laugh. "Most fun I've ever had."

Our gazes meet and the air between us grows heavy with the memories of all we've done with each other— and anticipation of all we have yet to do.

"Maybe we shouldn't talk about the experiment when we're in friend-mode," I suggest.

He grimaces, breaking the eye contact. "Is it weird?"

"More like… uncomfortable." In fact, the discomfort is getting to me right now. I shift in my seat, attempting to relieve the pressure of my zipper pressed against my thickening cock.

Heat sparks in Patrick's gaze as it drops to the parts of me hidden below the table. "I'm right there with you," he admits with a smirk. "Okay. No touching and no talking about sexual relations over the lunch table. Got it." Silence falls, but his mouth is still moving. There's something else he wants to say. I wait a full minute for him to speak again.

"Before we move on completely," he begins, "I wanted to ask you something. It is kind of about sex, but it has nothing to do with me or the experiment." He sucks in a big breath, so he can keep going. "It's something I could as easily have asked you before all the other stuff began. But if you'd prefer not to answer, I completely understand."

I frown. What kind of question could possibly be worth such a longwinded introduction? "How about you ask and then, assuming you don't pass out, I'll decide whether or not to answer."

"Okay." Instead of laughing at my joke, he gives a serious nod. Perhaps he really will pass out. "When did you realise you were gay?"

Staring at him, I shrug. "That's it? That's your question?"

"Yes." Again with the serious. I have to break him out of that.

"There was this guy in high school," I tell him. "Me and a couple other people stayed at his place one night after a party. It was late, everyone else was asleep. We were sitting out on his back patio finishing a bottle of wine he'd stolen from his mum's wine rack. We were kidding around, talking about some girl he was dating. He wondered out loud what it would feel like to get a blow job. I offered to give him one."

Patrick's mouth falls open. "Just like that?"

"Just like that," I confirm. "Didn't even hesitate. One taste of cock and I knew I'd be a homo for life."

He bursts out laughing. "Seriously? That's your big, gay revelation story?"

"No, not seriously." I throw a wadded-up paper napkin at him. He's still laughing, but now it comes with added confusion. "Well, yes, that really happened, and it was pretty damned spectacular—for me anyway."

My so-called friend freaked out after coming in my mouth and avoided me from then on. "Why are you asking me about this all of a sudden?"

He sobers instantly. "I suppose I thought it might help me figure out my own situation. Also, I've realised lately how much I don't know about you. I figured I should make more of an effort, as a friend. That way, when the experiment ends and we take away the physical stuff, we'll have more to fall back on than Friday night bar hopping and games of pool."

"Huh." I suppose I can see where he's coming from. Strengthening our friendship can't hurt, and it could help when we do eventually go through the trauma of ending the experiment and retreating to friend-mode permanently.

Patrick's certainly not the first friend to ask this question. I've never hesitated to answer before.

"Here's the truth," I tell him, leaning forward across the table, "for some people it is a sudden and profound revelation. For others, there's no revelation at all; it's something they've always known. For me, it was more like a lot of little clues that added up to one big truth." Patrick's gaze is riveted to my face as he listens, his earlier amusement forgotten. "It can come from meeting the right person, where gender ceases to matter. Or it can be a sudden understanding brought on by an experience." I give him a pointed look. "Of course, that only happens if it's an experience of—"

"Seismic proportions," he finishes for me.

"Exactly." After a short pause, I add, "The point is, everyone's story is different. The same way every childhood is different, every love story is different, every friendship. The commonalities are there, but you can't compare one story to another, that's not the way it works." I meet his gaze, wanting him to know I understand if he's struggling, and it's okay. "Your story will be different, too. But it will be important, Patrick, because it will be yours."

He releases a deep breath. "Thank you. I appreciate you sharing with me."

My answering nod is slow and deliberate. I'm glad I made the choice to open up to him. "Anytime."

A wide smile curves Patrick's mouth and he reaches for my hand, his fingers curving around mine.

My skin burns at his touch and I flinch, jerking away.

We both freeze, staring at his empty palm on the table between us. Rejection sours the air. His fingers curl into a loose fist before he withdraws.

"I need to get back to work," he murmurs, standing to push his chair in.

I follow suit and we leave the cafe.

"You'll be at Stacey's dinner thing tomorrow night?" I ask as we reach the point where we usually part ways. "She's invited me and Naomi."

"Yes," Patrick replies. "I'm bringing dessert." There's a short pause. "And you'll still be at my place on Saturday night?"

Turning my head, I catch a glimpse of uncertainty before he looks away. I hate that I've hurt him, that I've made him doubt me, but we're walking a dangerous line here and I'm the only one who knows better than to cross it.

"I'll be there," I tell him. "Nothing could keep me away."

He gives a sharp nod. "Good." With a quick goodbye, he rushes off in the direction of his office.

I make my way back to the library, shaking myself free of the tension of the past hour.

Lunch with Patrick is way more complicated than it used to be.

PATRICK

W hen I arrive at Stacey's the following night, I hold tight to the large, plastic container I used to transport dessert. Having my hands full is the perfect excuse to avoid any sort of physical greeting with Logan, and I'm not about to let it go. After my repeated screwups yesterday, I don't want to give him more reasons to be uncomfortable around me.

"I'll put this in the fridge for you," Stacey says, attempting to relieve me of my burden.

Evading her hands, I suggest an alternative. "How about I do that, while you pour me a drink?"

She shrugs a shoulder. "It's a deal. Let's go." With a wave of her hand, she leads me in the direction of the kitchen and I fall into step behind her.

Stacey lives with some housemates in an old house. The kitchen is a separate room of its own, but we still need to pass through the living room to get to it. And there's Logan, sitting on a couch chatting to Naomi.

"Patrick!" Naomi jumps up and bounds over to me. Completely disregarding my plastic body armour, she lifts onto her toes to touch our cheeks together with an air kiss. "It's good to see you."

"You, too." I smile at her before my gaze shifts to Logan. "Hey."

He gives his usual up-nod. "How's it going?" His tone is casual, but his eyes drink in every part of me.

"Good." An awkward silence settles in, before I raise my burden a fraction. "I'm gonna go deal with this," I mutter, before escaping to the kitchen.

Ian arrives soon after and we gather around the table for dinner. I make sure to sit diagonally across from Logan, so there's no chance of us bumping limbs under the table by accident.

We all launch into a variety of conversations, laughing and talking over each other. That is, until Ian decides to get nosy. "How did your experiment go, Patrick?" he asks during a lull in the conversation. "Did you get the answer you were after?"

All movement at the table ceases as four sets of eyes stare at me. Three of them curious, the last crinkled in amusement.

Chewing the food in my mouth, I manage to swallow before replying. "I'm still gathering data."

Ian pulls a face. "It's been a month. How much data do you need to decide if you're queer?"

"These things can't be rushed," Stacey tells him. "Going too fast would only mess everything up."

"That's not always true." The pique in Naomi's voice draws my attention. Her lips have tightened into a thin line and her body is tense. "Caution has its place, but sometimes we have to say *fuck it* and take a chance."

The two women stare at each other. Logan, Ian, and I look between them. We're definitely missing something.

Finally, Ian turns to Logan. "You're the other half of this experiment. What do you reckon? Is Patrick playing for team bi?"

"No point asking him," Naomi grumbles before Logan has a chance to reply. "He's refusing to provide details."

"Because it's none of your business, Na," he insists, not looking at me.

"You told her about our first kiss," I point out. After that, I figured he told her everything. "When I lost the bet."

Naomi shakes her head. "Nope. He only told me he kissed someone he shouldn't have." She stabs a piece of carrot. "It didn't take a genius to guess the someone was you."

"Why?" I ask, frowning. "Was I that obvious a choice?"

Logan shakes his head. "No."

"Yes," Naomi says at the same time.

"How about some dessert?" Stacey jumps up from her chair and starts to clear the empty dishes. We all rush to help, showering our hostess with compliments about the meal.

"I'll dish up the dessert," I tell Stacey after everything is delivered back to the kitchen. "You go sit."

She shakes her head. "I'm not letting you do it all by yourself."

Logan lifts his head as he and Ian put the last of the stacked dishes in the sink. "I'll give him a hand."

I look at him. He looks at me.

Naomi eyes us both off before clapping her hands together. "Excellent idea. You do that and we'll go polish off the last of the wine." She coaxes the other two out of the room, going so far as to close the door behind her.

"Thanks, Na," Logan scoffs. "That wasn't obvious at all."

With a snort, I take my plastic container out of the fridge while Logan hunts down some plates and forks. He joins me at the counter as I lift the cake plate out of the container.

"Damn," Logan says with delight, "that looks good enough to eat. What is it?"

"Black Forest Cherry Cake," I tell him proudly. "I made it this morning." My cake looks nothing like the picture on the website where I found the recipe. I had to use frozen cherries on top for a start, and their juice bled all over the freshly whipped cream. Then, my attempts to add shavings of dark chocolate around the sides of the cake resulted in weird clumps where there should be a delicate scattering. "Not the most attractive cake in the world," I say with a shrug, "but I tried."

Logan's grin is as lopsided as the swirls of cream I couldn't get right. "Well, the good thing about cake is, it doesn't matter what it looks like, it always tastes delicious."

I return his smile, my insides bubbling with pleasure. That's one of the things I've always admired about Logan. He goes out of his way to make other people feel good about themselves. A kind word here, a small gesture there. He sprinkles that shit around like it's confetti. It's part of what makes him such a great friend.

"Can I have the slice with this cherry?" He points to the largest cherry on the cake.

I fight a laugh at the idea he wants a particular part of my cake monstrosity. "You can have that cherry."

We dish up the cake, with me cutting and Logan lifting the plates to accept the slices. I do my best not to touch him as we work, but there's only so much I can do when we're standing this close. He doesn't seem to notice me shuffle a little further away each time our arms brush together.

After we're done, I put the leftover cake back into the fridge and wash my hands. Picking up two of the plates, I head towards the dining room.

"Can we talk for a second?" Logan asks from behind me. When I turn around, he's leaning back against the counter with his arms crossed, his face pensive.

"Sure." I put the plates back down and stand beside him. "What's up?"

He turns his body to face me, swallowing hard before he begins. "I'm sorry about yesterday. The way I reacted... when you reached for my hand."

Then again, maybe he did notice me going out of my way not to touch him more than necessary. Yep, I'm that subtle.

"I've been trying to stick to the ground rules we set," he goes on. "You took me by surprise, and I reacted without thinking. I don't have a problem with you touching me." He huffs out a laugh. "Quite the opposite."

Grinning at his confession, I decide to add one of my own. "It's harder than I thought it would be. The whole *no contact outside experimental sessions* rule."

My hand is resting on the counter and Logan places his there too, so our fingertips are only a few centimetres apart.

"Why is it hard?" he murmurs.

Licking my suddenly dry lips, I try to find a way to explain. "It's like, now I'm conscious of not being able to touch you, unless we're doing the experiment, it's only made me more aware of you. So, I end up thinking about touching you more than I ever would have if I'd never made the *no contact* rule in the first place."

Logan smiles and uses his fingertips to walk his hand closer to mine. Now, if either of us was to stretch our fingers out, we'd be touching. "Is this your roundabout way of telling me not being allowed to touch me makes you want to touch me more?"

"No." The response comes too fast—it's a reflex. I force myself to consider the real answer. "Maybe," I say in the end. "All I know is, suddenly I can't touch you at all without wondering if I'm doing the wrong thing."

"The rule doesn't say no contact at all," he points out. "It only says no *sexual* contact." There's a roughness to his voice that wasn't there before, an intimacy in the way he steps closer to me. "If you were to touch my hand right now, would that count as sexual contact for you?"

My gaze snaps to his. He's standing so close and my heart begins to race. Heat trips across my skin. Blood pulses in my groin. "It really would," I breathe, overwhelmed by my response to him. "Would it count as sexual contact for you?"

His grin is wide and unabashed. "Hell, yes."

A violent shiver runs through me and his chest rumbles with a deep sound of satisfaction. But then, he closes his eyes and steps away. "And it's probably better if we keep our hands to ourselves." His head tilts to one side and his lips quirk upward. "At least until tomorrow night."

Heaving a sigh, I let my head fall forward. Logan's chuckle is low as he drops an affectionate kiss on the top of my head.

"Come on," he says, loading up on dessert plates, "let's feed the masses."

I nod, hoping my arousal will calm before anyone notices. Logan waits by the door while I pick up the extra plates and follow.

We manage to get the door open and walk back into the dining room—and stop dead. Turns out, Logan and I weren't the only ones taking advantage of a few minutes alone.

Naomi is back in her seat at the table, only now Stacey is straddling her lap. Their bodies are pressed together, breast to groin, while hands roam and mouths devour. The sight is hot as hell and does nothing to relieve my arousal problem.

Logan recovers from the shock first, speaking loud enough to make our presence known. "I don't think these two have a *no contact* rule."

Stacey gives a loud squeal of surprise as she scrambles backward off Naomi's lap. She starts to fall, and Naomi reaches out to grab her, but overbalances. They land together in a tangle of limbs before Naomi glares up at us. "Have you heard of knocking?"

"It's a dining room," Logan replies with a laugh. "You were supposed to be expecting us to come back."

She tuts in disgust. "That's no excuse for such an ill-timed interruption."

Ian barrels in through the doorway to the other hall—obviously on his way back from the bathroom. "I heard a scream. What did I miss?" His gaze darts from us to the women. He takes in Naomi's mussed hair and the redness of Stacey cheeks as they pick themselves up off the floor, before returning to Logan and me in the doorway with plates of cake in hand.

"Damn it!" He throws his hands in the air, gesturing to Naomi and Stacey. "Now you two are gonna start dating as well? I'm on the verge of being the fifth wheel here people and I don't like it." He stomps across the room to snatch a plate out of my hand before dropping into a chair at the table. "I need to get a girlfriend."

"We're not dating," Logan says, gesturing between the two of us as we all sit down to eat cake. "Still just friends."

I resist the urge to roll my eyes. Ian knows we're not actually dating. Everyone in the room knows we're not dating. Heaven forbid someone forget. If they did, Logan would be sure to remind them. Holy hell, I'm not that bad a catch.

Naomi looks at Stacey with a hopeful expression. "Are *we* dating?"

I've never seen Stacey smile the way she is now, her face glowing with happiness. "I think we are," she whispers.

"Really?" Naomi stands, pulling Stacey upright into her arms.

Stacey releases a long breath and cups Naomi's face in her hands before pressing a light kiss to her lips. "I have a girlfriend," she says with wonder in her voice. Spinning around, she faces the rest of us with an enormous grin. "Everyone, Naomi's my girlfriend." The words burst free in a rush of excitement.

We all cheer and the two women laugh out loud before stealing another kiss.

Before long, the five of us are settled back in around the table, eating dessert as we celebrate the new couple among us. Naomi and Stacey hold hands. They look at each other with the joy of newfound love in their eyes. The stark contrast between Stacey's situation, and my own, has never been more apparent. She's shown a willingness to throw herself into her experience. There has been some hesitation, sure, but she hasn't held back the way I have. And she certainly hasn't used logic and science to analyse every feeling and second-guess every reaction.

Maybe it's time for me to stop letting the experiences of the past have control over my present. What do I have to be afraid of, anyway? That I'll hit my limit? That Logan and I will finally do something that turns me off the way I've been turned off by men in the past? I've never gotten this far with anyone else, and I'm beginning to suspect my desire for Logan may be limitless.

There's only one way to find out. It's time to start pushing further outside my comfort zone. I want Logan to know how good my touch can be.

LOGAN

I barely make it through the door before he's on me. His mouth slanting against mine, his tongue pushing between my parted lips. Hands shove the hem of my shirt up, delving beneath to rake blunt fingernails across my skin.

Hissing in a breath, I pull him against my already lengthening cock. "Hello, to you, too," I manage to gasp between kisses.

His reply is muffled as he trails wet kisses across my neck and down my jaw. By the time he returns to my mouth, he seems calmer, though his arms are still locked tight around me, his body restless against mine. "I've been thinking about this all day," he whispers, his panting breath warm on my face.

A deep-seated satisfaction unfurls inside me. "Show me, Patrick." I lick at his lips, easing between them to touch the tip of my tongue to his. "Show me everything you've been thinking about."

Heat flares in his eyes, but instead of kissing me again, he bites down on his lower lip and backs away. "Soon." Taking my hand, he leads me into the living room. The scent of roasting meat is heavy in the air. I would have noticed it sooner if I hadn't been otherwise occupied.

I glance at the dining table to see it's set for two. Nothing flash. There are no romantic whims by way of flowers or candlelight. He's definitely planning to feed me, though, which is more than any hook-up has ever done. I never pictured food as part of the experimental process, but Patrick does keep providing and I'm not about to turn down a homecooked meal.

"Honey," I drawl, teasing him. "You cooked for me."

"I did." Walking into the kitchen, he gets a bottle of white wine from the fridge. "Would you care for a glass?"

My eyebrows lift, but then I nod. "What happened to alcohol being off limits?"

With a shrug, he cracks open the bottle and pours a generous glass. "I think we can ditch the idea I was only into you that first night because of the vodka." Handing me the glass, he pours another for himself—even more generous than the first. "I'm into you, even when I'm stone cold sober. So, why not relax and enjoy ourselves?" He takes a long sip before looking at me again. "Besides, sometimes a little lubrication makes it easier to do what we already want to do, but are reluctant to ask for."

The words are my own, said to him the night we started this. Hearing them now makes my cock ache. What is it Patrick wants to do? Whatever it is, I already know I'll enjoy it, wine or no wine.

Holding his gaze, I stalk around the bench to join him in the kitchen, stopping when we're toe-to-toe.

Lifting the wine bottle, I add a little extra to his glass. "By all means, drink up. I'm pretty damned sure I'm going to want you to get what you want—whatever that may be."

He trembles in front of me. His eyes wide and his lip parted. I can hear the soft panting of his breath and I want to kiss him again, right now. Say forget dinner, and strip him naked. Do wicked, wicked things to him that he hasn't even thought of yet.

But he cooked. Which tugs at my heart in ways sexual favours can never touch. Damn, I'm in so much trouble.

"Can I help with dinner?"

He releases a shaky breath and I know whatever it is he wants, he's not quite ready to ask for it. He needs time and I'm going to give it to him. At this point, I'd give him anything.

Dinner turns out to be chicken, complete with roasted potatoes and steamed vegetables. It's delicious. We both devour every morsel with murmurs of appreciation. We talk as we eat, chatting about what we did today, and arguing over which of us was the first to realise Stacey and Naomi would get together eventually. It's easy and relaxed, the same as it's always been.

This is the reason we became friends in the first place. Not because the sight of him made my mouth water from the moment we met. Not because I suspected he secretly got off on watching me make out with guys. We became friends because we enjoy each other's company.

I'm glad we haven't lost the easy friendship we've built over the past year. But I'm reminded why I need to be careful about how this whole thing progresses. Because as much as I enjoy being part of Patrick's journey of discovery, this right here is what I'm trying to protect. Our friendship.

We clear the dishes together, and that's when the energy between us starts to change. One minute we're laughing, tipsy on the bottle of wine we finished a little too fast. The next, we're standing on opposite sides of the small kitchen staring at each other.

"Thank you for dinner," I tell him, my voice rough with lust. I can hear the sound of my own breathing. It quickens when he smiles at me.

"You're welcome." There's a look in his eyes now. He's reached the place he needs to be. He's ready for me.

I lick my lips as he approaches, one step at a time. It doesn't matter what he wants. I'll give it to him. Any experiment he wants to conduct. Any barrier he wants to breach, he can do it with me. And I will want it. Because I'm his. Fuck, I'm done for.

"I want to try something." He's standing right in front of me now, but refuses to meet my gaze. I would think him reluctant, if he hadn't gone to so much effort to get us here. "I don't know if I can go through with it." His voice is so quiet I can barely hear him.

"You mean, you don't know if you want to?" I suggest, hoping to clarify his thinking. "You might not like it?"

He nods, his head lowering. "It won't be because of you, though. If I don't like it. I just..." He runs his hands up my arms, squeezing my biceps as if he wants to comfort me.

Cupping his face, I place a light, gentle kiss on his lips. "It's okay if you want to stop," I tell him. "That's the whole point of this, right? You wanted the chance to try things out, find out what you do and don't like. You're not going to like everything, and you're not going to hurt my feelings if you stop. I want you to feel free to try."

He sinks forward, resting his forehead on my shoulder as his arms find their way around my waist. With the lower half of his body pressed against me, I can tell he's only semi-erect. He's afraid of this. I don't ever want him to be afraid when he's with me.

"Hey," I brush my lips against his neck, wrapping my arms around his shoulders so I can hold him close. "There are so many ways we can enjoy each other. You're not going to like all of them. That's not a bad thing."

With a heavy sigh, he lifts his head to look at me. "Why are you doing this for me?" he asks quietly. "What are you getting out of all this? And don't tell me it's curiosity. I never bought that bullshit."

I'm baffled by the question. The force of the orgasms I've experienced with him this past month have left me boneless, speechless, utterly incapable of thought—every time. How can he even ask me such a question?

"I get the chance to have you," I tell him, "and you are worth having. Any and every way I can have you. But only if you like it as much as I do." Patrick smiles and I grin back at him. "Plus, I really don't trust anyone else to take care of you the way I do," I add, trying to play down the possessiveness that will not be denied. "That part is still true."

He doesn't respond with words, but I see the appreciation in his gaze—the love. It's the love of one friend for another, maybe, but it's love all the same. I'll take it.

"I want to suck you off."

My body reacts without conscious thought. Arms gripping him tighter, my eyes close as my mouth falls upon his. I usually work up to this type of kiss. Where our tongues are filling each other's mouths. Where we clash in a fury of teeth and spit and lust. These are the kisses that are supposed to come after we're already insane with the need for each other. But I can't stop, not with those words echoing in my head. I want this. I want my cock in his mouth. I want his cheeks hollowing as he sucks the life out of me. But he might not like it. He might try it and decide it's not for him. I have to keep myself under control.

"I take it you like the sound of that?" He tugs me with him towards the living room until we're in front of the couch, the place that has been home base for every one of our experimental sessions.

"Yes," I rasp. I can feel my hard length pressing against the confines of my clothing, desperate for freedom, desperate for him. "I want to fuck your mouth."

Patrick's groan comes on the back of a gasp. As if he wants it, but is shocked to want it. He's always so surprised by this side of himself. I've never understood why. But that's a conversation for another time.

Reaching for my belt buckle, he pulls it undone and pushes my pants down, taking my underwear with them. My cock springs free, eager and weeping for him. He stares at it for a long moment.

I hold still, letting him look, letting him take his time. Even so, he darts a nervous glance at me. "Don't push me down, okay? Let me do it at my own pace."

My hands curl into fists as rage ignites. Whoever made him feel it necessary to make such a request, I want to break them. Tamping down on the sudden anger, I look Patrick dead in the eye. "I will never push. You only do this if it's what you want. You know that, right?"

His throat moves as he gulps. "With you I do."

I kiss him again, only this time it's a kiss of reassurance. As thorough as our earlier kisses, but slower, more comforting.

He pushes me back onto the couch and I land on the cushions with a whoomph. I have no time to react before he's falling to his knees in front of me. He pulls my shirt off and then yanks my hips forward until I'm half-reclined on the couch, my cock swaying hopefully in front of him. My knees are parted, but my ankles are still bound together by my pants and underwear.

Patrick leans over me, his gaze intent on my cock. He's staring it down like it might attack him. Apart from slapping him in the face, there isn't much it can do other than sit up and beg. It does so prettily.

Leaning down, his tongue emerges to lick the tip, lapping at the pre-come glistening in my slit. Chest heaving, I grit my teeth and resist the urge to buck up into his mouth. This isn't about me. This is about Patrick trying something new, preferably without me choking him with my overly eager prick.

He swirls his tongue around the head, trying different angles and pressures. My cock moves at his command, batting at his tongue, leaking for him, begging for more of his tremulous attention.

By the time he licks the broad flat of his tongue up the underside of my aching cock, I'm trembling. Sweat trickles down my left temple and the odd whimper escapes me without permission. I'm desperate to feel the inside of his mouth, to be engulfed by him. But I can't ask for it. He has to want it. He has to be the one to take it.

Then his mouth encases me, and I give a shout of pure exaltation. He closes his lips around me, halfway down my shaft, before slowly drawing back up and off me. He does it again, opening his mouth wide each time he takes me in, so I only get half the effect. The fourth time, he pauses while I'm still deep inside his mouth, swiping his tongue along the length of me, caressing me with wet heat. Frustration curls my hands into fists at my side, I want to feel him sucking me. Still he does that engulf and slow withdraw.

I have to cut him some slack. He's never given a blow job before. But seriously, I need some suck or I'm going to blow a fuse here.

"How am I doing?" A smirk betrays his amusement at the way I'm fisting the couch cushions and trying to swallow instructions on how to give a proper fucking blow job. It hits me. The bastard is driving me insane on purpose.

"You're doing great," I grit out, wearing a cocky grin, "for a beginner."

He laughs out loud, rising on his knees to catch my mouth in a wet kiss. "Let me try something different," he teases. "Maybe you'll enjoy it better."

Dropping back down, he wraps his lips around the head and proceeds to suck a single inch of my wet cock into his mouth. His cheeks hollow as he pulls back up, lips still clamped around me like a vice. He takes another centimetre on the next downward stroke. Then, another. And another. Finally, he pauses to hum loudly around my now throbbing length. The vibrations ripple through my entire body, and I can't help gripping on to his short hair with one hand. Not pushing, just holding.

Patrick reaches down to undo his own pants before wrapping a hand around the base of my shaft. He starts jerking me off in time with his mouth. The steady movements of his other arm tell me he's getting himself off, too.

"Fuck, yes," I mutter in a throaty whisper. "Like that." I can feel my orgasm building, ready to blow like a goddamned geyser. "Holy fuck, Patrick."

He shudders as he comes, and his long moan has me shooting my own load without warning. I know I should feel bad about not giving him a chance to pull off if he wanted to, but he gulps down every drop without hesitation. When we're finally done, he drops his head onto my thigh, nuzzling his face against my groin as he releases a long, contented sigh.

My hand strokes his cheek and a smile lingers on my face. That was fucking phenomenal. He may like to torture me, but he sure does make up for it in the end.

PATRICK

This is usually the part where Logan bolts.

He tries not to be obvious about his need to escape, but I've learned to read the signs.

He's always relaxed and mellow right after sex. The curve of a smile on his lips and his eyelids heavy. Then something will happen. I'll turn in to his side or kiss his shoulder. He'll wrap an arm around me, pulling me close. Just as we're getting comfortably entangled, he stiffens, as if realising what we're doing. Within minutes, he's dressed and out the door.

I try not to let it bother me, but I can't help wondering what the problem is. The women I've been with always seemed to enjoy my post-coital affections, as I enjoyed theirs. I know it's not strictly part of the experimental process but, damn it, being held after sex feels good. Why shouldn't we enjoy it?

A covert glance at Logan's face confirms he's still in the mellow phase. It's lasting longer than normal. That could be the effects of the alcohol. Or maybe I sucked his brains out through his dick. I stifle a snort, liking the second option better.

His eyes snap open at the muffled sound. I swear, I can see the instant his brain engages.

I lurch upright, beating him to the punch. Pulling off my t-shirt, I use it to clean the drying come from my hand before doing up my pants. He gets dressed as well, but when he starts to push up from the couch, I wag a finger at him.

"Don't even think about it," I tell him as I go into the kitchen to get us some water. "You've been drinking. You need to hang out at least another hour before driving home."

Sighing, he drops back against the couch cushions. "You're probably right."

I hand him a glass and sit back down, leaving a good half a metre of space between us. We're quiet for a while, as we drink our water.

"You could crash here tonight, if you want." I'm not sure why I make the offer. It's probably inappropriate given our situation. But I don't want him to leave.

He doesn't respond, but I can sense the sudden stiffness in his sprawl.

"It's not a big deal. I have a big bed and I promise not to snuggle." The last is said with an edge of amused sarcasm, though it's a promise I intend to keep—at least while I'm awake.

Lapsing back into an awkward silence, I mentally curse myself for even making the suggestion.

"Okay." The word is quiet, half choked in Logan's reluctance. I turn my head to look at him. His lips twitch. "I'd say *no homo bro*, but I'm totally a homo, so..." A few seconds of dead silence elapse, before we both burst out laughing.

We get up from the couch, ridding ourselves of the now broken tension.

"You mind if I take a shower?" Logan asks.

"No problem." I grab him a fresh towel, toothbrush, and a pair of my pyjama pants, and leave him to it.

I finish cleaning up the kitchen while Logan showers, then take a quick shower of my own after he's done.

Before I know it, the light is off and we're lying side-by-side in my bed under the covers. I wasn't lying about the size. It's a king. We don't need to come anywhere near each other if we don't want to.

I want to. But I know Logan doesn't.

"Thanks for letting me crash," he says, his voice reaching out to me in the darkness. "I should have stopped drinking after the second glass."

"It's fine. I wanted you to enjoy yourself."

He huffs out a laugh, turning onto his side to face me. "Mission accomplished."

I smile, even as my body reacts to the memory of his dick filling my mouth. I never expected to enjoy it so much. The feel of him, steely hard and yet velvety soft at the same time. The smell of him. The sounds he made as he came. "Thank you, for tonight." I turn my head towards him on the pillow, but his facial features are barely visible in the dark room.

"You're thanking me for being on the receiving end of a blow job," he points out, and I can hear his smile even if I can't see it. "You know how crazy that sounds, right?"

"I mean for not pushing me, for being patient."

The space between us grows heavy with the weight of his questions, though it takes time for him to form the words. "Patrick, can I ask you something?"

I know what he wants to ask. This has been coming since the beginning. I'm only surprised it's taken so long for him to get around to it. "Ask."

"What happened the first time you tried to figure out if you're bisexual?"

Sighing, I sit up in the bed and reach for the lamp on the bedside table. Dim light floods the room, making us squint momentarily.

"It's fine if you don't want to talk about it," Logan says as he pulls himself upright. "Not like it's any of my business."

I give him a look. "Of course it's your business. You've been in this with me every step of the way. Besides, it's not like it's all traumatic or anything."

He raises his eyebrows at me. "Are you sure? It turned you off the idea of even kissing a guy for years. Clearly someone hurt you, or scared you, or something."

"No, no, no. It wasn't like that." Phantom hands grab at the back of my head and I clamber out of the bed, running my hands through my hair to dispel the sensation. "Maybe it could have been bad, but I stopped it before anything like that could happen." I'm standing beside the bed now, my arms crossed in front of me. "I didn't like it, that's all." I shrug, as if it's no big deal. It wasn't a big deal. "I just didn't like it."

"Patrick." Logan's voice is calm, gentle. He's sitting up against the headboard, looking all gorgeous with his bare chest and the covers twisted around his hips, and he's watching me with those hazel eyes that see everything and accept it all without hesitation. "Why don't you start from the beginning?"

My head bobs as I nod—repeatedly. "I can do that." I lick my lips, moving back and forth on my feet as I begin. "When I was in Grade 9, I had a major crush on this girl in my class, Carla," I tell him. "She was gorgeous, with a great body and long, shiny hair. Plus, her laugh sounded like bells ringing. That shit killed me." I give a small chuckle at the memory. Yeah, I would have given up my wanking arm for the chance to kiss Carla. "That should have settled it, right? I was into girls, one hundred percent."

Logan's smile is knowing. "Except?"

"Except, then there was Jimmy Peretti." I grin as I say his name, though he's probably long forgotten mine. "Carla and Jimmy were dating, and I caught them making out backstage once during drama. I remember sitting there with a clipboard covering my lap because, naturally, spying on them gave me a massive hard-on. But the strange part was, I couldn't help noticing the way her hand stroked the length of his arm and wondering what his bicep felt like. Then, I wondered what it would feel like to have his body against mine, how his mouth would taste if I kissed him. Apparently, my dick was one hundred percent into him, too." My face is warm as I sneak a look at Logan. "When I realised I didn't know which one of them I wanted to make out with more, I decided it was time to ask myself some serious questions."

My heart rate has slowed, and I feel calmer. This is easier to talk about than I thought it would be. I climb back onto the bed and sit facing Logan with my legs crossed. "It was this enormous revelation for me, and I spent the next few months playing around with the idea. I checked out boys as well as girls, to see how I reacted to them. When I jacked off, I'd allow my mind to wander wherever it wanted to. It went back and forth between boys and girls, never quite getting stuck on either one."

"You weren't scared at all?" Logan asks. "About what it might mean? How people might react?"

"Not really." I shake my head. "I knew my family would be okay with it and I thought it would be kind of cool, actually. I figured it would give me twice as many people to choose from when I started dating but I still didn't know for sure because I'd never so much as touched a guy. Not like that, anyway." I thought I'd like it, but how could I know for sure?

"I tried some subtle flirting with people I liked at school, but only the girls ever responded. I mean, it's not like guys were going around announcing they were gay, or bi, or whatever. No way was I going to be the first—especially when I didn't even know for sure if it was true. What was the point of outing myself if I turned out to be wrong? Right?"

Logan looks like he wants to argue with my logic. Instead, he pushes the covers away and moves towards me, crossing his legs so we mirror each other, our knees almost close enough to touch. Resting his elbows on his thighs, he clasps one of my hands between both of his, bringing it up to press a kiss against the back of my fingers. "What happened, Patrick?"

He can tell I'm getting to the not-so-fun part of the story. And he's expecting the worst, I can hear it in his voice. He's going to feel silly when he realises nothing bad happened to me. It really wasn't a big deal. Which is why I was so convinced I'd hit upon the right answer.

"Okay, so my chance finally came about halfway through Year 11. I was sixteen years old, pissed off about my parents' separation, disillusioned with the whole damned world, and hornier than an antelope in mating season."

Logan lets out a laugh. "Sounds like fun."

"Exactly," I say, nodding. "My friend Crystal threw this birthday party and it got a little wild. Crystal was one of those girls who was active in everything. Not just school, but sports and music, the whole bit. So, this party was full of people I'd never met before." I pause for a second, swallowing. "Mark was one of them."

"Mark." The name falls from Logan's mouth with mild disdain. "I hate him already."

I huff a short laugh. "Yeah, well, I didn't end up liking him either. Although, I didn't know that until... well, later." I thread my fingers through Logan's, playing with them absently. "It was hard not to notice

Mark. With his shaggy brown hair and green eyes. He was close to me in size. Athletic, beautiful." So beautiful my gaze kept searching him out and every time it did, he was staring right back at me. "You asked me that first night if I had a guy type. I do, and he was it." I glance up at Logan. "Then again, so are you."

He waggles his eyebrows at me, and I smile. Dropping my gaze back to our joined hands, I take a deep breath before I continue my story. "The way he watched me, like he couldn't take his eyes off me, it made me all antsy and uncomfortable. I couldn't think straight, couldn't concentrate on what my friends were saying." I frown. "It confused me because I didn't know if I liked the way he was being so obvious about it, eyeing me off in front of everyone. But I didn't know if I disliked it either." I release a sharp sound of derision. "The semi in my underwear had already cast its vote.

"Eventually, it got to be too much. My hard-on was getting worse and I was scared someone would notice. I used my jacket to cover myself and muttered something to my friends about needing to use the bathroom before taking off." The words are coming faster now and I'm snatching breaths of air in the spaces between. "I didn't know he'd followed me until he pushed into the bathroom behind me and locked the door."

Logan waits silently as I collect my thoughts. His hands are on my knees now. Not moving or squeezing, just resting there. The simple touch grounds me here in the room, with him.

"I didn't object," I tell him. "I was glad he followed me. It was exactly what I'd been waiting for. The perfect opportunity to get an answer to the question that had nagged at me for well over a year: Am I into guys or not?" An echo of that old exhilaration shoots through me. At the time, I knew the anticipation for what it was. It's only now I recognise the panic that bled into it.

"I figured I had maybe ten minutes to get my answer. At least sixty teenagers were crowded into the backyard and we were in the only available bathroom. It wouldn't be long before someone needed to take a leak."

"But hey, no pressure," Logan scoffs, eyes widening with disbelief.

"No, it was the ideal situation," I insist. "Long enough to get the answer I needed, but not long enough to get carried away and do something stupid with a total stranger."

Logan holds his breath, waiting. "What went wrong?"

"Nothing went wrong, exactly. I mean, he was an arsehole but..." I don't know how to explain it. The way I'd wanted it to happen, or thought I'd wanted it... until I got it. "He just... he came at me too fast. I didn't have a chance to think... and then his tongue was inside my mouth and one of his hands was grabbing at my dick. I know my hips bucked up against him so I guess part of me must have liked it, but he was crushing me against the bathroom wall, and I couldn't breathe."

I can't look at Logan, but my hands clutch at his where they still grip my knees. He's squeezing hard and I know he's pissed. But there's no reason. It wasn't that bad. I just didn't like it.

"I told him to stop and he did stop kissing me, but his body still trapped me against the wall. And it was weird because my hands were on his chest and I remember liking the way his muscles felt under my fingers. I wanted to touch him, but I didn't want to set him off again, you know?"

Logan is rigid in front of me, his lips pressed into a thin line, but when I look at him for reassurance he nods. "It was confusing. I get that."

"Right, exactly," I say, releasing a long breath. "I asked him to slow down because I'd never kissed a guy before. He thought that was pretty funny. He started going on about how guys are so much more fun than girls." I bark out a laugh. "Can't say I agreed with him, but I figured that's what I was there to find out and I'd never know if I didn't try. So, I started kissing him again." I meet Logan's gaze, wanting him to understand. "I wanted to like it. He was hot and I was willing. I should have liked it."

"But you didn't," Logan finishes for me.

I shake my head. "He kept grinding against me, and I could feel how hard he was through his jeans. But I wasn't hard anymore and it was kind of uncomfortable. Not that he noticed, he was too busy shoving his tongue down my throat." I grimace, swallowing around the lump lodged there. "When he pulled away, I thought we were done and I could leave, but then I heard a noise and realised he was undoing his belt buckle."

Logan swears under his breath, raking his dark hair away from his forehead.

"Don't freak out, it's not that bad." I don't know why my hands are shaking. Nothing bad happened to me. It wasn't a big deal. Logan needs to know that. I don't want him to think it was more than it was. "It wasn't that bad."

I keep talking, but I'm not really there with Logan anymore. I'm locked in a tiny bathroom with a guy I don't know. The faint clink of a belt buckle fills my ears and, when I try to jerk free, my head bangs against the wall. "What are you doing?"

Mark bites down on my lower lip, just hard enough to hurt. "I want you to blow me," he growls. The rough timbre of his voice is supposed to turn me on. It's happened before with guys. Not this time.

"No." I shake my head. "I'm not doing that."

"Come on, Patrick. You've thought about it haven't you?" He's got his cock out now and he's stroking it slowly. "You've wondered what it would be like?"

"Yeah, but..." I glance down at the flushed head before looking away, my stomach churning. I do not want to put that in my mouth.

"Don't worry." He wraps a hand around the back of my neck. "I'll return the favour later." He doesn't yank that hard, but it's unexpected and I go down. Pain shoots up through my knees as I land on the hard tiles.

"Whoops," he says with a chuckle. "Sorry about that." His fingers are gentle as they stroke my cheek before sliding down to grip my chin. "Open wide."

The tip of his erect dick prods at my closed mouth, trying to push its way inside. My jaw stays clamped shut. I know I'm supposed to want this. I've jacked off thinking about it. The reality isn't anywhere near as appealing as I thought it would be.

I turn my head away. A thin string of clear liquid stretches between my lips and the tip of Mark's penis. Pre-come. My gut lurches and bile rises in my throat. I manage to swallow it back down as I scramble to my feet. Rubbing at my mouth with the back of one hand, I glare at Mark. "I said no."

"All right, all right." Rolling his eyes, Mark tucks himself back into his jeans. "You don't have to be so dramatic about it. What did you think we were gonna do in here, drink tea?" He looks at me like I'm some kind of halfwit. "Are you into guys or not?"

I pause to take stock. The boner I struggled with earlier is long gone. I'm hovering at least two metres away from the hot guy I came in here to make out with. If the room were bigger, I'd happily increase the distance. I don't want to kiss him anymore, and I sure as hell don't want to do anything else with him. In fact, right now I'm pretty sure I'll hurl if he touches me.

"Apparently not," I murmur, surprise seeping into my voice. "I'm not into guys."

Mark falls back a step, exasperation rolling off him in waves. "Whatever," he mutters. "Cock tease." Flicking the lock, he storms out of the room, slamming the door closed behind him.

Shock keeps me in the bathroom a while longer. Turning to the sink, I rinse my mouth out, glad to be rid of Mark's taste. I dry my face on a hand towel and meet my own gaze in the mirror. "I'm not into guys." I say the words out loud, testing the truth of them. The roiling in my gut starts to settle, leaving behind a sense of relief. "I'm not into guys."

It's a weird realisation, considering how many hours I've spent fantasising about them. Maybe even more time than I've spent fantasising about girls. But there's no denying my reaction to the reality of Mark's touch. I didn't enjoy any part of it, even before he started asking for more than I was ready to give.

I huff out a laugh. At least I don't have to wonder anymore. I'm not bisexual and I never was—not really. I like the idea of guys maybe, but it's nothing more than that. The thought of being touched by one again makes me shudder.

By the time I leave the bathroom, I'm proud to have figured out this piece of the puzzle. The experience itself might have been unpleasant, but it's not one I ever have to repeat. Because I know for sure now.

My name is Patrick and I am a confirmed heterosexual. It's one more thing I know about myself that will never change.

LOGAN

I t's been a while since Patrick stopped talking.

He's not agitated anymore. He doesn't seem distressed in any way. He's just—somewhere else.

Lifting the hand still clutching tight to mine, I brush a soft kiss across the back of his knuckles. He'll come back when he's ready. I can wait.

A minute or so later, he blinks several times in quick succession. When his gaze lifts to meet mine, a subdued smile steals across his face. "And that's the story of how I came to the conclusion I was straight." His voice cracks over the words and he clears his throat. "See? I told you it wasn't that bad."

Not that bad? I want to scream. *It's not that fucking good, either.*

He'd told me nothing bad happened to him. He'd said he wasn't traumatised. But sitting here, hearing him talk about it, watching him relive it? That was fucking painful. Patrick's story may not be violent enough to shock or disturb the disillusioned masses, but I can see what it's done to him. How that one experience shaped his entire adult life, making him reject a part of himself he'd sought to understand.

Mark was an arrogant, selfish, overbearing arsehole. I want to rip off his penis and feed it to him, sautéed perhaps, and served on a bed of his own freshly steamed fingers. But holding on to that kind of anger won't do anything to help Patrick. If he's never seen himself as a victim of what happened that night, I'm not going to be the one to alter his perception.

"I get it now," I tell him, rubbing a soothing hand up and down his arm. "I understand how you came to the conclusion you did."

His shoulders slump as he releases a breath. "Good. I thought you might think it was a bit stupid."

My teeth grind together, but I pull my lips into a tight smile. "Not at all." We're silent for a moment before I ask the next question. "You never doubted your conclusion?"

"Oh no, I definitely did," he says, nodding. "As I got older and started university, I realised my first experience kind of sucked. I wondered if I would have a better reaction to a more positive experience. It made sense to try again. Because, honestly, being a straight man who was attracted to other men, but couldn't do anything to satisfy that craving, was too freaking confusing."

"What happened?" I want him to say his next attempt resulted in a better outcome but, if it had, we wouldn't be here.

"There were a couple of times in uni when I'd meet some guy at a party or in a bar and the attraction would be there. Some of them seemed like genuinely nice guys, but every time I tried to kiss one of them," his face twists in distaste, "I could never get past the nausea. I thought that sick feeling was proof I'd gotten it right the first time. I liked the idea of guys but had no desire to actually be touched by one. Eventually, I gave up trying."

He shrugs his shoulders dismissively. "I don't know, I guess in the end it turned out to be some kind of classical conditioning thing. Kissing a man was the stimulus; nausea became the conditioned response. Retesting only strengthened the association, until finally I could barely even think about doing one without triggering the other."

I snort. "You sound like a head shrink."

"I am a head shrink."

"True."

He pushes up from the bed. "I need tea. You want tea?"

"Sure." He's halfway to the kitchen before I even make it off the bed.

"It's not like being straight has been hard on me," he says as he puts the kettle on to boil. "I like women. In fact, women and I have had a lot of fun together."

"Until I came along and fucked everything up?"

"Pretty much." He plonks a couple of teabags into mugs.

"Why do you think it was different with me?" I ask as I lean my back against the counter beside him. "What's your theory, Professor?"

Patrick stills for a second, his eyes closing as a shiver ripples through his body. When he looks at me again, he's wearing a lascivious grin. "I'm going to be an actual professor one day and I'm going to insist you always call me by my proper title."

The idea sparks all sorts of intriguing possibilities, except that's years down the track. The experiment will be a distant memory by then. Instead of pointing that out, I lean closer. "I'll keep that in mind," I drawl in my best sexy voice, "Professor."

He makes a rumbling sound of pure satisfaction, before dropping his gaze back to the mugs. "I… um," his tone is quiet now, hesitant and a little rough. "I care about you."

Hope punches at my chest and my body turns towards his, wanting to reach for him. "I care about you, too."

"Exactly." He smiles, sneaking a glance up at me. "I think that's what broke through the conditioning."

"What?" Frowning, I tilt my head to get a better look at his face.

"You wanted to know my theory," he says with a shrug. "In the past, the men I kissed were always strangers. I had no connection to them." He turns to lean his hip against the counter, so we're face-to-face. "But you're my friend and we care about each other. I think that connection was strong enough to break through the old response and give me a new one."

"Oh." Nodding, I try not to show signs of actual deflation. He wasn't confessing his feelings for me. He was only telling me his theory. I should have known, given I asked for it. "That's good then."

"It's better than good," Patrick insists. "Logan, you set me free. I never would have figured this out if it weren't for you... and our stupid bet," he adds, laughing.

"Does this mean you've decided you *are* bisexual?" Not sure how he could deny it now, but it happens. I've seen it happen.

"I think this means..." He pauses, pretending to consider his answer. "I am bisexual as all hell."

He holds his hand up for a high five and I laugh as our palms slap together. "Glad to hear it, man. Welcome to the queer club."

"Thank you, thank you." He gives a small bow. "I plan to register for my club card immediately."

"You deserve it," I tell him. "You've been brave, trying again after so long. I'm proud of you."

Smiling, he pulls me into a hug. "Thanks, man. I'm proud of me, too."

I wrap my arms around him, drinking in the feel of him against me. I *am* happy for Patrick. This is an issue he's struggled with for a long time, I realise that now, and I'm glad he's finally putting it to rest. At the same time, my chest is tight and there's a sinking feeling in my stomach. Now Patrick has the answer he's been searching for, he'll no doubt want to bring his experiment to an end.

That means no more experimental sessions. No more explorations and first times. No more us.

He'll go back to being my friend and I'll go back to pretending I don't want more—even if I want it so badly it makes me quiver. I want to be and do and have everything with this man. Because I don't love him as just a friend—I don't think I ever have.

The boiling kettle turns off with a quiet click and a conspicuous kind of silence settles on the room. The kind where I don't want him to tell me he's done with me.

Pulling back from our hug, I look into his blue eyes. They're bright with emotion, but also with what I think is regret. "Logan, I—"

"Did you still want tea?" I cut him off. *Don't say it. Not yet.*

His mouth opens and he glances absently at the mugs on the counter beside us before shaking his head. "Not anymore."

"Good." I take his hands in mine and start backing up in the direction of the bedroom. "Let's go back to bed. I'm going to snuggle the crap out of you." This may be my last chance, and I'm taking it.

Eyebrows lift and his smiling mouth falls open. "You hate snuggling."

"No, Patrick," I tell him with a slow shake of my head. "I really don't."

We enter the bedroom and I flick off the lamp before climbing onto his enormous bed. I tug on his hand and he comes willingly into my arms. We pull the covers up as we lie down together. His back is to my chest, his arse nestled in the cradle of my hips. My knees tuck up behind his and I drape my arm over him. Taking a deep breath in, I relax against him as I exhale.

"You give good snuggle," Patrick murmurs, his fingers stroking the back of my hand. "I can't believe you've been holding out on me all this time."

Opening my eyes, I press a light kiss to the back of his neck. He's right. I have been holding out on him—in so many ways.

My reasons for trying not to get emotionally involved with Patrick are solid. They've been a necessary part of protecting myself during this whole process. Patrick knows nothing about Ben, or what happened between us. He has no idea how closely our own situation mirrors the one relationship that almost broke me—even if the similarities are only superficial. Those are the kinds of intimate details you share with a lover, not with a friend.

But now, my commitment to my own safety seems profoundly unfair. Patrick has been open with me in every way. He's given me his body, his trust. He's showered me with his curiosity and his eagerness, without ever making me feel insignificant or replaceable. Then, tonight, he divulged memories that were obviously distressing, so I would understand him better. He did it because I asked him to.

What have I given him in return? Access to my body, yes, but nothing else. He's taken every possible risk and I've repaid him with hasty exits and constant reminders of the limits of our arrangement. He deserves more. Surely, I can give him something. Some small part of myself. Something real.

"I've wanted to hold you like this," I tell him, "every time we've been together."

His head turns a fraction and I can see his profile in the darkness. "Why haven't you?"

"Because I didn't want to cross any lines that couldn't be uncrossed. I've done that before, with a friend." I pause before adding, "It didn't end well."

He grips my hand tight against his chest. "He hurt you."

My throat constricts and I have to swallow before I can speak. "Yes."

Turning over, he lies with his face close to mine. One hand lifts to trace the deep lines of my frown. "Are you still friends?"

I shift my head on the pillow. "No."

Patrick cups my cheek in his hand. His lips brush against mine. Not to arouse, but to soothe, to comfort. "I don't want to hurt you," he whispers.

My eyes burn and I close them, glad for the cover of darkness. "I don't want to lose you," I whisper back.

It's his arms that wrap around me this time, hugging me close. My head settles in the crook of his neck. His lips brush against my forehead. One hand threads through my hair, while the other strokes the length of my arm.

"You're okay," he murmurs, echoing the words I said to him the first night we kissed. "I've got you."

I fall asleep right there in his arms for the first time—knowing it's probably the last.

PATRICK

I 've spent the last hour attempting to clean the latest data from my research study so I can begin running the necessary analyses but, for the first time, the numbers aren't holding my interest. Every few minutes, I realise I'm staring at the screen, an index finger hovering over the left button of my mouse, while my brain occupies itself by replaying the feel of my arms wrapped around Logan's body as we went to sleep Saturday night.

Telling Logan about what happened with Mark had left me rattled. It was the first time I'd ever spoken about it out loud to anyone. Following that with a blunt admission of my newly acquired sexual identity had pumped fresh adrenaline through my system. The realisation of what my admission meant for me and Logan finished me off. By the time Logan had pulled me back to bed, I could hardly keep my eyes open.

Falling asleep with him, holding him close, had felt good in ways I wasn't prepared for. The touch of his lips against my neck, his leg tucked between mine. The smell of him—masculine like me, but so different. It felt right.

Logan had left soon after breakfast the next morning, neither of us mentioning the drama of the night before. We'd been hesitant with each other, awkward. Maybe we were both afraid of what the other might say.

It was only one night, and yet in the three that have passed since then, my bed has felt lonely without him in it. The thought of ending the experiment, of never holding Logan again, makes my heart clench in unexpected ways. But I don't really have any other choice. I can't keep him tied to me forever.

"Patrick?"

My head snaps to the left, where Stacey's sitting at her own desk.

"Are you okay?" A small frown mars her face as she looks at me.

"I'm fine." Glancing behind us, I see Ian is missing, his chair pushed away from his desk.

"He went to get a caffeine fix," Stacey explains. "He asked if you wanted anything."

My eyebrows lift. "He did?"

"Yeah." She huffs a laugh. "You even replied. It was a vague sort of grunted no."

"Oh." I clear my throat. "I haven't been sleeping well. Guess I'm more out of it than I thought."

She tucks her hair back behind her ears. "You're not the only one."

It's then I see the dark circles under her eyes, the escaping locks of her normally tidy hair. "What's going on, Stace?"

"I um… I want to talk to you about something. If you don't mind talking about it."

"Of course." I nod, rolling my chair closer to hers.

She glances at the open door before getting up to close it. Returning to her seat, she flattens her hands out on top of her thighs, her breathing quick and shallow. She reminds me of me—right before a public speaking event.

"Stacey, whatever it is, I'm here for you. I promise."

She nods, only meeting my gaze as she starts to speak. "So, you're bisexual, right?" I gape at her. "I know you said last week you're still gathering data," she rushes to add, "but come on, it's been more than a month and you and Logan are still getting jiggy with it so, you must know by now." Her eyes widen as it seems to occur to her, I might not know. "You do know, right?"

"Yes," I jump in, putting her out of her misery. "I've concluded I am bisexual. Yes."

"Okay, good." She smiles as she breathes a relieved sigh. "So, here's the thing. I need to know how you're so calm about that." Expectant brown eyes stare at me, awaiting my response.

"What do you mean?" If I were to describe my emotional state over the past month, calm is not the word I would choose. "You think I'm calm?"

"I haven't seen you freak out about it even once," she says. "When it first came up you seemed so excited by the idea. And now you're just accepting it—just like that." She waves impatient hands at me. "Why aren't you scared?"

"Are *you* scared?" I ask, feeling some confusion of my own. "Because from the outside it looks like you've dived into dating Naomi with gleeful abandon." I shake my head in awe. "You're the bravest person I know."

She barks out a laugh. "Yeah, right. I'm so brave. Do you know how many people know we're dating? Five," she announces, holding up one hand so she can count us off on her fingers. "You, me, Naomi, Logan and Ian. The people who were there for dinner last Friday night. The worst part is, I don't plan on changing that any time soon. I'm actively hiding my girlfriend from everyone else in my life."

"That's okay," I assure her. "It's a brand-new relationship. There's no need to shout it from the rooftops if you aren't ready." I doubt my words are helping, but I have no idea what else to say. "How's it going?" I ask in the most casual way possible.

"Fine," she says, before giving me a tiny smile. "Spectacular, actually." I do a fist pump in delight and she laughs. "She's the most amazing person I've ever met and the things she makes me feel…" She stops talking, as if realising she's sliding into the territory of *too much information*. "The better it gets, the more terrified I am." With a heavy sigh, she runs her hands over her face before crossing her arms. "You know, my parents voted against marriage equality in the plebiscite." Our eyes meet and she swallows hard before continuing, "They didn't make a big deal out of it or anything. They simply mentioned it in passing one day over lunch, as if it wasn't important, a nuisance task they dismissed the instant they dropped the voting form into the post. They have no idea I'm… the way I am."

Tears gather at the corners of her eyes. She wipes them away before they have a chance to escape. "I'm falling in love with her," she whispers. "I don't want to be scared of that."

Standing, I tug her out of her chair and into a hug. She holds me so tight her fingernails dig into me through my shirt. "For what it's worth," I tell her, "I think you make a great couple."

"Thanks. I think so, too." Her laugh is watery as she pulls away. "What about you? You can't really be as unaffected by all this as you seem?"

I release a sigh as we sit back down. "Being bisexual doesn't worry me. I already know my family will be fine with it." My brother and I grew up knowing we would be loved and accepted by our parents, no matter what. I'm luckier than Stacey in that regard. "It's the fact I didn't know that bothers me."

"It's hardly uncommon to figure these things out a little later in life," she says. "You know that."

"When did you figure it out?" I ask, curious.

"I was sixteen when I realised I like girls as well as boys. I didn't want to know," she adds. "You may have noticed I ignored it for as long as I could, but I always knew."

"Which is exactly my point," I insist. "As a teenager, I thought I knew, too. But I never tried to ignore it or deny it to myself. I deliberately set out to find proof, one way or the other. Bisexual or straight." I had no idea, at the time, how rigid my thinking was, though it seems so obvious now. "Based on the results I got at the time, and for a long time after, I believed I was a straight man. With a few odd quirks maybe, but for all intents and purposes, I was straight. To find out I've been wrong all this time… it makes me wonder what else I'm wrong about."

I glance at my monitor and its display of research results. My entire PhD thesis is based on the idea that self-experimentation can help young people figure out who they are. I believed I was living proof of the validity of my theory. Now, I don't know what to believe.

"I've always prided myself on living an authentic life. But what if it turns out I'm a fake?" Avoiding Stacey's gaze, I stare down at my clenched hands. "What if…" My voice is little more than a rasp now, as I confront the one question I never expected to face. "What if I don't know myself at all?"

Stacey reaches out to place a hand on my knee, putting a stop to the bouncing I didn't realise it was doing. "If you don't know everything about all the nooks and crannies of your own psyche, that makes you human, Patrick. We're messy and complicated. Always growing, always changing."

"Not the fundamentals," I insist. "They don't change like that."

"What makes you such an expert on what's fundamental and what's not? You don't even have your doctorate yet," she scoffs. "You boys and your egos. It's time to get over yourself and admit you are not in full control of your own head."

I huff out a laugh. "I'm discovering that." My sense of self is officially in a tumultuous state of flux. I have no idea who I'll be by the time my equilibrium is restored.

At least I'm not in any kind of long-term relationship. It's the one thing I can be grateful for in all this. No one wants to watch the person they love grow into a total stranger. I've seen what that can do to even the strongest relationship. I don't ever want to cause that kind of pain—not in myself and certainly not in anyone else.

"What about Logan?"

My heart stumbles in my chest. "What about him?"

Stacey gives a slow shrug. "Does this mean the experiment is over?"

I don't want it to be over. There's so much Logan and I haven't done yet. So many things I want to try. I can't imagine doing them with anyone else, or even wanting to. But the original question posed by the experiment has been answered, and I can't expect Logan to keep giving himself to me indefinitely. Especially now I know he's been hurt in the past by getting involved with a friend.

"We haven't discussed it yet, but... I guess so." I sit up in my chair, doing my best not to look disappointed. "Which means we'll go back to being friends."

She raises a single disbelieving eyebrow. "How do you think that will go?"

"Fine." It doesn't feel fine. "We've been careful to keep doing the friend thing." Except for the part where

I can barely stop myself from touching him. "He's been beyond patient with me, but I know he's eager to put this thing behind us before we mess it up." I think I'm going to be sick.

Stacey stares at me with an amused smile but says nothing.

"Ending it is the best thing to do," I add, filling the silence. "The friendship comes first." My desire to climb onto Logan's lap at every given opportunity for frottage purposes comes second. "Obviously."

"Okay, then," Stacey says, nodding. "That's good to know."

I press my lips together, in case my mouth feels the need to dig me in deeper.

"In that case, I'm going to round up the gang." She grabs her phone from her desk as she makes the announcement. "We're going out tonight."

Frowning, I wonder what she's playing at. "We are?"

"Yep." She's too busy typing into her phone to bother looking at me as she answers.

"Why?" I ask.

With a last jab, she sends off whatever message she's been typing. "Because I think we should celebrate your newfound bisexuality in an appropriate manner." When I grimace, she laughs out loud. "I haven't told them that's why we're going out. I would never do that. But this is a big deal and it deserves a toast, even if you choose to keep the reason for the toast between us."

Her phone pings and she picks it up. "What do you know," she says, cheerfully, before turning the screen around so I can see it. "Logan is the first one to say yes."

LOGAN

He's going to end the experiment. Why else would he and Stacey be inviting everyone out for drinks on a random Wednesday? Patrick must have told her he has an answer to his question, and now he's planning to announce it to the rest of the group.

It makes sense to reveal the results of the experiment to the people who were there when it began. They've all been curious. God knows, I've fielded enough questions from Naomi about it. At least I won't have to deal with those anymore.

There's only one problem with Patrick bringing the experiment to an end: I promised him I would continue being his friend after it was all over. I promised him we'd be able to go back to the way things were before all this began. I promised him a lot of things, but I don't know how to keep any of them.

Pushing thoughts of Patrick away, I refocus on the two monitors in front of me. I'm at home today, finishing up a web development job I've been working on the past couple of weeks. It's taken longer than I would have liked, due to some extra hours I put in at the library—and all the time I've been spending with Patrick.

I'm looking forward to finishing, though. I'm proud of the work I've done for this client. The website is slick and clean, it functions well on all the usual devices, and the user interface is simple and intuitive. People don't realise how much technical detail goes into pulling off functional simplicity, but when it works it is a thing of beauty.

It's good to be doing the kind of work I had in mind when I was studying for my degree. But, more and more, the strain of trying to balance my two jobs is wearing on me. Though my brain and interests continue to urge me in the direction of working for myself, I still worry about getting caught in the isolation that caused me so many issues in the past. If I'm going to make the switch back to working for myself full-time, I'll need to find ways to make sure I stay out of my own head and connected to the world outside my apartment door. But do I actually want to leave the library? The position I have is easy work and I'm surrounded by people when I'm there. I never have to be alone.

With a frustrated groan, I rub my hands over my face. Speaking of getting out of my head, if I don't finish this work I can't go out and play with my friends tonight. Adulting sucks.

I work steadily through the remainder of the day, pausing only to grab something for lunch, and manage to finish a little after five. I shoot off a quick email to the client, so she can check over the most recent changes before the website goes live at the end of the week. After a quick shower, I throw on some clothes and take a cab to the bar.

Pulling open the door, I scan the crowd for familiar faces. Naomi catches my attention, waving to me from the other side of the pub, where she and the others are sitting in a small booth. I hold up a hand in acknowledgment and then point to the bar to indicate I'm going to get a drink. She gives me a thumbs up.

I order a scotch and coke. "Make it a double," I tell the bartender. If I'm going to make it through Patrick ending things with me in one piece, I'm going to need at least a couple of drinks under my belt.

"Logan, hey." Patrick shows up at my side, his chest brushing against my bent elbow. "Thanks for coming."

"No problem." I wait for him to order his own drink before gesturing to where our friends are sitting, talking among themselves. "I take it this is what I think it is?" He raises his eyebrows in question, so I clarify. "You came out to them?"

"Oh, yeah." He clears his throat as he nods. "It was like the words leapt out of my mouth the second everyone showed up. It's weird, but I couldn't *not* tell them."

I smile. "What you see is what you get, right?"

He laughs, nodding. "That's the idea. Not sure how well the execution is going, but I'm giving it my best shot."

"No one can ask more than that," I assure him.

Patrick's drink arrives and we make our way to the booth and join the others.

"Logan, man, I applaud you," Ian says with a laugh, holding up his beer glass. "The touch of your expert lips really can make a man switch teams."

I put a hand over my heart in mock modesty. "What can I say, it's a gift. If you ever want to test the theory, I'll be happy to gayify you."

"Yeah, nah." Ian pulls a face. "I'm happy with chicks, but thanks." He reaches out with one hand and we bump fists.

I grab a chair and drag it up to the end of the table.

"Speaking of testing theories," Naomi says as I get settled, "does this mean the experiment is over?"

Stacey gives me and Patrick a forlorn look. "No, you can't. You guys are so good together. I'd hate for you to give up now." She leans back against Naomi's side as she speaks. Naomi wraps an arm around her shoulder and drops a kiss on her cheek.

"It wouldn't be giving up, Stace," Patrick points out. "The experiment was intended to answer a question and that's been done. If we do end the experiment, it will be because it's reached its natural conclusion."

If.

He said *if* we end the experiment.

"Besides," Patrick adds, "I'm sure Logan is anxious to be done with the newbie." He chuckles, but it sounds forced. "Right, mate?" He looks at me for confirmation, his expression carefully blank. I have no idea what answer he's hoping to get.

"That was you being a newbie?" I exclaim. "Fuck me. Get a little experience under your belt and you may give me a heart attack."

The table erupts in a chorus of cheers and laughter. Patrick flushes red, but he's smiling as he covers his face with one hand. I take a sip of my drink, grateful to have successfully avoided his question. "This is a celebration," I add, standing up. "Who wants to dance?"

"Me!" Stacey and Naomi speak at the same time. They shuffle out of the booth and follow me onto the sparsely populated dance floor.

The next couple of hours pass in a blur of loud music, dancing, and round after round of drinks. Even Patrick goes back to the bar more times than usual. Somewhere in the middle, we order enough deep-fried food to cover the table. It's fun, hanging out together. These people make me happy, and I'm grateful to have found them.

As the night winds down, we say goodbye to Naomi and Stacey, who leave hand-in-hand. Ian is off on the dance floor with some woman he's picked up. Which leaves me and Patrick alone for the first time tonight, sitting together on one side of the small booth. We nurse our drinks, a comfortably inebriated silence between us. He's switched to water. I'm on my last scotch and coke.

Patrick drops a hand down to his thigh, turning his body slightly towards me. "There are benefits to ending the experiment," he blurts out, as if we're already in the middle of the conversation, instead of just getting started. "For example, we wouldn't have to abide by the ground rules anymore."

"We already got rid of one of the ground rules," I point out, gesturing with my drink. "You decided you want me all the time, remember? Even when you're stone cold sober." Winking at him, I take another sip and lick my lips.

His heavy-lidded gaze locks on to my mouth and he hums in pleasure. "I remember."

Drunk Patrick is adorable. Drunk Logan wants more. "Which reminds me, there's something I have to know." I lean my head against the back of the seat as I gaze into his blue eyes. "How many drinks *does* it take to make you horny?"

He snorts a laugh. "This many…" Nabbing the glass from my hand, he takes a long sip before returning it. "Minus at least three. I'm not sure." Brow furrowing, he asks, "When did you arrive? It was about that many."

My laugh mixes with a groan and I drop my forehead to the curve of his shoulder, banging it repeatedly. "I shouldn't have asked that question. Knowing you're horny gives me all sorts of ideas I'm not supposed to have when we're in public."

"That's another thing about ending the experiment," he exclaims suddenly. "We can go back to touching each other without constantly second-guessing our motivations or worrying if we're doing the wrong thing."

"We hardly ever touched each other before the experiment began. That's what you want to go back to?"

"Not necessarily." He wags a finger at me. "I know we used to be pretty hands-off, though I'm not sure why."

I know exactly why. I'm only surprised he noticed the safe distance I used to keep between us.

"It's not like we *have* to go back to *exactly* the way we were before." Drunk Patrick is fond of emphasising pertinent words. "To try would seem, I don't know, wrong somehow." He glances at me out of the corner of his eye, gauging my reaction. "The things we've done together mean a lot to me. Even when we do go back to being friends, I don't want to act like it never happened."

My eyebrows lift. I assumed that's exactly what he would want. It's what Ben wanted. I should know better, though. Patrick is nothing like Ben. He never hides who he is, not from anyone—including himself.

"So, we'll be friends who were lovers for a while?" My voice comes out softer than intended, and Patrick leans closer to hear me over the loud pub music. "And we'll touch each other in the knowing, but non-sexual, way past lovers sometimes touch?"

"I guess that's supposed to be the idea." His brow crinkles as he attempts to concentrate. "Ideas become fuzzier after the fourth drink."

"Tell me about it." The alcohol is leading me in directions my sober self would refuse to go. Then again, maybe that was the idea. While I'm not anywhere near as self-aware as Patrick claims to be, I do know one thing: When it comes to the man beside me, I'll lie to myself a thousand times over if it gets me closer to what I want.

"What do you think?" The breath Patrick takes is slow and quiet, as if trying not to draw attention to itself. "Could it work?"

Not in this reality. At least, not for me. I don't want it to work for him, either.

"How about you try it out?" I dare him, my words ripe with innuendo. "Go ahead. Touch me, all friendly like."

The man full-on giggles, covering his mouth with one hand and everything. "I can't do it if you make it sound dirty."

I join in with his laughter. I swear teasing Patrick is my new favourite thing to do. "All right, I'll be good." Turning side-on to him again, I nudge his shoulder with mine and pretend my skin isn't already twitching at the thought of his hands on me. "Put your arm around my shoulder."

His hand lifts and he waggles his fingertips before reaching around me. The weight of his arm settles easily across my shoulders.

"There," he drawls, looking all smug. "How's that for platonic?"

Meeting his gaze, I give him time to realise how close our faces are before allowing my eyes to trail down to his mouth. I lick my lips again. "Feels good to me." The low rumble of my voice reaches for him, and he shivers on contact.

"Arsehole." He shakes his head, but his arm tightens around me. "You're sexing it up on purpose."

I shift to slide an arm around his waist, wrapping it around his middle—exactly as I would a friend. "Nah, simply spending time with my buddy. This has nothing to do with my desire to have your dick in my arse," I say, casually. "Nothing at all."

I expect him to laugh at my bawdy comment, but instead his eyes slide closed, and he presses his forehead to mine with a groan. "Is it bad that I hate how we didn't get that far?"

My heartbeat falls in sync with the throbbing of my cock. Both want the same thing. Him. "Do you think you'd like to try it?"

"I don't know. I think I do, but you're the only..." His lips twist into a grimace and he backs off, removing his arm from around me. "I'm not asking you for more, I won't do that to you, I promise. I just wanted—" He cuts himself off more abruptly this time. Turning away, he rests his elbows on the table as he rakes his hands through his brown hair. "I'm gonna shut up now."

I don't want him to shut up. I want him to tell me everything he desires. Then, I want to fulfill every one of those desires and a million more he hasn't thought of yet. Every part of me is hungry for him, despite knowing each taste consumes more of me. Patrick has the power to fuck me up in ways I've never imagined.

Way more than Ben ever did. Right now, in this moment, I don't give a shit.

"Maybe you getting an answer to your initial question isn't a sign we should end the experiment," I suggest, feeling my way around the idea as the words leave my mouth. "Maybe getting this first answer simply means it's time to move on to the next phase of the experiment."

Patrick's gaze snaps to mine, his eyes wide. "The next phase?"

"Yeah. I mean, discovering you're bisexual, all by itself, raises a whole host of new questions about what you like and don't like. I did promise to drag you as far down my end of the spectrum as I could. I think you know we haven't come close to hitting your limit yet, which I'll remind you was part of the original experiment. Phase Two will give you a chance to ditch the stupid ground rules and um," I don't bother trying to hide my leer as I finish, "probe deeper into the issue."

Patrick's staring at me, his limbs restless and his lips parted. I have a feeling, if we were alone, he'd be in my lap by now. "Are you sure?"

"Am I sure I'm not done with you? Fuck, yes!" I huff out a laugh. "We've barely scratched the surface. I mean, you haven't even experimented with kissing me in public yet."

His mouth drops open. "Yes, I have!"

"Our first kiss doesn't count, we were in a gay club. The second one, when we sealed the deal on the experiment, was barely a peck. Kissing me here, right now, would be different. It could be like a mini-experiment in itself." His expression is as dubious as my reasoning. "After all, you could potentially be uncomfortable with kissing me so publicly, but you won't know until—"

He presses his lips to mine, his hands rising to cup my face so I can't escape. He deepens the kiss and, as our tongues twine together, I moan deep into his mouth. It's several minutes before we finally part.

"I'm proud to kiss you," he whispers, breathing hard against my lips. "I'm lucky to be kissing you. That you're choosing to kiss me back."

I smile at his words, at his lack of hesitation in saying them. "Such a sweet talker."

"Although, for the sake of honesty," he adds teasingly, "one part of me is starting to get uncomfortable."

"Me, too." I lean in to lick his bottom lip, but avoid his attempts to lure me into another kiss. "Maybe you should take me back to your place so we can take care of that."

His eyes flare with heat and need... and relief. "I'll take care of yours if you'll take care of mine."

"It's a deal." Chuckling, I take his hand in mine. "Phase Two starts now."

DATA GATHERING

PHASE TWO

PATRICK

L ogan heads for the kitchen as soon as we enter my apartment. "I need water. You want some?"

"Sure." I follow him, my heart pounding at the thought of what the night may bring.

I was so sure Logan would be eager to end the experiment. He's never made a secret of wanting this situation to be temporary. For him, our friendship is more important than anything else that could happen between us. It was for me too, at first. Now, the thought of losing access to any part of him makes me want to dig my nails in deeper to prevent his escape. I'm not entirely sure what those feelings mean, or what I even want from him. I only know what I don't want to lose.

He moves around the kitchen with ease, knowing where everything is almost as well as I do. My gaze meanders over the length of him before locking on to his round, firm arse. What would it be like to fuck him there? To push inside his body and feel the heat of him surrounding me. I've been unsure whether I want to try it, or if the whole *dick in arse* thing would be a turn off. Surely, there'd have to be an ick factor involved—at least sometimes. But then, if I think about it, there's been the occasional ick factor involved in having sex with women, too—on both sides. Because life isn't a porno and our bodies are designed for more than just sex. Those occasional, minor issues never once stopped me from enjoying sex with a woman. Why would I assume they'd interfere in my enjoyment of sex with a man?

Plus, I've been doing research on gay sex, and how the prostate is supposed to be orgasm heaven. I want to see the look on Logan's face as I fuck him, nailing his prostate over and over until he comes all over me. It's become a firm favourite in my rotation of wanking fantasies. Given all our other experiences together, the fear of being turned off is fading fast. Curiosity is taking its place and, after our earlier discussion, anticipation is coming a close second.

"Something caught your interest there?" Logan's question yanks me out of my reverie.

He's standing still, watching me over his shoulder. Amusement tugs at the corners of his mouth, but his eyes are bright with interest. "You can come closer if you want. To see what happens."

My mouth waters and I swallow hard. My cock starts to thicken as I take a few steps forward, coming up behind him.

His hands flatten out on the counter as he waits for me to make the next move. He always does that—lets me decide the pace and the destination. Never pushing me beyond what I'm ready for. He gives me total control, allowing me to explore without fear of reprisal.

Gratitude swells in my chest as I place my hands on his hips. I want to make him feel good. I want to give him pleasure in ways I never have before.

My palms slide down onto the roundness of his arse cheeks. There's a slight intake of breath and his muscles clench beneath my touch, but otherwise he doesn't move.

Slipping under his shirt, my hands begin to travel upward, tracing the lines of his back and shoulders. He reaches over his head to pull his shirt off before dropping it onto the counter beside our forgotten glasses of water. The broad expanse of his back meets my gaze and my lips make contact, trailing over him. My tongue sneaks out to lick tiny wet lines across his skin, and I'm amazed once more by the heat radiating from him. Wrapping my arms around him, I press myself against his body, so we're connected from shoulders to thighs. For a long moment I stay there, absorbing his warmth, his presence.

Then one of my hands slides down to cover his groin and he lets out a harsh sigh. He's long and hard beneath the denim and, holy hell, I want him.

When I go to work on his belt buckle, he takes his phone and wallet from his pockets. Flicking open the wallet, he takes out a condom and a small packet of lube. "Just in case," he murmurs over his shoulder before placing them aside, but within easy reach. No expectations, only opportunity.

I nod, kissing the top of his shoulder.

His puts his hands back in place, flat on the counter, and rubs his arse back against me. "Patrick, please."

I realise then, he gets off on this—giving himself to me. He's being generous with me, yes, but part of him is also loving every minute of it. The realisation sends a fresh wave of arousal shuddering through me and my chest rumbles in approval.

My hands start moving again and I have him unzipped in seconds. Slipping my fingers into his boxer briefs, I curve one hand around his arse cheeks, while the other wraps around his hard cock. He hisses in a breath, eyes sliding closed as I start to jack him. His hips move, the motions slight and jerky. He's trying to control his response, but he's failing. I want him to fail. I want him to lose control.

"I love touching you like this." My lips brush against the back of his ear as I murmur the words. "I love to watch you. So hot, so fucking sexy."

My hands are roaming all over him now, unable to get enough. Blunt fingernails run through the hair on his chest, down over his stiff length, beneath to cup his balls. Returning both hands to his arse, I cup his cheeks, easing them apart. His whimper makes me bare my teeth as I teeter on the edge of a full-on growl. Need claws at my insides and I take the side of his neck between my teeth. Not biting down, just holding him, laving at him with my tongue.

I start to ease a finger down into the top of his crack, but he reaches one hand back to grab my wrist. Pulling it up to his mouth, he sucks three of my fingers deep into his mouth and circles them with his tongue. I gasp as he sucks and moans and sucks some more. Finally, when my forehead is against his shoulder and I'm trying my damnedest not to hump his backside, he drags my fingers from his mouth. Swirling his tongue around them one more time, he returns my hand to where it came from.

Moving to his side, I stand close, my chest against his arm. My heart thunders as I slide my wet middle finger down into his crack. Down, down, not stopping until it brushes across his hole. The tight ring clenches at the lightest touch, his whole body tensing. Hands curl into fists and a single bead of sweat slips down his temple. Fuck, he's beautiful.

This time, when I touch him, I press more firmly. Rubbing back and forth over his opening. It's good, but it's not enough to satisfy. Changing the angle of my finger, I take a deep breath and push into him. He lets out a strangled cry, his eyes closing.

I push deeper before withdrawing. Then I do it again. Logan's shaking, heaving body moves with me— pushing back as I push forward. Every sound he makes lifts me higher, every movement encourages and welcomes me. Finally, I shove all three fingers inside and he roars his approval.

I'm smiling. I can feel the grin stretching my open mouth. I kiss his shoulder as I press myself tighter against his side. Watching his face closely, I take hold of his long, beautiful cock.

My fingers wrap around him and he collapses forward until his forehead rests against the kitchen cupboards. He quakes and shudders as I jack him off on one side and thrust my fingers into his arse on the other.

He doesn't turn his head to look at me, doesn't speak. He simply offers himself, in all his panting, trembling glory. Whatever I want to do to him, I can do.

My breath stills in my chest. I know what I want.

Looking down to my left, I see the condom and lube waiting for me. It's a good thing one of us knows what we're doing, or we'd never get anywhere.

I gently withdraw my hands from Logan's body, and he cries out in protest. "Shh, love," I whisper in his ear. "Trust me."

Lowering myself to my knees behind him, I grip on to the waistband of his jeans and boxers, tugging them down. His bare arse is revealed, along with thick hairy legs and muscular calves. The musky scent of him hits me and I lean closer, breathing deeply as my face nuzzles him.

"Fuuuck." It's the first word he's spoken in several minutes, the guttural sound torn from his chest.

Silently, I rise to my feet and shed my clothes. Logan follows suit before moving back to his original position. The second we're both naked, I grab the condom packet. Tearing it open with shaky fingers, I sheath myself before ripping into the packet of lube. Some of it spills onto the floor and I swear under my breath.

Logan lets out a light laugh before turning to nab the packet. "Allow me." Pouring some of the cool liquid onto his hand, he reaches down to stroke it over my covered cock.

Oh hell, that feels good. "No, no, stop." I'm thrusting into his hand, even as I speak. "You'll make me come."

"We wouldn't want that." The words are said against my mouth and my lips part for the invasion of his tongue. The kiss is wet and messy and so damned needful I can't stop myself from keening.

"Fuck me, Patrick," he demands. "I want to feel you inside me."

"Yes," I hiss. Grabbing my hand, he drizzles the last of the lube onto my fingers before turning his back on me again. I reach down to find his entrance, sliding my fingers into him. There's no hesitation this time, no doubt. All I can think about is getting my dick inside him—right, the fuck, now.

Logan leans forward as I pump my fingers in and out, making sure he's nice and wet and open for me. I pull free, quickly replacing my fingers with the tip of my cock. A single push, and the head is enveloped in the sweetest, tightest heat I've ever experienced in my whole freaking life. My hips jerk, desperate for more, and we both cry out in relief.

I never planned on being the one to lose control here, but I fucking lose every ounce of control I've ever possessed in my life. I pound into Logan like a freaking wild man. All sense of finesse and composure disintegrate beneath the power his tight grip has on me.

Logan doesn't seem to mind. If anything, he's as far gone as I am.

It doesn't take long for the pleasure to break us. Logan comes first, shouting his release. Thick jets of come shoot out of him, splashing against the lower cupboards and across the counter. My arms wrap around his torso as I follow close behind, emptying into the condom deep inside him.

When we're done, our legs give out and we sink to the floor. He turns, dragging me into his arms until I'm sprawled across his lap. We're still breathing hard as I remove the condom, tying it off.

About a minute later, Logan lifts his head to look at me, a wide grin on his face. "That was hot."

I let out a full-bellied laugh, sounding only mildly hysterical. "Are you sure? 'Cause I feel like I went full-on berserker on your arse."

"You did, and I loved every beastly second of it." He laughs too, and his hot breath washes over my throat, making me shiver. "You make one hell of a top."

Lifting onto my knees, I straddle him, draping my arms around his shoulders. "You make one hell of a bottom."

He grips on to my hips as he kisses me. "Let me know if you ever want to try it the other way around."

My cock gives a telltale pulse of interest and I buck against him in reflex.

His eyes widen and he slides his hands up my back. "I think you like that idea."

"I think you might be right," I reply, nodding slowly.

With a low chuckle, he starts to move, urging me off his lap so we can both stand. He swipes the condom and tosses it in the bin while I grab my shirt to mop up his come. It's hardly thorough, but it will do for now.

When we're done, Logan reaches for my hand. "Let's go take a shower, get each other all sudsy and clean. Then, we can snuggle."

Sounds perfect. "Lead and I will follow," I tell him as we make our way to the bathroom.

Holding him in my arms as we fall asleep a short while later, I wonder if there is anything I don't want to do with this man. I could spend years searching for that limit I was so sure was there. But I realise now, I'd never find it.

LOGAN

I stand in the middle of the department store and stare at the vase my sister pointed out. Smooth and shiny beneath its very own store spotlight, the bulbous curves of the glass vessel swirl with a half dozen shades of blue.

"It reminds me of a partially open flower," Paula says with some vague hand gestures. "What do you think?"

I think it's a vase. "It's very nice."

Tutting, she rolls her eyes at me. "Whatever. Do you think Mum will like it?"

The number of vase-centred conversations I've had with my mother over the years lies between zero and... well, zero. "Honestly, you'd know better than me."

"True." Stepping forward, she eyeballs the blown glass more closely, before giving a decisive nod. "It's pretty and it's within our budget. Plus, Mum's birthday is next week so we're running out of time." Reaching for the vase, she eases it carefully off the high shelf and looks around for a sales desk. "If she doesn't like it, she can always bring it back and exchange it for something else."

"Like that would ever happen," I scoff. "Mum would never return a gift we gave her."

Paula sighs. "I know, but the thought makes me feel better."

The lady at the register boxes and bags the gift and we each hand over half of the necessary cash. Another parental birthday, done and dusted.

"Let's grab some lunch before we go," I say as we leave the store and step into the central corridor of the shopping centre. "I'm starving."

"You're a boy. You're always starving."

I shrug. "I'm in a good mood. Good moods make me hungry."

Her face is alight with curiosity as she looks up at me. "I've noticed you bandying that smile about today. What's going on?"

I try to smother my grin. It's useless. Nothing can throw me off my joy game. "Food first. And coffee. A really big coffee." Sleep has been taking a back seat lately, and for once it's not due to looming deadlines. Since discovering the pleasures of gay sex, Patrick has been intent on indulging at every given opportunity. I've been more than happy to provide an ample supply of those opportunities. Who needs sleep anyway?

Minutes later, I'm moaning in pleasure as I bite into my foot-long sub. "Damn," I say after swallowing. "I needed this." We're in one of the main food courts. It's loud and obnoxious, with hard plastic chairs and more people than space. But the food is fast, and we need to be gone in the next half hour if we're going to avoid paying for parking.

"Okay, you have food, you have coffee. Now, tell me about him," Paula demands, before taking a bite of her own sub.

"About who?" I ask, pretending ignorance.

She circles an index finger in front of my face while she chews. "The guy who's putting the smile on your dial. Is he your boyfriend?" She singsongs the words in true brat sister style before laughing out loud.

"More friend than boyfriend, but we've been," sucking each other off at regular intervals, "enjoying each other's company."

Paula's face falls, the smile vanquished. "Oh no, you're not back with Ben, are you?"

"Fuck no!" Several tables worth of shoppers glance our way at my outburst, including a glaring mother with two small kids, and a handful of giggling teenage girls. I clear my throat and continue in a lower voice. "His name is Patrick. I met him through work, you may have heard me mention him."

"I suppose I have. He's a close friend, isn't he." There isn't even a hint of question in her tone. I nod anyway. "And you're sleeping together, but not dating." Another nod. "Please, Logan, at least tell me Patrick is gay. Like fully, openly, happily gay."

The ears of the teenage girls seem to be growing, along with their eyes.

"He's bi, actually." She narrows her gaze at me, and I snap, "And he's nothing like Ben."

"I'll be the judge of that and do you girls really not have your own gossip to deal with?" She swings her head to the left to glare at our audience, who mutter apologies. Grabbing their empty food wrappers, they bolt from the table, falling into hysterical laughter as they rush off.

Paula turns back to me with a sigh. "I need details," she demands. "Then I'll decide whether or not to stomp all over your love life."

I heave a sigh, but give her a quick, PG-rated overview of my newly changed relationship with Patrick while we eat. Myriad expressions cross her face as she listens, especially when I describe the experiment, but she manages to keep her commentary to a minimum until I'm done.

"Why would anyone be so invested in knowing every little bit of themselves?" she asks as we get up from the table and toss our empty wrappers into a nearby bin. "Most people don't even want to look at themselves in the mirror, let alone know the intricate corners of their own head."

"I don't know. As far as I can tell it's just part of his personality." We wander towards the lift that will take us down to the car park. "It's not a bad thing to want to know who you are and be honest about it. I mean, people go on about living authentically all the time. Patrick actually makes a conscious effort to do it."

"Hey, no one is more authentic than me," Paula says, putting a hand over her chest, "until I realise how full of shit I am." We get into the lift and she jabs a finger at the button. "Seriously, Logan, people lie to themselves all the damned time. It's not because we want to, sometimes we have no idea we're doing it." She looks me up and down before continuing, "Look at you, for example. You talk like this is some sort of glorified friends with benefits action, when clearly it's more—at least for you."

I don't bother trying to deny it. Paula is my sister; she knows me too well. "I know it's more, but I didn't have a lot of options to choose from when it all came up. He was going to do this thing with or without me." The mere thought of another man putting his hands on Patrick the way I have makes me want to lash out. "I wanted him to be safe."

"Because you're in love with him," she says softly.

My jaw tenses as I glare down at her. "Yes."

A small quirk of a smile appears as the doors to the lift open. "At least you're not lying to yourself about that."

We approach the car in silence. I put Mum's birthday present in the boot, taking care to surround it with a bunch of reusable grocery bags so it won't slide around too much. Paula doesn't speak again until I climb behind the wheel and close the door.

"Logan," she says in a quiet voice, "you know you can't keep this whole experiment farce up forever. What happens then?"

It's the question I've been trying not to ask myself these last few weeks. Patrick seems genuinely okay with his new sexuality status. Not that I expected him to have a meltdown or anything, but I've never seen anyone be so blasé about it. It's like he's ticked a box on some mental personality checklist and moved on. As if nothing about his life has really changed.

"I don't know." I make no move to start the car and we sit together in the dim light for a few moments. "I know, when this began, Patrick still assumed he would end up with a woman, no matter how the experiment turned out, but now... I don't know, maybe that could be changing. Maybe now, when he imagines his future, he'll be more open to the full range of possibilities."

"You thought Ben would change, too. But he didn't and it ended in disaster." She reaches out to put a hand on my arm, squeezing gently. "I don't want to see you go through that again."

"It wasn't so bad." Speaking of lying, there's a whopper right there. "I still managed to finish off my last year of university, and graduate near the top of my year level."

Paula raises her eyebrows as she turns towards me. "What about after you graduated? When you barely left your apartment for weeks at a time. I practically had to break the door down to get you to talk to me."

"I was working."

"You were hiding."

"Ahh," I wag a finger at her, "but I also made a shit ton of money while doing it."

Sinking back into her seat, she sighs. "There's a difference between making money and making a life. You need to do both."

"That's why I went to work at the library, remember? To get a life."

"I know that was true at first," she grumbles. "Now I wonder if maybe you've just found a way to hide in plain sight."

I turn my body to face her. "Look, I know this thing with Patrick is a risk, okay? It could all amount to nothing and I'll have no one to blame but myself. But, quite frankly, being with him is worth any risk I have to take."

"Does he have any idea how you feel about him?" she asks.

"No, and I don't want to rush things." I frown, adding, "You're right, though. I can't hang around in limbo again hoping things will change on their own." Frustrated with my lack of action, I reach out a hand to start the car. "I know what I want. Maybe I should take a leaf out of Patrick's playbook and do something about getting it."

"Damned right you should," Paula agrees, before adding, "It would be the authentic thing to do."

I throw her a dirty look, but she's too busy laughing at me to notice.

PATRICK

We need to get the hell out of this apartment. Over the last few weeks, Phase Two of our experiment has devolved into little more than a sexfest. We've barely gone outside, except to go to work and occasionally in search of sustenance. Most of our time is spent naked and crawling all over each other. I've never been blown so many times in a week in my freaking life.

Logan lies beside me, staring at the ceiling. We're both still panting from that last round. How Logan did that thing with his tongue, I have no idea—but I've already put it on my mental list of fun things to learn and do.

"Have you ever heard the saying about how people are basically houseplants with more complicated emotions?" I ask him.

"No. Why?"

"I think this houseplant is in need of sunlight."

He laughs, turning his head to look at me. "You mean, man can't live on orgasms alone?"

"Unfortunately, not." I take a deep breath that ends with a grimace. "Although, if I did have any actual plants in here, I'm pretty sure they'd all be dead by now." The room stinks of sex. Lots and lots of sex. I need to wash the sheets—again.

"All right, I'm calling it." Grabbing hold of Logan's hand, I pull him with me as I climb out of bed. "We need a shower, and food, and daylight—in that order."

"Aye aye, professor."

The title has me turning a slow circle to narrow my eyes at him. "Don't start that again."

His chuckle is all deep and throaty and my tongue is on the verge of reaching for his, but instead of kissing me, he smacks me on the arse on his way to the bathroom. "Remember, we must be on our best behaviour, so we don't starve to death."

We manage to keep our hands to ourselves as we shower. I shave, Logan trims—which is a good thing because I've become addicted to running my fingers over his short stubble. By the time we're dressed we look vaguely human.

It's almost noon so we head to the kitchen in the hope of finding something edible. Managing to locate some ham and salad stuff, I throw together sandwiches. Logan makes iced coffees, adding way more sugar than I want to know about. We sit down at the dining table to eat. Logan's quiet hum of appreciation while he chews makes me smile.

"I have an idea," he says after finishing his last bite of sandwich, "about how we could improve our chances of survival."

I swallow a mouthful of iced coffee before speaking. "Tell me."

He bites down on his bottom lip before he speaks, as if he's psyching himself up for whatever is about to come out of his mouth. "What would you say, if I asked you out on a date?"

Blinking, I stare at him. "A date."

"Yes."

The staring continues. After all the times he's reminded me, reminded everyone, we *aren't* dating, his suggestion comes as something of a surprise.

"Here's what I'm thinking," he says, breaking the overly long silence. "Generally speaking, bisexual people are open to having relationships with both men and women. You're bisexual, but so far you've only ever dated women." He pauses to look at me. "I thought you might like to experiment with dating a man."

Pressing his lips together, he sits back in his chair and waits. The implication is clear. He's done talking. It's up to me now.

I clear my throat, forcing my mouth to open in the hope something vaguely sensible will come out. "What you're saying is," because I want to be certain we're on the same page here, "you want to fake date me?"

"No." There's no hesitation in his response. "I would be asking you out on a real date."

Now I'm confused. Not only are we not on the same page, I'm not even sure we're reading the same book anymore. "You want to experiment with going on a real date with me."

A smile breaks out on his face. "Okay, I get how that sounds weird." When his gaze meets mine again, the hazel is warm with determination. "The experiment is how we began, and I guess I figured the idea would seem less overwhelming if I put it in those terms. This wouldn't be a make or break thing, it's just dating. No pressure, no expectations. We could give it a try and see where it leads. Same as we have with everything else."

Giving things a try has led us to some interesting places. A few of my favourites come instantly to mind. "I suppose it could be a good idea to try dating a man... to see what it's like." And it would be Logan, so it wouldn't be such a big deal. I wouldn't have to worry about getting in too deep when my mind is still a mess. Dating Logan would be fun, if kind of surreal. With all the fantasises I've had about men over the years, not one of them ever included candlelit dinners or strolls along the beach. But I can imagine doing those things with Logan. I'd like to try it, I think, but only with him. "Are you sure you're okay with doing this with me, though? I know it's the opposite direction from where you ultimately want to end up."

Logan tilts his head to one side, looking puzzled. "Where is it you think I want to end up?"

"Come on, you've made no secret of the fact you want us to go back to being just friends when this is all over." I clear my throat, trying not to sound put out about his ongoing dedication to that goal. "I get it and it's fine. I'm not exactly the type of guy you normally go out with."

"What type of guy is that?" he asks, eyebrows lifting.

"You know, guys more like you." I gesture to him. "Guys who are all over-the-top gorgeous, with big muscles and sex-eyes and lots of experience with… you know, being gay."

His expression is half amusement, half frown, and all surprise. "Well, yeah, I pick up guys like that when I want to get laid. We have a good time, get each other off and then we go home. Patrick, I screw those guys, I don't date them."

"Well, that's the only type of guy I've ever seen you with." Logan hasn't had a boyfriend since I've known him. He's never so much as mentioned any past boyfriends, though surely he must have exes out there somewhere. "What type of guys do you normally date?"

He pulls his lips between his teeth as he fights a grin. "What if I told you, when it comes to dating, I'm a total fool for academic types." My gaze snaps to his and he winks at me. "I like a man who can talk to me about all the big ideas in his head. A man who'll invite me over for sex, but then cook me dinner first. Someone who is open to life and learning new things." We stare at each other for a long moment before he smiles. "Hard as it may be to believe, I do want more from a partner than a well-practiced dick."

That's it. My heart is melting into a big, wet puddle. Pulling back on the feelings overload, I flash him a teasing smirk, "I'm sorry, but my brochure clearly stated all gay men are interested in dick and nothing but dick. Now, you're going to tell me feelings are involved?" I huff out a breath. "My mind is blown."

He laughs out loud. "In that case, I guess two things have been blown today."

I reach across the table to take his hand before I realise what I'm doing. Not only does he not jerk away, but his fingers thread through mine until our palms press together.

"We make great friends, Patrick," he says in a quiet voice, "and I don't want to lose that. But we make pretty amazing lovers, too. If you're open to the idea, I would like to put those two together and see what else we could be to each other."

A full-body smile ripples beneath the surface of my body. It tugs at the corners of my mouth and sets my skin to tingling. I hesitate to give in to it, because I'm still a mess and I know this can't work long-term. But I want it. I want to have this with him—even if it's only for a short while. "I'd love to go out on a date with you." I reach out with my free hand so we can shake on it.

"What is that?" His gaze drops to my outstretched hand. "Every single one of our deals so far has been sealed with a kiss."

I rise from my chair, making a sound somewhere between a groan and a laugh. "If you kiss me, I'll kiss you back. Then we'll be having sex again and I'm not sure my penis can take it." Nor am I sure how convincing I am, considering I'm lifting a leg over him as I speak. Settling onto his lap, I grip the front of his t-shirt in my hands. "We're supposed to be heading out to get some sunlight right about now."

"We'll get there." He laughs as his hands squeeze my butt cheeks. "Eventually." Standing up with me still in his arms, he deposits me on the edge of the table and stands between my spread thighs. "How about I kiss you, but I promise not to have sex with you." Leaning down, he licks the seam of my lips before whispering, "And I promise not to touch your penis."

Snorting, I lift my legs and wrap them around his waist. "Don't make promises I don't want you to keep."

Our mouths fuse and before long we're lost to the world and its offerings of sunlight.

Logan does end up touching my penis. But only as much as I touch his.

LOGAN

For our first official date, I meet Patrick after work on Friday and drive us up to the Sunshine Coast. We stop for dinner at a restaurant at the Noosa Marina. It's there I hand over an envelope containing our plans for the evening. Tickets to a concert for an upcoming local band I've heard Patrick gush over the last few months.

His eyes widen as he reads the tickets. "Holy shit," he exclaims with a laugh, "how did you even get these? They sold out a month ago."

"I have connections in all the right places," I tell him. "One of the guys in the supporting band is an old friend of mine. One phone call to my mate, Ned, and the tickets were mine." One phone call and a promise to revamp the band's website. Their existing site is an old, outdated piece of trash so I'll have to chuck it and start from scratch, but the extra work is worth seeing the excitement on Patrick's face.

"This is awesome. Thank you." He rises out of his chair to land a quick kiss on my lips. It's such a normal couple gesture, my heart soars with hope for all that could be ahead of us.

After dinner, we head to the concert venue and find a good spot near the stage, which is good because the place quickly fills to capacity. When Ned's band comes on stage, the energy of the crowd surges upward. Ned spots me in the crowd as he stalks to the centre of the stage in black leather pants and a tight black t-shirt. I hold up a hand in acknowledgment and he grins and blows me a kiss.

"That's your old friend?" Patrick raises his eyebrows at me. "The sex-god who's flirting with you?"

I shrug, giving a nod. "Yep."

"Of course, it is." His gaze narrows and he shakes his head. "You and he?"

Catching the flare of jealousy on his face, I want to crow in delight. While I'm tempted to tease him further, I never would. "No. We've only ever been friends."

My words don't seem to make him feel any better. With another glance at the stage, Patrick turns to wind an arm around my waist, the front of his body brushing against my side. It's a blatant sign of possession if ever I saw one, and it sends a ripple of satisfaction through me.

We soon get caught up in the heavy beat of the music and, by the time the main act comes on stage, Patrick and I are dancing like a couple of idiots, along with about five hundred other people. The rock is deafening and the crowd near the stage is crushing, but we stick close to each other, linking hands when the heaving mass of bodies threatens to pull us apart.

A bigger guy starts failing his arms too close to Patrick's head for my comfort and I yank him closer to keep him out of striking range. Once he's in front of me, I wrap an arm around his torso, coming in under his arm and stretching up towards his other shoulder. "This place is crazy," I say into his ear, so he can hear me over the wailing guitars and crashing drums. "I don't want to lose you."

Reaching over his head, he wraps a hand around the back of my neck and leans back to yell into my ear. "You won't lose me. I won't let you." His eyes are bright and his arse rubs against my groin with every movement. He captures my lips with his, his tongue thrusting deep into my mouth as his fingers rake across my scalp.

My own fingers curl against him, fisting his shirt. By the time the kiss ends, my erection is pressed hard against the curve of his butt. He goes back to watching the band on stage, his gyrating hips torturing me. My guttural groan is drowned out by the music and I have to move back a step to prevent embarrassment.

Looking back at me over his shoulder, Patrick laughs at my predicament. I sling an arm around his neck and smack his cheek with a kiss. We rejoin the chaos of the dance floor, and I've never had so much fun on a first date in my life.

By the time the concert ends, and we spill back out onto the streets of Noosa, it's after ten. We're pumped from the concert, but still stop by one of the major petrol stations to grab some bad coffee and doughnuts in preparation for the two-hour drive home along the darkness of the highway.

We spend a good half hour talking about the concert and how much we enjoyed it, before moving on to discuss our favourite songs and the albums that changed our lives. As always, the conversation twists and turns to cover a dozen tangents.

"The supporting act wasn't too shabby either," Patrick says, after a lull in the conversation.

I chuckle at the reluctance in his admission. "Yeah, they were good. It's been ages since I saw Ned perform."

"Now there's a man who knows exactly how good looking he is," he adds dryly. "Am I right?"

"Oh, yeah. He was always a bit of a poser, even when we were teenagers. I'm glad it worked in his favour though. There's a good man beneath those leather pants."

Patrick's sudden silence draws my attention. When I turn my head, he's giving me a pointed look.

"Not that I've ever been in his pants," I add, my pointedness every bit as sharp as his. "Platonic friends all the way."

"Ha!" he scoffs. "Up until about two months ago we were platonic friends, too. Look how that's turning out."

Reaching out a hand, I place it on his thigh. High up on his thigh. High enough to make him squirm. "Patrick, baby, we may have been friends, but it was never truly platonic—at least, not from my side." Glancing at him, I lick my lips. "I was always one kiss away from wanting you."

He stares at me while I go back to staring at the road. I have yet to move my hand.

"Really?"

I nod—with extra exaggeration. "Fuck, yes."

There's a short silence, before he says in a quiet voice, "I didn't know."

"Of course, you didn't. I barely acknowledged it to myself." Removing my hand from his leg, I put it back on the steering wheel where it's safer. "When we met, if I'd allowed myself to even think about you that way, I couldn't have become friends with you. I've done the unrequited love thing already and it was too damned painful." I heave a sigh, hoping to expel some of the sudden tension running through me. "But I wanted us to be friends. I liked you."

"I liked you, too," he says with a smile in his voice. "Is that what happened with your other friend? The one who hurt you? Were you attracted to him when you met, and became friends with him anyway?"

"No." My knuckles turn white and I shake my head. "I wasn't attracted to anyone at the age of six, so…"

"Christ. You really were friends a long time."

"Yep." I don't know how much I want to tell him about Ben. Revealing that kind of information—it's a big deal.

As the silence lengthens, Patrick clears his throat and sits up straighter in his seat. "So, how about that local sporting team?"

I snort a laugh. When I glance at him sideways, he grins back at me.

"Thank you for tonight," he says, reaching out to tangle his fingers in the hair at the back of my neck. I've avoided cutting it for weeks now, because I know he likes to play with the loose curls that have formed there. "I had a great time. You totally get a gold star in the first date column."

"Phew. What a relief."

The silence returns but it's the relaxed, comfortable kind. Patrick seems to have accepted my reluctance to share about Ben, thank goodness. The fallout from that relationship brought out the worst in me. Sharing those pieces of myself would imply a closeness well beyond the boundaries of any friendship. Despite our new dating status, I'm not entirely sure Patrick wants us to get that close. Ben didn't. I've never invested enough of myself in anyone else to bother trying.

Do I want to invest so much of my heart in Patrick? It's a choice I have to make. To take the risk. To trust in this tenuous bond we've formed and hope for the best.

"Ben and I met in primary school," I tell him. "We were best friends for years. It wasn't until we were teenagers that I started to look at him differently." Puberty hit me like a truck and my first wave of lust settled itself on Ben's young shoulders. Suddenly, I didn't see him as a friend anymore. He was the boy I daydreamed about and wanted and got hard for. "I hid my feelings for him for years. Sometimes, I even managed to think I'd gotten over it, usually by developing a crush on some other boy. Unfortunately, while crushes generally didn't last, my love for Ben was always there below the surface. When I came out in senior year, he watched my back from day one. Ready to jump on anyone who dared to object or give me a hard time, and he was big enough to do it. His support meant the world to me and made me fall for him all the harder."

I glance at Patrick. He's watching me silently, probably psychoanalysing every word out of my mouth. He wouldn't be Patrick if he didn't.

"When we graduated high school, Ben and I both enrolled in the same course at university. In our second year, we decided to move out of home and get an apartment together, so we'd be closer to the campus. It was only after we started living together things changed. Not right away," I clarify. "It was more of a gradual thing. At first, it was nights when we hung out together watching television and he'd end up with his head on my shoulder. Or he'd get all up in my personal space when we were both crowded into our tiny kitchen. One day, he accidentally walked in on me in the shower..." His gaze had lingered on my naked body through the transparent curtain. I'd been hard within seconds, despite my mortification at the fact. "Let's just say, he took way too long to leave." I can't help but smile at that particular memory.

"He kissed me first," I tell Patrick, as if it makes a difference. "I never would have dared. I'd convinced myself the vibes I was getting off him were the mad wishes of my overly horny mind. But no, he definitely made the first move." I wink at Patrick. "I made the second."

He gives a shadow of a smile. "How long were you together?"

"We never were, officially. Outside the walls of our apartment we were nothing but friends, but within those walls... we were a lot more." I can't keep the traces of bitterness from my voice, though the anger I once harboured has long-since cooled. "I didn't care about the secrecy at the time. Ben was the love of my life—or so I thought—and against all chance and hope, he finally wanted me back. It was a dream come true."

In some ways, those were the happiest months of my life. I'd believed my relationship with Ben was blossoming, that we were moving, ever so slowly, towards something beautiful and enduring. If there were times when I got the feeling our relationship was based less on feelings and more on the fact I was a convenient body to rut against, it didn't matter. I knew I could make us work. If I made Ben happy enough, he couldn't help but fall in love with me.

A gentle weight lands on my thigh and I look down to see Patrick's hand there. His thumb moves back and forth in a soothing caress. I smile. Ben never would have done that. He touched me in all sorts of ways, from rough and grabby to soft and teasing, but only when he was looking to get off. I'd seen him use casual gestures of affection with plenty of girls he'd dated—but he never used them with me.

"It didn't last, of course." I shrug a shoulder at the inevitability of it all, though I was blind to it at the time. "His desire for me waned and he started to avoid coming home. Honestly, I think as the novelty of it all wore off, he realised he didn't want to be in a relationship with me, or any man. But he didn't know how to tell me."

It was a conclusion I had to come to all on my own—in slow, agonising degrees. When he stopped greeting me with kisses. When I became the only one giving oral sex. When he started to freeze up every time I touched him.

Ben and I only had penetrative sex a few times. He had zero interest in bottoming, and when he topped me, I knew I got more out of it than he did.

"Eventually, I ran out of ways to ignore the truth. Ben didn't want me anymore and he would never fall in love with me—not the way I loved him. About six months after our first kiss, I suggested we go back to being friends." It broke my heart to say the words. I wished so hard he would tell me I was crazy, that he loved me back and wanted to make us work. No such luck. "He jumped at the chance to go back. Told me how relieved he was I felt that way, too."

Patrick hisses in a breath. "That must have hurt like hell."

I bark out a harsh laugh. "Only in the way it hurts to be gutted from the inside out."

After a brief silence, Patrick says, "It's no wonder going back to being friends didn't work for you and Ben." Something in his tone makes me look at him. He's staring at me intently, his hand still tight around the top of my thigh. Is he trying to assure me we'll be okay if we make the same attempt? I'm not so sure.

"It worked well enough for him. It was like he just set aside the part of himself that had been attracted to me, like it was a coat he shrugged off." I'd never understood how he could turn those feelings off so easily, unless there'd been no substance to them in the first place. "The switch was much harder for me. I still loved him and pretending not to hurt like the devil. Then, a few months after the relationship we never officially had ended, he confessed his love." I put a hand over my chest as I continue the story, knowing it will be easier to get through if I add some dramatic flair.

"He did what now?" Patrick cries, playing along.

"Yep. He'd met some girl at uni. Her name was Vicki and, apparently, they'd started dating not long after we broke up. Ben had been reluctant to tell me because he thought it might be awkward."

Patrick's eyebrows go up. "He thought being replaced would be awkward for you?"

"Pretty much." At least Patrick appears as appalled as I was. "Anyway, his new girlfriend was gorgeous and nice, and she loved him back. I tried to be okay with them being together, but then she started staying over at our place a few times a week and it all became too much. Knowing he was in the next room, making love to her in the bed we'd shared. Knowing he'd fallen in love with her so quickly, when he'd found it impossible to love me..." My voice catches and I pause briefly. "I started to hate him for it, and I didn't want that. So, I moved out. That's when I got the place I'm in now."

The night I packed a bag and told Ben I was leaving, I went to my sister's house and confessed the whole sordid tale. She'd had no idea what was going on between me and Ben, no one did. After I'd filled her in, I practically had to sit on her to stop her from marching back to the apartment to kick Ben in the gonads.

"Is that when you stopped trying to be friends?"

I nod. "We were finishing our last year of university by then. I managed to avoid Ben for the most part and he didn't exactly come looking for me. By the time we graduated, we rarely spoke." I huff out a laugh. "We're still Facebook friends, if you can believe it. That's how I know he and Vicki are still together. They look happy."

Patrick looks at me like I'm crazy. "Masochist."

My laugh is more genuine this time. "Maybe at first. But I'll have you know I did get over Ben—eventually. Starting work at the library with Naomi helped. Then I met you, and then Stacey and Ian. Making new friends was good for me. It stopped me from being alone so much."

The streets around us begin to brighten as we enter the outskirts of northern Brisbane. The drive has been more emotionally draining than I expected, but at least the heavy conversation made the time pass quickly. I feel lighter now, like I'm not hiding all my bullshit from Patrick anymore. Who knows, maybe I'm learning to be more authentic, too.

"I can't believe, after all that, you actually agreed to do my stupid experiment with me," Patrick cries, throwing his hands in the air. "Are you a crazy person? Doesn't this feel like some kind of messed up déjà vu or something?"

"Not so much." I chuckle at his expression of disbelief. "I get that there are similarities on the surface, but our relationship started in a completely different place to the one I had with Ben. For one, I wasn't in love with you for like five years before it even began." I'm in love with him now, but there's no need to point that out. "And two, when I offered to do the experiment with you, it was because I wanted to get my hands on your dick, not because I was picturing our tenth anniversary. Do you see the difference?"

"I suppose." He sighs and I can tell my words have stung, though that wasn't my intention. "What about now?" he asks grudgingly.

"It's still different," I say without hesitation. "Entirely, fundamentally different."

"How is it different?"

A smile tugs at my mouth. He's still huffy. That's okay, a little more truth will fix that. "Because I never feel like I have to seduce you into wanting me. With Ben, a part of me always felt like I needed to convince him." Which is part of the reason why I always let Patrick take the lead when we're together. Not only because he was skittish to start with, but because I need to know he's with me because he wants to be, not because I promised to suck him off if he kissed me.

"Well, that makes no sense," Patrick snaps. "You're freaking gorgeous, and you do that sexy thing with your eyes that drives me crazy. Anyone in their right mind would want you."

"I know, right?" I'm laughing now, because he's so goddamned adorable when he's pissed off on my behalf. "And I have a stunning personality to boot."

"Exactly."

Before long, we're nearing the turn off for Patrick's place, but as I flick on my indicator, he sits up suddenly.

"No," he says in a clear voice. "Let's go to your place tonight."

I frown at the odd request, but turn off the indicator and keep driving, heading in the direction of my apartment. "Why?"

We've never spent the night at my home. I've always met Patrick at his place. Maybe because that's where the experiment started. Maybe because keeping Patrick out of my personal space has been one more way of protecting myself from him. If so, the strategy hasn't been as effective as my unconscious hoped.

"I want to sleep in your bed." He turns his head to look at me, the intensity in his blue eyes clear, even in the darkness of the car. "I don't know how this whole thing between us is going to end and I don't know what we'll be calling ourselves six months from now. For right now, though, I don't want you to doubt your bed is exactly where I want to be. And I'm going to fuck you while I'm there, all slow and deliberate like, to drive the point home."

"You see that?" I say in a low voice, a smug grin on my lips as blood rushes for my groin. "Entirely, fundamentally different."

PATRICK

W atching Logan sleep is a creepy arse thing to do. He did invite me into his bed, and has continued to do so on a regular basis in the month or so since we officially started dating, so technically he knew this was a possibility. Still, I've been staring at him for at least ten minutes so… yeah, creepy.

He stirs, finally, and blinks open sleepy eyes. Seeing me lying there beside him, his lips curve into a lazy smile. A long arm snakes beneath the blankets that ward off the late-Autumn chill. Wrapping it around my waist, he pulls me closer, humming in pleasure as his body curves around mine.

"Good morning." The words are muffled as he nestles his face against my neck, inhaling deeply.

"Morning." I go one step further, sliding an arm under him and dragging him on top of me. With a deep, satisfied sigh, he settles with his head on my chest, his torso cradled by my hips and our legs tangled.

It's early on a Tuesday morning. Work looms, but we don't have to get up for a while yet. I can feel Logan's morning erection pressed against my thigh, but neither of us makes any moves towards sex. If he touched me in any of the ways he's done so many times, I know I would be ready and eager for it in a heartbeat. For now, though, I'm content to lie here, threading my fingers through his hair, tracing them down over the long lines of his back.

I love touching him like this, even when it's not about sex. I love kissing him, even when it's not leading to more. I love talking to him, knowing what he thinks about a million different things that matter and don't.

Because I love him.

I'm in love with him. As a friend, a lover, as everything I've ever wanted in a partner—even though I never expected that partner to be him.

The realisation brings me no joy. I never meant for it to happen and I would take it back if I could.

Logan and I have crossed a lot of lines in the months since the experiment began. We've always done so with the belief we can edge back over to the other side if needed. That if things don't work out between us, we can still hold on to the friendship that brought us together in the first place. But this, falling in love with him, is a line I can only cross in one direction. Now I'm here, I can't go back.

Eventually, the alarm goes off and we drag ourselves out of bed. We begin the simple morning routine we've fallen into on weekday mornings, whether we're at his place or mine. He makes coffee and pops bread into the toaster. I cook up some eggs. Conversation begins to flow as our brains kick into gear and we talk about our plans for the day.

We plate up our breakfast and sit down to eat. I watch him bite the end off a piece of toast and wonder if I should tell him I'm in love with him. It doesn't seem like the kind of thing I should keep to myself.

If he were in love with me, I would want to know.

Is he in love with me? If so, he hasn't mentioned it. It hasn't come up in casual conversation.

The last time either of us mentioned the word love, was the night he told me about Ben. When he told me how deeply and how long he'd loved another man. At the time, he said he was willing to do the experiment with me because he *wasn't* in love with me when it began. But I'm trained to notice the things people don't say, and he never clarified whether his feelings had changed by then or not. He could be in love with me now. Or at least, he could be in love with whomever he thinks I am. Given I don't know these days who that is, it would be impossible for *him* to know.

Damn it, I'm thinking in circles now. It's not helpful and it's giving me a headache.

"I won't be able to come over tonight," Logan tells me as he finishes his meal and stands to take the dishes to the sink. "I have to finish setting up a website for a client after I get home from the library. It's a bit of a rush job, but they get me lots of word-of-mouth business so I want to stay in their good books."

"Okay." Spending the night home alone sounds lonelier than it used to be. Maybe because it's been so long since I did it. Logan and I started spending most of our nights together back around the time we began Phase Two of the experiment, before we even started officially dating. It hasn't always been about sex or experimentation, though. Some nights we simply hang out watching television, or reading, or talking until all hours of the night. Other nights we've gone to the movies, or out to dinner. Dating Logan is fun, and comfortable. And I don't want to spend the night without him.

This is getting ridiculous. I've been in relationships before, but I've never been this… attached.

"I've got a bunch of assignments I need to mark for my Abnormal Psych students. How about I bring them over here and we can work together?" I nudge his shoulder as he finishes cleaning his mug. "I promise not to distract you."

"As if having you in the room isn't distraction enough." Smacking a kiss to my forehead, he wipes his hands on a tea towel. "Sounds good. You want to leave your car here and get a lift to the uni with me?"

I shake my head. "I'll need to swing by my place after work to get more clean clothes." We head for the bedroom to get dressed. "How about I pick up some Thai on the way back here, so we don't have to cook?"

Logan grins. "You have the best ideas."

An hour later, I'm walking across the university campus with a smile on my face. I'm still not happy about being in love with Logan. But at the same time, there's a bubble of exhilaration trapped under my ribs. It keeps bouncing around down there, looking for a way to escape and cause havoc with my nervous system. I'm tempted to set it free, I want to enjoy this, but I have to be careful.

It's all happening too fast and too soon. I've only just figured out the whole thing where I'm an unexpected bisexual. Who knows what other personality traits are hidden away in the outer regions of my psyche, waiting for the most inopportune moment to reveal themselves? I need to find a way to restore some sort of equilibrium to my sense of identity. I need to know who I am. Until then, my love for Logan has to be contained. It's the only way to ensure I don't mess it up.

My phone rings, interrupting my musings. I check the screen before answering. "Hey, bro. How's things?"

"Bloody perfect," Charlie growls. "If you don't count the fact it's my birthday next week."

I frown in confusion. "You're turning twenty-three. That's way too young to see birthdays as a bad thing."

"Don't be so sure. Has Mum told you, she and Dad are insisting on taking the whole family out to dinner to celebrate? Both of them."

My steps slow. "Oh." My mouth forms the sound and then freezes as I consider the implications. "As in sitting at a table together? For a whole meal?"

"Yep."

"Crap."

"Exactly," he cries. "Now you get why I'm pissed."

I'm about to reach the door for the psychology building. Instead, I turn and walk the other way. This could take a while. "They're mellowing out in their old age," I say, in a vague attempt to assure him this isn't the disaster-in-waiting he's imagining. "Maybe it won't be so bad."

"That's bullshit and you know it," he insists. "Which is why you need to bring a date."

Frowning, I shake my head. "How will that help?"

"I figure they might try to rein in their crazy if they think it could hurt your chances of having an actual love life."

"Or it could make them crazier." I run a hand over my face. "I'm dating Logan."

"Oh, hell yes! That's perfect." Charlie's exclamation has me pulling the phone from my ear with a grimace. "They'll be so focused on you and your new boyfriend, they'll barely even notice me."

"Why is them noticing you on your birthday a bad thing?"

"Because I quit my job and if they find out they're going to spend the whole damned night arguing about it."

"Why did you quit your job?" I ask. "When did this happen?"

"Last week and that's not the point," he insists. "The point is, you have to bring Logan to dinner. Consider it your birthday present to me."

I try to tell him I already bought him a present, but he's lowered his phone so he can call out to Penny. "Hey, babe. Patrick and Logan are official. I owe you ten bucks." Rolling my eyes, I wait for the distant sound of Penny's squeals to recede and Charlie to put the phone back to his ear. "I guess this means your experiment was a success?"

"The experiment is still going, technically." It's lip-service at this point, but it helps me feel like I still have some sort of control over the situation. "It's evolving as needed."

"Riiight," Charlie says, dragging the word out. "And when you decide to have babies, will you refer to them as experiments, too? Because Penny has assured me that's not appropriate child-rearing behaviour."

"Slow down, little brother. We've been dating for a month."

"No, you've been dating for three months," he insists. "You've only been admitting to it for a month."

"Fine, we've been dating for three months." It's semantics anyway. I know what's going on between me and Logan. What do I care what Charlie wants to call it? "Either way, it's too soon to start introducing him to the family."

"I'm family, and I've already met him, multiple times."

"Mum and Dad haven't met him."

"And this is the perfect opportunity," he says with exaggerated patience. "Why wait?"

"Because we're keeping it casual. No pressure, no expectations," I say, borrowing Logan's words. "We're not even using the boyfriend label. It's still part of our... experimental partnership or something."

Charlie snorts so hard he starts coughing. "That's the most romantic thing I've ever heard. Logan, baby, will you be my... experimental partner." A long peal of laughter follows. "Freaking hilarious."

Turning around, I head back in the direction of my office. I have a sneaking suspicion this conversation is about to come to an abrupt end.

"Seriously, though," Charlie says as his laughter slows to a chuckle. "That's a pretty shitty thing to call the man you're in love with."

I stop dead. "How do you know I'm in love with him?"

"Because if you weren't, you would have denied it."

A rude sound erupts from my mouth. "Arsehole." Pulling open the door to my building, I stomp up the stairs instead of taking the lift. "Fine. Maybe I am a little bit in love with him."

"You can't be a little bit in love with someone, you idiot. Either you're in love with this man, or you aren't. Don't go half-arsing it, or you'll lose it all together."

"What the hell, Charlie?" I stop outside the door to the office I share with Stacey and Ian. "You sound like a romcom."

"Hey," he cries. "I'm not responsible for the ball-shrinking romantic fluff my girlfriend makes me watch. Now, are you bringing your experimental partner to dinner or not?"

"All right, I'll bring him." If only to shut Charlie up. "But if our parental units go bat shit and Logan dumps me before dessert hits the table, I'm blaming you."

LOGAN

I'm scrolling through Facebook during my morning tea break when I see it. At first, I don't realise the post I'm staring at belongs to Ben. Somewhere in the last two years, my brain has trained itself not to pay attention to his posts. But the diamond ring catches my eye. It's big and flashy as it's held out for the camera.

Ben is engaged. He's marrying Vicki.

They look happy, their heads touching as they pose for the photo. It's obvious this picture was taken in the moments after his proposal. Ben's smile is bright like the sun. It's the same smile he had when he got his first gaming console when he turned fourteen. The one he wore for three days straight after he got laid for the first time. I know that smile. It's the one he wears when he's totally, blissfully happy.

I'm smiling too, I realise with a start of surprise.

It's not that I ever wished him ill, not really, but there was a time when I believed the idea of seeing him marry someone else could only mean misery for me. As it turns out, not so much. My heart has healed, as hearts do. I can be happy for him now. I am happy for him.

When my break finishes, I head back into the library to find Naomi behind one of the computers at the front desk. I do a doubletake when I see her. "What the—?"

"Shut up," she snaps without looking up.

"Not going to say a word."

Her dark gaze flicks upward and I draw a zipper over my lips.

"Good," she says.

Taking a seat at the other end of the long desk, I go back to the project I've been working on the last few days. Every now and then I sneak a glance at my friend. I try not to, but I can't help it. I've never seen her with brown hair before. Green, purple, sometimes pink, but never brown.

"I met Stacey's parents on the weekend," she says, still not looking at me. "I wanted to look respectable, so they wouldn't hate me."

A few torturous moments pass before I ask, "Did they hate you?"

Her gaze slides to mine and I see uncertainty, but also a flash of hope. "I don't think so. They were so painfully polite it was hard to tell."

My lips curve. "Painfully polite is good. It means they're trying," I point out, before adding, "By the way, I like the hair. It looks nice."

A reluctant grin tugs at her lips. "Thank you."

We both turn back to our work and I try not to sigh at my monitor. The project I'm working on is useful enough, but it's so goddamned boring. I'd much rather be working on my own stuff. Still, it's a job and it keeps me from going crazy on my own at home so... best to keep at it.

The next couple of hours are uneventful. Naomi and I happen to take our lunch break at the same time, so we head over to the cafe to grab some sandwiches. Naomi starts to fidget as we make our way across campus. "How are you and Patrick going?" she asks finally, an odd note of concern in her voice. "Are, um, are you guys okay?"

"We're good." We're still dating, at least. We're dating so hard we're practically living together. It has to be a good sign. "Why?"

She swallows, as if she's not sure whether her next words should come out of her mouth, or just hole up there and die. "I found something out yesterday..."

Of course, she did. Because we went to uni together and she has a bunch of the same Facebook friends I do. "Ben's engaged. I saw the post."

Naomi heaves a sigh of relief. "Oh, thank goodness. I saw it and I didn't know if I should tell you, or if you already knew or... because I know it's a big deal for you."

"Actually, it's not a big deal anymore." I understand why she would think it is. Naomi saw me in the depths of my despair after Ben and I broke up. She knows how bad I got, how bad I allowed myself to get. "I'm over it. Really."

Her face breaks into a smile. "Good. I'm glad." We enter the cafe and join the end of the line. "Patrick is much better for you anyway," she says while perusing the pre-packed foods visible through the glass at the counter. "I didn't know you and Ben were together when it was happening, but I did know both of you, kind of." We were more like distant acquaintances, than friends, at the time. "You always seemed kind of miserable back then. Honestly, I thought maybe you were one of those naturally depressive types or something."

"Naturally depressive? Gee, thanks." If anything, I was situationally depressive. Coming to the slow realisation the man you love doesn't love you back isn't exactly uplifting.

"You know, that day I ran into you, after we graduated, I almost didn't tell you about the job here at the library. I wasn't sure I wanted to be around you that much. But you seemed to need it so desperately, I decided to take a chance. Of course, when you got here you perked right up. Thank god!" she says dramatically, before smirking at me. "Then, I got my reward for being all selfless and shit."

I tilt my head to one side. "What reward?"

"Stacey." She rolls her eyes at my inability to make the simple connection. "If I hadn't told you about the job, you wouldn't have been here to meet Patrick. And if you hadn't met Patrick, I might never have met Stacey." Her hands wander back and forth through the air as she spells out the logic of it all. "Don't you see? My selfless act proved to the universe that I deserve the love of the most beautiful girl in the land." She winks at me with a joyful giggle. "Karma isn't always a bitch."

"Well then, I'm glad my glum mug didn't stop you from telling me about the job," I tell her, "because I definitely needed the change of scenery. You probably saved my life that day."

"I know I did, darling," she gushes, a hand over her heart. "I'm a saint."

We laugh, but I'm not sure I overstated how dire my situation was. I'd been so out of it from working too many hours for too many weeks. Barely eating or sleeping. It's a wonder I hadn't already stumbled into the path of an oncoming truck while searching for the grocery store, or fallen asleep behind the wheel of my car.

It's strange to look back on it now. I was a different person then.

"I'm surprised you're still working here, though," she says after we buy our food and sit down. "I love the library. It's an actual forest of knowledge, what's not to love? You though..." She shrugs. "With your side business and all, I didn't think you'd make it to the end of your first year, and now you're finishing up your second."

"I like working at the library."

"No, you like being at the library," she points out. "You find the work tedious and we both know it."

Breathing out a sigh, I put down my sandwich. "Yeah, you're right. It was only ever supposed to be temporary. Something to help me get back on my feet."

Taking a sip of her iced tea, she shrugs at me. "You did that ages ago. What's keeping you here?"

I shrug, which pretty much sums up my approach to life these last few years. "I don't know. Sometimes I think about quitting, going back to my business full-time. Then I think, what's to stop me falling back into the downward spiral of overwork and isolation." I don't want to believe it would happen, but I'm not sure I'm willing to put it to the test. "I don't want to be alone like that again." The idea makes me panic, every single time, and then I put off taking any action at all.

"Do you mean to tell me starting a business by yourself, with a broken heart and a giant hole where your best friend used to be, isn't the perfect recipe for happiness?" She makes a gasping sound, her mouth falling open in supposed shock. "I'm flabbergasted, Logan. Really."

I roll my eyes at her and she laughs. "Come on, you can't tell me there aren't ways to work for yourself and still be the social butterfly you've become."

"That's true," I concede. "Not the butterfly part." There are ways I could stop myself from becoming too isolated. Networking events for small businesses like mine happen around the city all the time. I ignored those opportunities the first time, preferring my own misery to the company of others.

"Besides," she continues, "you now have an advantage you didn't have before." I stare at her in question and she spreads her hands with a flourish. "You have me."

"Ah, yes. The queen of the knowledge forest." Her smile widens with delight at the title and I laugh warmly. "Na, you know you'll be running the place someday, don't you?"

She bows her head in a stately manner. "I do."

I love seeing Naomi so happy. It suits her. She seems more herself than I've ever seen her before. Comfortable in her own skin. Authentic, Patrick would say.

It strikes me that everyone is moving forward with their lives, finding their niches in the world. It's not just Ben and Naomi. Patrick will finish his PhD at the end of the year and move on to the next stage of his career. So will Stacey and Ian.

Meanwhile, I continue to be stuck. Halfway between two jobs. Halfway into a relationship I'm not sure is quite real.

How can I expect my life to move forward if I don't do something about it? Take a chance. Commit to something.

And let go of all that's been holding me back.

Pulling out my phone, I put it on the table between us and pull up the Facebook app.

"What are you doing?" Naomi asks.

I tap on Ben's name to open his profile. "I'm moving on." Ben and I were great friends once, the best. But that part of my life is over now. I have no desire to rekindle our friendship. It would be awkward and messy, and I don't want to go there. I have new friends now, and a new life. It's a life I want to share with Patrick.

Unfriending Ben takes all of about five seconds. Turns out, ending a friendship of almost twenty-years is not as hard as I thought it would be. I do feel it, deep in my chest, the tug of that last tie severing. But it doesn't hurt, and when I take a deep breath and smile at Naomi, I'm not sorry it's gone.

LIMITATIONS OF
THE STUDY

PATRICK

I'm ensconced on Logan's couch, marking my sixth essay on the assessment and diagnosis of mood disorders, when Logan bends over the back of the couch to wrap an arm around my chest from behind and buzz my cheek with a kiss.

"You're sexy when you're being all critical of other people's work." He strokes a finger between my eyes. "It think it's the frown that gets me hot."

Trying to hide a grin, I kiss him back. "How's your work going?" I save my file and dump my laptop on the coffee table. "Better than mine, I hope."

"I'm done." He goes into the kitchen to refill his water glass.

"Already?" Yawning, I stretch my arms over my head and glance at the wall clock. "That was quick."

"Sometimes, if I'm a good little web developer, the Internet Gods shine down upon me and everything works right the first time. It's a rare occasion and therefore worthy of celebration." His grin turns suggestive. "Want to celebrate with me?"

"I'd love to, but..." This is the perfect opportunity to do the thing I've been thinking about all damned day. If I don't do it now, I'm not sure I'll find the courage later.

"But?" he echoes, cocking his head to one side.

"First, I need to talk to you about something." My heart kicks into overdrive, unsure how this conversation is going to play out. "It's about the experiment. I've um... I've discovered some limitations of our study." Phrasing this in terms of the experiment is a chicken shit thing to do, but it's the only way I can think of to broach the subject.

Logan stills at my words. "You've hit a limit?"

"No," I assure him. "It's not that kind of limitation." When it comes to exploring his body, I'm still sitting at *barely scratched the surface*. "I'm talking about some unintended consequences that kind of interfere with my," I clear my throat, "objectivity."

"Okay," he lowers himself to the couch. "What kind of consequences?"

"Well, you know I already cared about you when we started this." I want to smack my own forehead at the level of *duh*. "You were my friend, of course I cared about you."

Logan is still and tense as he sits beside me. "That's what allowed this whole thing to start in the first place, right?"

"Right. At least, I think so." My hands are sweating, and I rub them against my thighs. The denim is rough against my fingertips and why does every cell in my body feel like it's on high alert? "The thing is, I've recently realised my feelings have changed. I figure I should tell you, in case it affects your desire to continue with the dating phase of the experiment."

Logan's gaze is locked on mine, his expression wary. He's pushed himself back into the far end of the couch and I'm suddenly positive he knows what I'm about to say and he doesn't want me to say it. Oh crap, what if I'm wrong and he doesn't feel even a little bit the same way. What if this is it?

Swallowing past the lump in my throat, I try to say the words, but find myself rambling instead. "I want you to know, if you want to end the experiment, and go back to being friends, I'll understand. That's why I need to tell you. It would be wrong of me to hide it from you."

He snaps. "Say it, Patrick."

"I'm in love with you."

Everything goes quiet, and then, incredibly, he starts to laugh. Big, gulping laughs that turn his face red. He collapses forward as the tension leaves his limbs, his head landing in my lap. "Fucking hell." The words are muffled by the fact he has his face buried in my groin. "You gave me a goddamned heart attack." The sounds of his voice cause a faint vibration I can feel clear through the denim of my jeans. Normally, his position would have caused a quick and obvious reaction, but I'm currently too busy dealing with my own horror at his response to get turned on.

"I didn't mean to. Fall in love with you, I mean." My hands want to play with the dark waves at the back of his head, but my bruised ego refuses to allow it. "I know it's not particularly professional of me." The words strike me as ridiculous, but I push on regardless.

"It goes against all scientific protocol, but apparently I couldn't help myself."

Logan manages to drag his head out of my lap as he releases another chuckle. "I agree," he says, his smile beaming. "You're a terrible researcher. Maybe I should take over the experiment from now on."

My eyebrows lift, along with my hope. "You're still in, then?" I ask. "You don't want to use your *get out of bed free* card or anything?"

Sitting up, he edges closer to me, folding one of his long legs up on the couch between us. "Why would I do that?" His hands land on my knees before beginning to wander upward. "Things are just getting interesting. Besides, do you really think I still want to go back to being friends after knowing the taste, and the feel, and the smell of you?" Reaching down to take hold of my ankles, he lifts them high before wrapping my legs around his waist. "Not likely."

"Good." I smile in relief but can't stop myself from going on to voice my doubts, even though I know I'll sound like a crazy, jealous person. "I guess, I thought you might want to end it, to save my feelings or something—after what happened between you and Ben."

He frowns at the sound of Ben's name, even as he turns to sit against the back of the couch, pulling me over to straddle his lap. "Save your feelings," he murmurs. "What do you mean?"

"Well, you loved Ben, but he didn't—" I break off with a groan of frustration, trying to find a way to explain without reminding him of past hurts. "I know you'll never love me the way you loved him, but—"

"Patrick, baby, shut the fuck up." His fingers dig into my arse as he frowns up at me. "You know, for a smart man you can be a total idiot sometimes."

I press my lips together. If I'd known confessing my love for him would lead to laughing fits and insults, I may have kept the information to myself, after all.

"Ben's engaged," he says flatly. "I found out today. He's getting married and, you know what? I don't care." This laugh is brief, but it's light and free of pain. "Patrick, my relationship with Ben was enacted in my imagination as much as in reality. Loving him was like a bad habit I couldn't quit. Yes, he was the first man I ever loved, and he always will be. But he's not *you*." The feeling he pours into that final word, the way it bursts out of him with joy and wonder and—God help me, I hope it's love—makes my body tremble. This is all too soon, and I know it's risky, but I want him to love me back.

"You kiss me in public," he says, as if the fact is somehow amazing. "You fuck me like you'll die if you don't. I asked you out on a date and you said yes. You've never once denied me or what we've done, to anyone. You're open and honest and weird and incredible and I fell in love with you the first time you kissed me." More laughter, but this time I'm laughing to and the release of all those pent-up emotions feels like freedom in a way I've never experienced before, not in my whole life.

He cups my face in his hands, staring intently into my eyes. "Don't you ever feel like what we have somehow pales in comparison," he says, "because, for all the ground rules and labels we've slapped on this relationship, what we've shared feels more real to me than anything that came before—with anyone else."

He kisses me then, his lips brushing back and forth against mine. "You are everything I want," he whispers, still close enough to breathe my air.

My eyes close as I melt against him, my lips curving upward.

Gripping me tight, he bends forward at the waist and levers himself up off the couch with me still wrapped around him. Once he's standing, he cups his hands under my butt to help support me. "Christ, you're heavy."

I laugh out loud. "You're a big, strong man. You can take it."

"I'm your man," he says, with a lift of his eyebrows.

"Because you're in love with me," I add as he starts walking us towards the bedroom.

"And you're in love with me." He grins. "That's pretty amazing."

Amazing isn't the word I would use. Because, despite the happiness flooding my system, there's a clenching of dread in my gut. "It's terrifying," I murmur, tightening my hold on him.

His brow lowers into a frown. "Shh, darling." Lifting one leg, he kneels on the bed before lowering us both to the mattress, his body covering mine. He's heavy too, and the weight of him makes me sigh in pleasure.

"Don't be scared," he whispers as his hips start to roll against mine. "I've got you."

LOGAN

We wouldn't be running late for Charlie's birthday dinner if Patrick hadn't decided I looked really good in a suit, and even better with my shirt and tie still in place and my pants around my ankles. The resulting blow job was totally worth the daggers Charlie's eyes send our way as we approach the table.

Penny sits on Charlie's left, her face lighting up in relief at the sight of us. The young couple is flanked by an older man and woman who can only be Patrick's parents.

His dad sits at one end of the rectangular table. Dressed in a simple pair of tailored pants and a button-up shirt, his face is rough and tanned from years spent living a stone's throw from the beach. At the other end of the table is Patrick's mother. The faultless cut of her lush blue dress is also simple, but in a way that screams high-end elegance. Her alabaster skin and manicured nails suggest she has little interest in the ocean. She is the champagne to his seashells.

"Patrick, glad you could make it." Charlie comes all the way around the table to give his brother a back-thumping hug—extra emphasis on the thumping. "Where the hell have you been?" he mutters through gritted teeth. "This is torture."

"I'm here now." As Charlie moves away, Patrick starts to make the necessary introductions. "These are my parents, Lynn and Keith. Mum, Dad, this is my… friend—" He trips over the word before coming to an abrupt halt. Which is understandable, considering he swallowed my jizz not half an hour ago. The word friend doesn't quite cut it anymore. "I mean, he's my…"

The sentence hangs there for a while, as his parents watch us expectantly.

His reticence is something of a surprise. I know he's not worried about getting a negative reaction from his family, but apparently something is still holding him back. When his gaze flickers up to mine, I see confusion there, and maybe a touch of panic.

Giving him a nod of reassurance, I step forward to offer my hand to Keith. "I'm his Logan," I say with a warm smile. "Logan Delaney. It's a pleasure to meet you, sir." After we shake, I do the same with his mother before greeting Charlie and Penny with less formality.

Penny's smile is wide with excitement. "Good to see you again, Logan."

We take our seats. I'm opposite Charlie, beside Patrick's dad, while Patrick takes the spot opposite Penny and beside his mother.

"Sorry we're late," he says, regaining his voice. "Traffic was a bitch. There must have been an accident on the freeway."

Charlie snorts a laugh. "What was it? An overturned unicorn truck?"

Ignoring her younger son's crack, Lynn offers Patrick an indulgent smile. "It's not a problem, darling. You're here now."

"Which means we can order," Keith adds, picking up his menu. "I'm starving. Let's get this party started."

A waiter appears within moments to take our orders. After he's gone, Lynn turns her attention to me, her eyes bright with curiosity. "Logan, how do you and Patrick know each other?"

"We both work at the university." The answer is both polite and truthful but does nothing to explain my presence at their family dinner, or the nature of my relationship with her son. I'd prefer to claim Patrick outright, but if he's not ready to out himself, I'm not about to do it for him. It's a big step. No need to rush.

"Are you studying psychology as well?" Keith asks.

"No, I have a degree in IT. I run a web design business from home, but I also work in the university library a few days a week."

"Ah, the library," he says with an air of nostalgia. "Wonderful place. Lynn and I met in that library when we were in university." His gaze slides to Lynn, who purses her lips and fiddles with the stem of her wine glass. "We spent many an hour there, hunched over desks with our law books, pretending to study."

Patrick and I met in the same place as his parents. The thought makes me smile, though the connection would be more meaningful if they were still together. "You're both solicitors?"

"I'm a barrister," Lynn says. "Keith was also a barrister, once upon a time." She leans forward a touch, her lips quirking with a conspiratorial air. "Until he was lured away from the drama of the courtroom by the irresistible allure of..." she pulls a face, "contract law."

I give a quiet chuckle at her joke. The remainder of the table is silent. It's the kind of silence that comes from half the guests holding their breath.

Beside me, Keith lifts his wine glass in a mock toast. "There is always someone wanting to screw over the little guy—or girl," he adds with a nod to Penny before turning back to me. "Technically, I always worked in contract law. But when I was a barrister, I had flashy corporate clients with lots of money to throw at any legal problems that came their way. One day, I realised how much time I spent feeling like I was on the wrong side of the argument." He lifts his hands in a gesture of concession. "No one likes working for the bad guys. So, I quit. Started a firm where I could help people get the right contract from the start, so they never need to end up in a law court."

"Working for the bad guys," Lynn scoffs. "Don't be so dramatic. You were doing your job, it's what you were paid for. It's what I'm still being paid for."

On the far side of the table, Penny edges closer to Charlie and puts a slender arm along the back of his tense shoulders. I glance at Patrick, whose jaw is locked tight, his focus on his younger brother.

"While they do pay handsomely," Keith agrees, "these days I prefer to choose my conscience over deep pockets."

Lynn laughs as she tosses her long, dark hair over her shoulder. "Is that what you tell yourself when you curl up at night in your multi-million-dollar beachfront property on the Gold Coast?"

Keith's eyes widen. "My parents left me that house."

I look at Patrick. His chest moves in fast, shallow breaths. Reaching out under the table, where no one can see, I slide my hand onto his knee. He takes hold of it, drawing it into his lap so he can grip it tight between both hands.

Meanwhile, his parents continue to take thinly veiled pot shots at each other. I'm not sure if they're about to start a slap fight or let old passions take hold and go for it right there on the table. Is dinner with Patrick's parents always this intense? I glance at Penny to see her reaction, but she's only got eyes for Charlie, who's staring at the white linen tablecloth as if it's the most interesting thing in the room.

"For better or worse," Keith says, spreading his hands wide, "I'm where I'm supposed to be and I'm all the happier for it."

Picking up her glass of wine, Lynn takes a small sip. "So long as _you're_ happy, Keith." Her lips press together as she offers him a tight smile. "That has always been the most important thing… to you."

Keith sighs, shaking his head at his ex-wife. "My dear Lynn, you never change."

"The difference between you and I is, I never felt the need to change. But then," her voice falters slightly, "you did enough of that for the both of us."

I try to keep my face neutral as silence descends… and lengthens… and lengthens some more.

As the only outsider here, I absolutely cannot be the first one to speak. Keith and Lynn seem to have retreated to their corners. I'm not sure they'll return without prompting. Patrick doesn't look like he's up to breaking the silence and it's Charlie's birthday—he shouldn't have to be the one to save the day. My gaze turns to Penny. She's been with Charlie for years, maybe she can—

"I'm bisexual." The words shove free of Patrick's chest in a—no doubt louder than planned—declaration.

Can silence actually get heavier? I mean physically. Because this one is crushing the life out of everyone at our table.

And it's not just us. The tables around us have fallen silent as well. In fact, it's possible the entire restaurant has hit pause to deal with Patrick's unexpected confession. He grabs his wine glass, with the hand that doesn't already have mine in a death grip, and drains it dry. "I thought you ought to know," he croaks.

"That's awesome news, brother," Charlie announces. He reaches out to shake Patrick's hand. "I'm happy for you."

"Thanks, man." They offer each other tight grins and suddenly it's like they can breathe again, both of them drawing air deep into their lungs.

Patrick looks to his mother next. Her eyes are brimming with tears and her scarlet lips break out into a wide smile.

"Well, isn't this a treat," she says, placing her hand over his. "I'm so glad you told us." Patrick's shoulders slump and his hand relaxes around mine. His mother laughs in delight. "I knew all along, of course."

Keith picks up the bottle of wine and stands to refill everyone's glasses as our meals begin to arrive at the table. "For heaven's sake, Lynn, we all knew."

"I didn't bloody know," Charlie cries indignantly.

"Didn't you?" Keith sits back down, and takes a deep whiff of his lamb shank, his eyes practically rolling back in his head. "I guess you weren't there that night."

Charlie gasps. "What night?"

"No, he was at a sleep over," Lynn says as she lifts her fork. "He had no idea." Charlie glares at her and she shrugs. "It's not like we could go around sharing the news. If Patrick wanted you to know, he would have told you himself."

"Christ," Patrick drops his head forward, running his hand over the back of his neck. "I can't believe you guys even remember that."

"Remember what?" Charlie's exasperation is hitting supernova levels, but so far no one is paying attention to him.

"Honey," Lynn says to Patrick with a fond smile. "No parent forgets a conversation like that."

"You have to tell us," Penny begs, looking back and forth between the two older Seymours. "What happened *that night?*"

My own breath catches in my chest, hoping Patrick and his parents will eventually get around to putting the rest of us out of our misery.

Keith and Lynn share a secretive grin, and it's like their earlier argument never happened. Whatever came between them personally, they love their children. That much is obvious.

"Patrick comes into the living room one night as we're about to put on a movie," Keith begins. "He was thirteen years old and, I swear, his knees were knocking together, he was so scared. Out of nowhere, he announces he might be a bisexual. He doesn't know yet, but he suspects. He's still working it out."

Lynn rolls her eyes. "He was fourteen and he was not terrified. Honestly, knees knocking together, as if he ever needed to be scared." Finishing her reprimand, she continues telling the story, picking up where Keith left off. "We asked him if he wanted to talk about it, or ask any questions and he said no." She lifts her hands in a baffled gesture. "What were we to do? We invited him to watch the movie with us and left it at that. Keith and I separated about a year later. Patrick hadn't mentioned it again, so I suppose we didn't think too much of it." Her tone implies the whole thing was nothing more than a quirk in the long road of adolescence. "Then, one day, he mentions, completely out of the blue, he's discovered he's not bisexual after all."

My jaw tightens and the rice I'm chewing sticks to my throat. I know this part of the story. The part where he came to the conclusion he wasn't into guys. I wish I could go back in time and convince him not to go into that bathroom with Mark. I wish I could have made his first kiss with a boy special, and memorable, in a good way.

He glances in my direction and I get the feeling he's making a similar wish.

"We thought it was bullshit, of course," Keith says, recapturing our attention, "and we both tried to get more out of him, but he refused to talk about it. We didn't want to push so, we let it go. That was the end of it—until tonight." He waggles his eyebrows comically as his gaze darts back and forth between me and Patrick. "So, son, what changed your mind? Or should we say who?"

I grin as Patrick clears his throat, his eyes automatically shifting to me. I wink at him and he dissolves into a smile. "That would be Logan's doing."

"How romantic," Lynn croons, clasping her hands together. "Your first boyfriend."

We haven't used the word boyfriend with each other, not out loud, and I look at Patrick to see his reaction. There's a question in his gaze as it meets mine. Is he wondering if I'm okay with it? Smiling, I lean over to murmur in his ear. "Hey there, boyfriend."

He bites down on his bottom lip. "My boyfriend," he whispers back. "I like it."

Our lips meet in a brief kiss and suddenly I'm incredibly grateful I didn't meet Patrick's parents a couple of months ago. Knowing Patrick's obsession with transparency, he probably would have introduced me as his partner in sexual experimentation. I'm not sure that title would have received such a warm welcome. Plus, his parents would have thought we were getting up to kinky shit. Images of Patrick binding my hands to the head of his bed flash through my mind. Actually, we have been working our way up to some kinky shit.

Conversations start to spring up naturally as we eat. Patrick's parents take turns asking me questions about my work and family. Charlie begins to join in the conversation, laughing as he and Penny share stories of what they've been up to.

When Patrick visibly relaxes, I assume we're through the worst part, the part that had Patrick dreading this dinner all week. Until we get to the end of dessert.

"How's your new job going, Charlie?" Keith asks. "Are you enjoying it?"

Charlie is chewing on a bite of birthday cake when the question comes up. His Adam's apple bobs as he swallows, and Penny is already moving back into support mode. "I'm not working there anymore."

Lynn gasps in horror. "What happened? You've only been there a few months?"

"It turned out the job wasn't anything like they advertised. They hired me for high-level systems design, but then piled on the work of a low-level flunky. So, I quit."

"Charlie, you weren't even there six months. I'm sure you could have made it work."

"I tried, but with the bullshit micromanaging supervisor looking over my shoulder all the time, it was never going to happen. They said they wanted me to bring innovative ideas to the table, but every time I did this guy shot them down. If I stayed there, I would have been stuck doing the same crap I was doing two years ago. Which wouldn't have gotten me anywhere."

Keith nods, waving his fork in the air. "Good on you for realising and moving on. You need to be somewhere you can move forward and develop your skills."

Lynn narrows her eyes. "He needs to be somewhere that gives him a pay cheque." She frowns at Charlie. "Looking for something else is one thing, but quitting without another job to go to is madness in this economy."

"In this economy," Keith says, "staying in a job that won't further your chosen career path is madness."

They argue back and forth, ignoring Charlie's attempts to tell them about an interview he has on Tuesday.

I reach for Patrick's hand again. This time, instead of reaching back, he flinches and pulls away. Lifting his arms onto the table, he clasps his hands together in front of his mouth. I get the point and keep my limbs to myself.

When he looks back at me, I see regret in his eyes. "I'm sorry," he murmurs quietly.

I'm not entirely sure what he's referring to. Is he sorry for the behaviour of his parents? For bringing me here? For rejecting my attempt to support him? Or is it something deeper?

I'm reminded of the day I told my sister about my relationship with Patrick. She asked me why anyone would be so obsessed with knowing themselves inside and out. At the time I didn't know, but I'm beginning to think I've just had dinner with the answer.

PATRICK

After we say goodbye to my family outside the restaurant, Logan suggests we take a walk through the nearby Southbank Parklands. I jump at the chance to work off the stress of the evening. I don't understand why my parents insisted we all have dinner together in the first place. It never ends well.

The full moon hangs low in the sky as we make our way down to the boardwalk that runs alongside the Brisbane River. The lights of the cityscape shine on the far side of the water. A cold breeze announces the arrival of Winter and I do up the buttons of my jacket to stay warm.

Logan strolls along beside me, his hands tucked into his pockets. He hasn't tried to touch me once since I pulled away from him in the restaurant. I don't think he's upset with me. He's just trying to be there for me in whatever way I need him. Holy hell, I do not deserve this man.

"So, dinner was fun," he drawls.

I huff out a bitter laugh. "Wasn't it though?"

"Your parents are characters." His chuckle eases some of the tension inside me and I move closer to him, my arm brushing against his as we walk. "They love you," he adds, "and your brother."

"Yeah, they do." Sometimes the love gets overshadowed by the way they grate on each other's nerves, but there's no denying their basic parental devotion. It's always been there, even during their break-up.

"They didn't even blink when you told them you're bisexual."

I smile. "Never expected them to." Their reaction, or non-reaction, makes me proud in a way I didn't appreciate back as a teenager. "They're nothing if not accepting. Despite their problems with each other, they want us to be happy. In whatever form that takes."

Logan opens his mouth, as if he's about to say something about the form he'd like my happiness to take. "How long did you say they've been divorced?" he asks, instead.

"They separated when I was fifteen, but it took another four years or so before they signed the divorce papers." At times I wondered if they'd ever get around to making it official. "It was weird. Like they didn't want to be together anymore, but it was hard for them to let go. You know?"

He nods. "Love is messy. Letting go can be even messier."

"The thing is," I tell him, "I remember how happy they were when I was little, you know?" My childhood was full of picnics in the park, holidays at the beach, trips to the cinema that started with an overload of junk food and ended in sore tummies and sticky smiles.

There had been a time I'd worried whenever I heard them arguing. Near the end of primary school, when my best friend's parents got divorced and he talked about hearing them fight at night after he went to bed. My parents did that too, even though it wasn't often. The next time I heard them arguing, I'd crept out of bed and into the kitchen. Bending down to hide behind the counter, I'd watched them talking in harsh, hushed tones, their gestures sharp with irritation. My heart pounded in my chest as I wondered which of them I'd end up living with. My friend moved into a tiny apartment with his Mum, where he shared a room with his big sister. I didn't want to share my room with Charlie.

Then, Dad pulled Mum into his arms and held her tight. They'd whispered to each other, and although I couldn't hear what they said, the tones they used made me feel safe. I'd crept back to bed when they got to the kissing part. Their fights never worried me after that because I knew their love for each other was stronger than anything else.

"Their relationship wasn't perfect. They had their ups and downs, the same as every other couple. But they truly did love each other. I could feel the presence of that love in our home every day. They were unbreakable. At least, I thought they were."

The back of Logan's hand brushes against mine and I reach for him instinctively. Looking down, I see our fingers threading together, our palms touching. I like the warmth of his skin against mine. He feels solid, dependable. I know that feeling comes from both the depth of our initial friendship, and the bond that has grown between us since we became more. Logan makes me feel safe.

My parents made each other feel safe, too. They made Charlie and I feel safe. That security turned out to be more fragile than I ever would have believed.

"Dad was in a car accident," I tell him, my voice rough. "Some arsehole ran a red light and ploughed into the side of his car." I'll never forget the fear that streaked through me when I heard my mother on the phone to the police that afternoon. The way she burst into tears. "He was hurt, but not as badly as we first thought. A broken arm, whiplash, bruises, that kind of thing. If he'd been even a little bit further through the intersection, if he'd taken off from the green light even a tiny bit faster, the car that hit him would have gone straight through the driver's side door. At the speed the guy was doing, there's little doubt Dad would have been killed."

Logan's staring at me with wide eyes. "Holy shit, Patrick, that must have been awful."

"Yeah, it was, but he recovered well, and everything should have gone back to the way it was. Only it never did." I glance at Logan, wanting him to understand. "He changed after the accident, became a completely different person." And everything about our lives was forced to change with him.

"How so?" Logan asks with a frown.

"The accident wasn't his fault, but he didn't see it that way," I told him. "He'd been on his way to work when it happened, and he was late for a meeting. He'd been getting red light after red light and he was getting more and more frustrated by the delays. At that last intersection, when the light turned green, he slammed his foot on the accelerator, so he could get up to speed as quickly as possible. The way he saw it, his determination to get to work sooner put him in the path of that car." Technically, it's true. If he'd been able to go as fast as he wanted, he would have died.

"After he recovered, he quit his job. He declared he'd never wanted to be a barrister in the first place, but did it because his father expected it of him. What he really wanted was to start his own law firm, to help people and small businesses in his local area get better deals when negotiating with larger corporations. For him, it was like moving from the dark side of the business to the good side. The new firm was a success, but there was no way he'd ever make as much money as he did working for corporations. And because it was a new business, he worked long hours. The thing was, he looked happier than I'd ever seen him." But the happier he got, the unhappier my mother became. "He kept telling us how, for the first time in his life, he was the man he should have always been. The way he said it, it always sounded like he was saying the person he'd been before was some sort of fake. A false skin he'd waited too long to shed."

Logan is quiet for a moment. "That must have been hard to hear."

"Mum was gutted every time he said those words." I shake my head, remembering the pain I so often saw on her face, though she tried to hide it from Charlie and me. She didn't need to hide it from Dad, he'd stopped paying attention. "She missed the life they had together. High pressure cases and the drama of the courtroom. Grand parties and dinners with friends. She loved their old life, the life she still lived, and I hated seeing her go through that. It felt like my father had died, and someone else was walking around in his skin. She missed the old him." In some ways, I'd missed him, too. "At the same time, I watched my father transform from someone who hated his job and was constantly exhausted, to someone who walked with a bounce in his step and loved to talk about what he'd done that day. How could I ever wish for him not to have that?"

Heaving a sigh, Logan shakes his head. "Sounds complicated."

"Tell me about it," I say, nodding in agreement. "When they told us they were separating, I asked Mum if she still loved Dad."

Logan stops walking and, after a single step, I stop too. He turns to face me, his gaze locking on mine. "What did she say?"

I'm quiet for too long, I know. But I don't trust my voice, and I don't want to have to repeat myself. "She said, 'I'm not in love with who he is now, but I would give anything for one more day with the man he used to be.'"

LOGAN

P atrick is quiet on the way back to his place. But it's not the kind of quiet that comes from being tired, or resigned to a situation you can't change. The wheels of his mind are turning, reflecting, evaluating. I can only guess at the conclusions he's preparing to draw. But somewhere there, beneath the active silence of his thoughts, I can sense the future echo of my heart breaking.

The night Patrick confessed his love for me, he told me it terrified him, and he didn't mean for it to happen. I don't fully understand how the breakdown of his parents' marriage has influenced his view of how love works, but I'm beginning to realise he doesn't actually want to be in love with me. It is love, what we have, I don't doubt it, but he wishes it weren't.

This was only ever supposed to be an experiment. A way for Patrick to explore a part of himself he'd ignored too long. I was supposed to help him reach a deeper level of awareness, and then remove myself from his bed without fuss or upset. That was the promise we made to each other.

I knew the risks going in. The chance I'd come to feel more for Patrick than a friendship could allow was always there. I just never expected to fall this far.

Pulling up to the curb outside his building, I make no move to get out of the car. It's been nearly a month since we spent a single night apart, but I'm not entirely sure he wants me to stay this time. I'm reminded of the first night we kissed, when we found ourselves in a similar position. My hands gripping tight to the steering wheel as I watched him, waited to see what would happen next. I wondered, at the time, if he would kiss me again. He didn't, then. This time, he does.

But there's something in his kiss, in the extra pressure that comes before his retreat. It's longing, mixed with regret.

"Stay with me," he whispers against my lips.

My hands loosen their grip and I touch my forehead to his as I release a long, measured breath. "Always."

We make our way up to his apartment in silence. The air between us is heavy with need, but there are no stolen kisses or wandering hands, only the knowledge of what's to come.

The instant the door is locked behind us, he takes my hand and leads me into the bedroom. Turning around, he steps into the circle of my arms. He wraps himself around me, breathing deeply, as if trying to draw me inside himself.

"I want you to make love to me, Logan." The whispered words sound loud and harsh in my ear. I can feel his lips moving, his breath rushing across my skin. "Please, show me what it's like to be yours."

A shiver courses through me. I've dreamed of him saying those words to me. Of him giving me this final gift.

In that moment, every part of me gives in to loving him. All the little pieces I've held back, tried to protect, are his now. It doesn't matter if his own heart is reluctant or his mind is desperate to rebel. I am his and I want him to know it. My heart. My body. Everything I am, belongs to him.

"I love you." I say the words as I pull him more firmly against me. Again as I unbutton his shirt and push it back off his shoulders. Again as I undo his belt buckle and push his pants down over his hips.

"I love you," he whispers in return.

My body shudders in recognition. This is the man who is meant to say those words to me. The only man. They won't mean as much now, coming from anyone else. They are perfect only on his lips.

Capturing his mouth with mine, I encourage him to fill my mouth with his tongue before seeking to return the favour. With a quiet moan, he begins to tug at my clothing, his fingers clumsy with the rush. I smile as I lend a hand.

As soon as we're both naked, I guide him back onto the bed, pausing only to grab a condom and lube from the bedside table. My body covers his and I hiss in a breath at the heat and hardness of him.

His hands clutch at me, eager and desperate, but I capture his wrists and drag them up over his head.

"Shh, baby," I murmur against his throat. "Let me take care of you."

He trembles with need, and perhaps nerves, but my words seem to help calm the fury and he nods. When I release his wrists, his crosses them, leaving them above his head. It's a simple sign of submission. He's giving me control this time. Having told me where he wants to go, he's trusting me to take him there.

The possessiveness I've fought against for so long roars through me. I want to make him mine in every way possible. I want him to come undone for me. Spread out, boneless and wanting. Then, I want to put him back together in all the ways that feel right to him. The ways that fit with me, so he'll never leave.

I start to make my way down his body. My hands are firm and thorough, but unhurried. My kisses wet, but brief. I want this to last, so he knows how good we can be.

His cock is hard between us, the head flushed and weeping. My hands trace a path from his shoulders, circling around his length before continuing all the way down to his knees. My open mouth latches on to his left hip bone, sucking gently. I move to the right side of his waist, licking my way around the faint ridges of his abdominal muscles. Desperate for contact, he tilts his torso towards me, but I evade him with a low chuckle.

Turning my attention to his nipples, I lave each one with the broad flat of my tongue, before dipping down to do the same to the sensitive skin of his inner thighs.

He's shaking now, with restless hips and heaving chest. "Logan, please." The guttural sound clamours with desperation. "Need you."

I crawl back up his body, allowing my stomach to drag along the underside of his throbbing dick. The lower half of him launches off the bed as he seeks more contact and I lower my full weight on top of him, forcing him back down to the mattress. "Oh fuck, yes," he cries. "Please."

Bringing my mouth to his, I lick at his lips with tiny strokes until his mouth is chasing mine. "I like hearing you beg," I tell him. "Tell me, love. Where do you need me?"

"On me," he breaths. "In me." His hips jerk as he rubs our cocks together, desperate for friction. "Anything you want, please. Just fucking *fuck* me."

"If you insist." I grab for the lube before he's done talking. The time for teasing is over. Any trepidation he may have experienced is gone now. Drowned out by lust until all that's left is the sweat on his skin and the musky scent of his arousal. Slicking up one hand, I reach for his cock at the same time I take possession of his mouth.

With a loud groan of relief, his hands come down on me. One clutches the back of my head as he deepens our kiss, fusing our mouths together. The other reaches between us to wrap tightly around my cock, stroking the length of me before reaching down to fondle my balls. Holy fuck, maybe I shouldn't have let him bring his hands back into play. The man has the power to end me with a few deft strokes.

Pulling away, I sit up on my knees between his thighs. He tries to follow, but I splay a hand on his chest. "Stay right where you are."

He opens his mouth to object, but then I pick up the bottle of lube again, spreading the cool liquid over the fingers of both hands this time. Patrick's eyes widen as he watches, but then he relaxes back onto the bed, bending his legs up on either side of me in invitation.

"My very own intrepid scientist," I drawl, smiling down at him. "Open up nice and wide for me."

His lips part as he follows my instructions, wrapping his hands around his shins and pulling his legs back towards his chest.

My gaze runs over him, from his hungry eyes, all the way down to the luscious curves of his virgin arse. "Such a pretty hole, Patrick," I murmur. "I can't wait to fill it with my cock." I run a single, wet finger over him, and he gasps, every muscle clenching in response. Satisfaction rumbles from somewhere deep in my chest. "Hmm, so hungry for it."

"Only," he croaks, before licking his lips and trying again. "Only for you."

"Yes." I slide a finger into him, and his eyelids flutter closed, his head tilting back in pleasure. My other hand reaches for his cock, working him over with long, sure strokes. I quickly lose myself in the movements of his body, the changing expressions on his face. I want to see and learn every reaction, I want to know how to take him apart, how to make him need me, make him crave me.

"More." He's done with begging. He's demanding now.

The sudden change flips a switch and all I want in this world is to obey. Reaching deep inside him, I curl the tip of my middle finger over his prostate.

Patrick's hips lift off the bed as he yells. "Christ, fucking, argh."

Raising myself over him, I place my free hand beside his head so I can lean down and kiss his mouth while I stroke his prostate again. His reaction is just as enthusiastic, only this time, instead of swearing, he lifts his head to attack my mouth with lips and teeth and desperate swipes of his tongue.

"More?" I ask as he settles down once more.

"Hell, yes." The words are forced out through gritted teeth, and then he grabs the condom packet that's still on the bed beside us and slaps it onto the centre of my chest. "Use this thing to fuck the shit out of me, or I will use it to fuck you."

With a quiet laugh, I take it from him and tear it open. Within moments, I'm replacing my fingers with the tip of my aching cock. I've waited so long to be here, I want to slow down and savour the experience but, damn it, the instant I make contact I'm pushed into him. His body engulfs me eagerly and sweat rolls down my temple as I fight the urge to bury myself in him in one thrust.

"You feel so good," I manage to say through gritted teeth. "Want you so much."

Patrick's response has devolved into a series of continuous moans and grasping fingers. He pulls me down until I'm lying on top of him. He takes my head between his hands, fingers digging into my cheeks, and forces me to look at him. "More," he gasps between panting breaths. "Want all of you." His legs are bent back as far as possible and I angle my hips, sinking further into him. His mouth opens wide and his eyes close. "Yes."

Between his curling hips and my desperate need to stake my claim on his arse, I quickly bury myself to the hilt inside his fevered body.

"Oh, dear god," I groan against his throat. "I fucking love you."

A laugh spills from his lips as he kisses me. "I fucking love you, too."

We begin to move together, desperate for more, harder, deeper. Mouths whispering, demanding, joining. We both want it to last, this moment where our bodies writhe with pleasure. But the pull demands satisfaction and before I can stop myself, I'm reaching between us to wrap my hand around him.

"Mine," I growl as I drag him closer to orgasm, one stroke at a time.

"Yours." His reply is barely audible, lost within a shuddered gasp, but I drink it in all the same. I drown in it.

There is nowhere else I'd rather be.

PATRICK

I've been trying to remember when I first made the rule about not drinking too much when out with friends. There must have been a point when I came on to someone I shouldn't have or had a one-night stand I regretted. Something caused me to decide drinking enough to loosen my inhibitions was a bad idea.

The earliest incident I can come up with is the time I watched Logan make out with that guy at Stacey's party. It happened almost a year ago; only a few months after Logan and I first met. I wasn't even single back then; I was still with Robyn. I did get drunk that night, though, and I was horny as all hell. But did I go looking for my girlfriend? Nope. Instead, I sat on a couch mesmerised by the sight of Logan sliding his tongue into someone else's mouth. Right before I rushed into the bathroom and jacked off like a total pervert.

Did I want Logan, even back then? Was my attraction to him always there, beneath the surface of my consciousness? Close enough to affect my behaviour but not close enough for me to realise what it meant?

Which then begs the question, why did I really start the experiment? I claimed I was curious about my attraction to men, but what if the whole thing was an excuse to get my hands on Logan—the one man I wanted all along?

More and more, the latter is sounding like the real me. Doing shit for one reason, while telling myself I'm doing it for a different reason entirely. Is that who I am now? Is it who I've always been?

All these months, I've been convinced denying my own bisexual nature—however unintentional it may have been—was the biggest mistake I've ever made in my quest for self-knowledge. What if that's not true? Perhaps everything I think I know is bullshit. What if I made it all up? Chose qualities I wanted to possess and then pasted them onto my psyche with arrogance and wishful thinking.

Is that what my father did? When he made decisions based on someone else's dreams, did he convince himself he was the person others believed him to be? He sure as hell convinced my mother.

"You're up early." Logan yawns as he pads into the dining room in rumpled pyjamas and bare feet, a blanket wrapped around his shoulders. His eyelids are still heavy with sleep and his hair sticks up in every direction.

Tiny pieces of me spark to life at the sight of him, even as my brain seizes in fear. I'm so in love with this man. I have no idea how I ever thought I could get this close to him and *not* fall in love. He is my favourite place to be now. He is my home. And if I don't do something to put the pieces of myself back together in some sort of order, I risk losing him in the long run.

"What's going on?" he asks as he slides into a chair opposite me at the table.

"Just thinking." My hand finds its way to the back of my neck and Logan stiffens. I lower my hand back to the table, curving it around my mug of tea. I suppose it's too much to think he hasn't learned my tells by now. He loves me, after all. He loves *this* me. "You want some tea? I just boiled the kettle."

"No, thanks." He doesn't take his gaze off my face. "Thinking about what?"

"My dad," I reply with a heavy sigh. "I keep wondering what would have happened if he didn't follow my grandfather's wishes and become a barrister. What if he didn't need to have a near-death experience to find his true self, but followed his own path from the start and lived his life as that man all along? Maybe my mother would have fallen in love with him anyway. Only, she would have loved all the parts of him that seemed so new to us after the accident, instead of being disappointed and put off by them. Maybe he never would have felt the need to change, and they would have stayed together." I'm gasping for breath by the time I'm done.

Logan stares at me in silence for a long while. "That's a whole lot of maybes to force onto someone else's life."

Lifting my eyes to meet his, I give him a bittersweet smile. "I remember thinking, at least I don't have to repeat their mistakes." My parents always encouraged me to be myself and I took full advantage of their support. I set about figuring out exactly who I was and then did my absolute best to live those truths out loud. "I swore I'd never pretend to be anything I'm not. What you see is what you get and it's what you'll always get. That way, the people who love me will always love me, and they won't need to worry that I'll change and grow and all that bullshit.

"That's why I've always been so determined to figure this shit out *before* I fell in love with the person I'd spend my life with," I say with a groan of exasperation. "I wanted to make sure I lived authentically, being the most real me I could be, so I would attract someone I'm genuinely compatible with. Someone who would love me for the real me, for the parts of me that *won't* change."

"You did attract someone like that," he says quietly. "For better or worse, you attracted me."

"You're early," I tell him.

Logan shrugs, but there's no hiding his grin. "I couldn't wait any longer. Sorry about that."

I slump forward, my head propped on one upturned hand while the other finds its way halfway across the table. "The thing is, people always say you need to be a complete person before you can give yourself fully to someone else, but I barely feel like half a person right now." My voice quivers in an unfamiliar way. The sound of it sets my stomach to churning. "It makes me wonder how long I get to keep you."

Logan leans forward, the blanket forgotten on the back of the chair. When his hand joins mine, his index finger curls around the end of my middle finger. "How about a lifetime?" I hear the smile in his voice, the sincerity. "Does a lifetime work for you?"

My eyes slide closed, and I bite down on my lower lip. Swallowing past the lump in my throat, I ask him the question I've been directing at myself for weeks now. Maybe he'll have an answer because I keep coming up empty. "How can I expect you to love me for a lifetime, if I can't even be sure of who I am today?"

He huffs out a laugh as both his hands engulf mine. "We'll figure it out together." He looks at me, his hazel eyes clear and hopeful. "You can spend years exploring all the deep, dark secrets of that overly-complex brain of yours if you want to. I'm okay with that, and I'm not going anywhere."

"No." I shake my head. "I have to do this part alone. If I don't get it right, I'll only end up hurting you. Then, you'll stop loving me."

"That's never going to happen, Patrick."

"You might think that now, but the more I change the more of a stranger I'll become. You won't necessarily fall out of love with me, but one day you'll realise I'm not the person you fell in love with in the first place and we'll lose everything."

He releases my hand, draws his own back onto his side of the table. "Where are you going with all this?" he asks. "Are you breaking up with me?"

"No," I say in a guttural voice. "I'm trying *not* to lose you. We can make this last, I know we can. I just need to sort myself out first, or we'll never have a chance."

"Why not?" he cries. "You think you're the only one who's unsure of themselves? Look at me, Patrick. I'm a fucking mess. I've been a mess for years. I can't even make up my mind what I want, let alone who I am. You love me anyway. Right?"

I shake my head. "That's not the point."

"It's the only point worth making," he snaps. "We may not have chosen to fall in love with each other, but we're here now and the only choice left is how we react to it." He glares at me in challenge. "You can accept it or reject it. You can weep with joy over it or you can fuck it over until you kill it. The one thing you can't do is hit pause and come back to it at a more convenient time."

"And jumping in headfirst when I'm not ready is better?" I ask, my voice rising. "I'm pretty sure the divorce rate is damning evidence against that line of reasoning."

His eyebrows fly up so fast I worry about their ability to stay attached to his face. "We've only been together a few months and you already have us, not only married, but divorced as well? Since when are you such a pessimist?"

"Since my father decided to grow as a fucking person and broke my whole damned family apart in the process!" My chest is heaving as I glare down at Logan, my hands clenched into tight fists. I don't remember standing up, or the sound of my chair tipping backward onto the floor. Holy hell, where did that come from?

Bending down, I set my chair to rights and sit back down. I take a deep breath in and release it slowly. "They were like us once, Logan," I tell him, keeping my voice low and calm. "They took care of each other. The way Penny takes care of Charlie. The way you take care of me." I heave a sigh. "Now look at them. They can't even get through a single meal without getting on each other's nerves."

"I have a theory about those two," Logan says with a snort of amusement. When I give him a questioning look, he shrugs. "I reckon they'd get along a lot better if they got a room and banged it out."

I pull a face. "Eww. Dude, they're my parents."

"What? They obviously want to."

"Stop talking." I hold my hands up.

He winks at me, but drops the topic.

"What did you have in mind?" Logan asks after a brief silence. "In terms of sorting your shit out." He's staring at me, waiting for the other shoe to drop, or the axe to fall. I'm not sure either of us knows how much damage my next words will do. "How would that work?"

"I think…" My throat closes up, choking the words I'm reluctant to say. I hate the thought of hurting Logan, but the fear of losing him trumps all else. "I need to take a break from the experiment."

LOGAN

"**A** break." I repeat the words slowly, unsure how to interpret them. Not a break-up, but a break. Sounds like semantics to me, like being a little bit pregnant. Only, in this case, Patrick and my relationship would be a little bit broken. "And during this break, we would…" I allow the sentence to trail off, waiting for him to fill in the blank.

He swallows heavily. "I suppose we would go back to being friends for a while." If he's trying to convince me it's possible, he'll have to sound more sure of himself. "You promised we could go back, if necessary."

"I did promise that." Three months ago, when I was still kidding myself such a thing was possible. "How long would this break last?"

A flicker of uncertainty crosses his face as he shakes his head. "I don't know. Long enough for me to get back onto an even keel. So you know who it is you're dealing with."

I frown. I already know who I'm dealing with, even if he doesn't. "What would happen after that?" I ask. "I mean, assuming you manage to spank your inner moppet into submission. What next? Do you consider yourself done and stagnate for the rest of your life?

"It's not stagnation," he insists. "It's stability."

"But that's the ultimate goal, isn't it?" I want to believe I'm getting this wrong, but I don't think I am. "You want to be finished. The complete package with no need for add-ons or updates."

Patrick frowns. "That's not exactly the way I think of it, but I do want to have the foundations of my personality nailed down, yes." He's losing patience with me. The feeling goes both ways.

"What about me?" I ask. "Am I supposed to stop changing, too? Do you want me to be *stable* for you?"

"That's not what this is about." Confusion sparks on his face. Did he honestly think I'd never question how his beliefs apply to me? "I love you, Logan. I want you to be *you*—exactly as you are."

"But I don't want to be me, exactly as I am now." It's taken so long for me to get to the point where that's true, and now I'm finally ready to move forward with my life, Patrick wants me to stay where I am? "I've spent the last two years stuck in a rut I dug for myself. Not trying for something better because of fear of where I might end up. You know what snapped me out of it?"

Patrick shakes his head.

"You," I cry, gesturing to him. "The man who got turned on by kissing me and then dived headlong into the experience, just to see what would happen. You taught me *not* to be afraid of change."

"But that's not *me*, it's just part of the process," he says dismissively. "I know this whole thing has been unnecessarily complicated and I've been unpredictable as all hell, but I swear I won't be that way forever."

"I want you to be that way. Don't you get that?" I push up from the table, needing to put some space between us. Raking a hand through my hair, I turn back to look at him. "Do you want to know who you really are, Patrick? Because I can tell you." He stares at me in silence. I decide to go ahead and tell him anyway. "You are smart, and capable, and insatiably curious. You want every person in the world to feel safe and secure in themselves. You don't only want to bring out the best in people, you want to bring out everything about them. You've made it your life's work to teach people how to confront their fears, and all the places inside that scare them, until they run out of monsters to face. Until there's nothing left inside them but peace and comfort."

I approach him once more, leaning over to place my hands flat on the table as I stare down at him. "If you stop being curious about yourself, about other people, if you stop analysing and experimenting and adjusting and changing, that's when you'll stop being you. That's when you'll stop being the man I fell in love with."

"And then you'll stop loving me, right?" His leg bounces like a jackhammer under the table until he slams his hands down on the surface and stands up. "Damn it! This is exactly the situation I've spent my whole life trying to avoid," he cries, his voice harsh with frustration. "I need a break, Logan. My head is about ready to explode and I need my friend back." He pauses. Hesitating. Terrified. "Can you give me that?"

He's asking me to put myself right back where I was with Ben. In love with my best friend, pining for someone I can never truly possess. I did promise him we could go back, but when I said those words, I didn't know I was setting myself up for an impossible choice. Break my promise to a man I care for more than anything in this whole world. Or break my own fucking heart.

It's time I start putting what's best for me first. If I can't do that for myself, how can I expect anyone else to?

"No, Patrick." I have to force the words out, because if I don't, they'll never come. "I'm sorry I can't be what you need, but we're not just friends anymore, and I can't go back.

"I can't pretend I'm not in love with you. I can't stay the same for you. And I can't stand by and watch you give up on everything you have the potential to be, because you're scared of losing what you have."

His legs buckle and he drops back into his seat at the table. I do the same. Neither of us reaches for the other. The tabletop stretches wide and empty between us.

"Don't push me away, Patrick," I say, my voice thready and desperate. "You are the love of my fucking life. You're it for me. So, please, be open to me. Be open *with* me. We can share new experiences and fresh excitement. Let's grow and discover, but let's do it together."

"But we'll grow apart," he whispers.

"If we do, I'll pull us back together," I tell him. "Because I don't want us to be apart. Not ever."

He looks up, and the desolation on his face pulls at me. I want to comfort him. I want to tell him I'll do anything for him. But I can't. I've given all I'm willing to give. It's up to him now.

I stand and make my way to the bedroom. My limbs feel heavy as I get dressed. Grabbing my overnight bag, I start tossing in my belongings, but quickly run out of room. I hadn't realised how much of my stuff had found its way into Patrick's apartment over the last few months. I zip up the bag, ignoring anything that doesn't fit inside. He can keep it, or toss it. I don't care.

Patrick's still sitting at the table when I re-enter the living room. Breathing shallow and muscles clenched.

I come to a stop on the far side of the room, halfway between the bedroom and the front door. "The experiment is over, in case you didn't pick up on that." His gaze snaps up to mine, but he says nothing. "You have all the data you could possibly need to draw whatever conclusions you want, and it's time we both stop hiding."

"I never hid how I feel about you," he growls.

"Maybe not." A sad smile tugs at one corner of my mouth as I remember how bravely he confessed his love for me that first time. "But we probably could have been more honest with ourselves." I stare at him as I lift my bag, slinging it over one shoulder. I'm waiting for him to stop me. He doesn't.

"Good luck with your soul searching," I bite out as I start for the door. "Who knows, if you dig deep enough you might convince yourself this wasn't the real you, and you never loved me at all."

My hand is on the doorknob when Patrick speaks again. "You promised this wouldn't end with you hating me." He doesn't phrase it as a question, but the expectation of an answer hangs in the air.

I heave a sigh, not turning to look at him. "That's a promise I will keep. Always and no matter what." My eyes close. I can feel the hard metal of the knob in my hand. It's time to open the door and walk away.

Please, Patrick. Ask me to stay.

My ears strain, but there's only silence.

I leave, closing the door behind me.

DATA ANALYSIS

PATRICK

L urking is stupid. It's a creepy thing stalkers do. I'm not the type to stalk anyone, generally. But there's no way I'll ever convince a judge I'm standing by the corner of a building I've no intention of going into, clutching my takeaway coffee and staring at the entrance to the university library, for any other reason.

Logan appears on the path leading up from his usual car park. He's running late this morning, so he's walking faster than normal. His hair is shorter, the curls I enjoyed playing with so often are gone. He must have cut it over the weekend. At least he still has his stubble. My fingers tingle at the sight of his face, wanting to touch.

It's been over two weeks since we broke up and we haven't had any form of contact since. I miss him—in my bed, in my life. I miss sending him silly text messages and dropping into the library to invite him to lunch. I miss telling him about my day and hearing about his. I miss our morning routine. Waking up in his arms. Shower kisses. The humming noise he makes when he takes the first bite of a good meal. I miss everything.

He disappears into the library and I force myself to move in the opposite direction. Putting one foot in front of the other, I drag myself to the psychology building. I have a meeting with my supervisor in less than two hours and I'm woefully under-prepared. The end of my research project is drawing closer. The last of the data has been gathered and most of the analyses are now complete. Soon, I'll start working on the Conclusion section of my thesis.

If I wrote up the Conclusion for my experiment with Logan, what would I write? Heaven knows I've spent enough time over the last few weeks analysing our data from every possible angle. Replaying each experimental session in my mind. Every kiss we shared. Every touch. If I tried to write about it, I'd probably end up with some kind of bittersweet love letter, brimming with declarations of devotion and flowery descriptions of the one and only time he fucked me in the arse. And holy crap, don't I wish I'd found the guts to do that sooner.

I could still feel him inside me the next day, after he walked out, and I sat there in shock and wondered how I could have ruined us so completely. By the day after that, all sensory traces of what we'd done were gone, and I was left alone with my craving for more.

By the middle of the first week I caved and bought a dildo online. It provides some minor relief when I'm lying in bed, pretending Logan is still with me. Pretending I didn't destroy the best thing ever to happen to my life.

I keep telling myself it's better to have ended it now, than to watch what we had fade by slow, torturous increments. Maybe, this way, if I get myself back on track quickly, I might still have a chance to win him back—for good. Only I can't even begin to think about how to handle the mess inside my head when every available neuron is so thoroughly preoccupied with the ache of his absence.

Reaching my office, I'm glad to see Stacey and Ian haven't arrived yet. I can't take much more of their morbid looks and concerned questions about how I'm doing. I've driven away the only man—the only person—I've ever truly loved, because of my own messed up doubts and insecurities. How the hell do they think I'm doing?

Settling in at my desk, I try to get some work done. The morning passes slowly. When the others do show up, I give them a quick greeting but pretend to be engrossed in my work.

It occurs to me I'm doing a lot of pretending these days. I'm not sure I even remember the last time my external actions matched what was going on inside me. Every incongruency drags me further and further away from the sense of authenticity I need to achieve to be with Logan.

The alarm on my phone goes off at ten minutes to ten. Gathering what I'll need for my meeting, I take the lift up two levels to Prof Mitchell's office.

His greeting is quick and his smile quicker. We sit down at the small table he has tucked into the corner of his office and begin to go through the work I've done since our last meeting.

"This is all looking good," he says with a nod as he goes over the structure I've used to analyse the qualitative data I've collected through short-answer questions. "You have a lot of useful information here."

I thought so too, but now I'm beginning to question... pretty much everything. "All the data I've collected seems to support my hypotheses but, I'm not sure if it's because it's true or if I'm seeing what I want to see."

His brow dips in a frown. "The evidence is right here on the page," he points out. "You've managed to ask the questions in such a way these kids have given actual answers, instead of a few monosyllables. What's more, the responses seem honest and free of filters. It's impressive work."

Pulling a face, I shake my head. "I think I would feel better if I'd asked more questions."

"Then the questionnaire would have been too long, and more kids would have dropped out before they finished." He puts the printout down and clasps his hands on the table in front of him. "Your research is on track and your program is showing promise. Why the sudden crisis of confidence?"

It's not as sudden as it appears. This has been coming for a while, but I didn't want to admit it. I don't want to believe the theory I've spent my life developing is fundamentally flawed, but I can't hold it in anymore. If I'm wrong about this, I need to face up to my mistake.

"My entire thesis is based on the idea self-experimentation can help young people learn about who they are. So they can live authentic lives and be happy. I believed I was living proof it worked, but recently... well, I've come to realise I'm actually proof it's all bullshit."

He gives me a dubious look. "So, now you've decided teaching adolescents a simple strategy for becoming comfortable with their sense of identity is somehow a bad thing?"

"No, of course not," I say with exasperation. "It's just... I thought the process worked, that it provided real answers but... what if they use what I'm teaching them, but end up getting the answers wrong?"

His eyes narrow. "Ahh, now I see. I believe this is a question I've heard before." The faint lift of a smile appears on Prof Mitchell's face. "How is the young man who caused such a stir at my seminar?"

I sigh heavily. "I don't know. We haven't seen each other for a while."

"Those seminars are usually so dull and academic," he says with a brief laugh. "At least your presentation got everyone talking, though not about the research, which is a shame."

"The point here," I go on, hoping to draw his attention away from Logan and back to the subject at hand, "is that I'm wondering if I'm doing more harm than good, suggesting these kids can use self-experimentation to learn about who they are. What use are their conclusions if they don't last?"

"That's always been your biggest mistake, Patrick." He wags a finger at me. "Thinking the process of self-discovery reaches some kind of end point. I tried to steer you away from the idea, but you've always been stuck on it. I didn't push too hard," he goes on, speaking faster as he presents his reasoning. "There is evidence the foundational aspects of personality remain stable and those were the aspects you included in your research, so I let it go. But!" His voice rises with the last word. "You have always placed too much weight on the conclusions these kids reach, when in reality it's the *process* that's important. Self-awareness is not about locking down your personality and throwing away the key. It's an ongoing, organic process of discovery."

He picks up my data summary, becoming more animated as he gestures to it. "The skills your program taught these kids are ones they will, hopefully, be using their whole lives. To continue to reach new and interesting—and relevant—conclusions about who they are in… and this is the important part," he adds, jabbing a finger in the air between us, "in each stage of their lives."

Giving a decisive nod, he grins at me. "This is not the time to abandon your research theory, Patrick. But maybe you are finally ready to open up that mind of yours and start expanding on it."

I sit there, his words whirling in my head, thoughts and ideas coming apart and reforming in new ways. None of it makes a lot of sense right now, but one main point does manage to hit home. "So, my self-experimentation theory isn't bullshit?"

Prof Mitchell rolls his eyes at me, throwing his hands in the air as he collapses back in his chair. "Excuse me,

Mr Seymour," he announces with dignity and humour, "but I do not supervise research that is based on bullshit."

LOGAN

C oming to this particular club was a bad idea. It used to be my favourite place to meet guys for a night or two of casual sex. The music is always good, the drinks reasonably priced and the clientele eager to have a good time.

Now, every inch of the place is tainted with memories of Patrick, despite the fact I only brought him here once. The bar to my left is where he tried and failed to kiss Toni with an I. The table where he came up with the bright idea of locking lips with me instead, is on the far side of the dance floor. From the place I'm standing now, I can glimpse the door to the balcony where we shared our first kiss. No way am I stepping foot out there tonight. I may be something of a masochist at heart, but even I can't inflict that kind of cruelty on myself.

Stalking up to the bar, I order a beer and then find a seat on a couch at the edge of the crowded room. It's almost ten o'clock on a Friday night, so the place is packed. Plenty of men here are cruising for a hook-up. All I need is one.

This is the latest of many steps I've taken in the last few weeks in an effort to jumpstart my life. It's a goal that has occupied the majority of my waking hours since I walked away from Patrick. I told him I didn't want to go on being the same man I've been the last two years and I finally meant it. Saying those words, out loud where I could hear them, broke the spell of procrastination and indecision I'd lived under for so long. The fire inside me, the ambition I thought I'd lost, reignited and the thought of allowing my life to stagnate any longer became unbearable.

I'd handed in my resignation at the library a few days later. Next week, I'll work my final shift. After that, it's up to me to choose the kind of life I want and make it a reality. It will not be a life where I sit around my apartment pining for lovers who don't want me enough to put up a fight.

Turning my attention back to the crowd, I set about considering my options for the evening. It's a good thing I'm not as fussy as Patrick, or I'd be here for hours. But no, my requirements are few: a hard body, and a willingness to get well and truly fucked. Those are the only qualities I want in a man right now. Actually, eyes that are any shade other than blue might also help. Also, I should probably go for a blond, to be safe. Otherwise, I am determined to be easily satisfied.

Drowning my sorrows in the body of someone I don't give a shit about won't stop me from missing Patrick. But it might help to scrub his taste from my mouth, and it might obliterate the memory of his touch from my skin. At this point, anything that helps keep me focused on the future is worth a try.

"I haven't seen *you* here for a while." The sultry voice curls around my shoulders from somewhere to the left. Casting a glance in that direction, I find Toni staring down at me. "I thought for sure you'd been taken off the market by that tall, dark and homo-erotically challenged friend of yours."

I can't help but smile at his complicated, and somewhat accurate, phrasing. "I thought so too, for a while," I say with a half-hearted shrug. "Turns out, it didn't stick."

"Ugh." Rolling his eyes, he slides uninvited onto the other end of the small couch. "There's nothing worse than a straight boy playing at being queer."

The unexpected company should spark annoyance. Toni's presence beside me makes me look taken. Granted, I am taken in every way but the one that counts, but not by him. It's an easy fix. All I have to do is ask him to leave. Instead, I move over to make room for his skinny, cock-blocking butt.

"No, he's definitely queer," I tell him as he settles in. "It was the being queer with me part he had trouble with."

"Arsehole," Toni says with a shocked gasp. "I warned him not to break your heart. If I ever see that man again, he's going to cop an earful from me."

I open my mouth to tell him there's no way Patrick will be back here again, but the words die on the way out. Patrick and I are done. Which means there will come a time when he'll decide he's ready to meet someone else. Now I've gone and disabused him of the assumption the someone else will be a woman, it's entirely possible he could come back here. To meet another man.

Slumping back in the couch, I take a long pull on my beer. "This fucking sucks."

"I hear you, lovely." Toni heaves a sigh. "Men are awful." We look at each other and start laughing. "Present company excluded, of course."

"Of course," I agree.

He slaps a hand on my knee, moving forward to the edge of the couch. "I'm going to buy you a drink and you can tell me all about your schmuck. Then we can poke fun at his flaws. What do you say?"

"Oh, he has plenty of those." Like letting me walk out the door for one. "Even if he is like super smart, and fun, and his dick is, holy crap, a thing of beauty. And he's really…" I should shut up now or I'll be cock-blocking myself. "He's nice." *Not too nice to fuck me over.* I pout as I vaguely remember thinking the same thing about Ben. Maybe the two of them aren't so different, after all.

"Fuck it, you're right," I grouse to an amused Toni. "Patrick is a goddamned wanker."

Patting my knee some more, he gives a low chuckle. "Make that two drinks," he says before getting to his feet. "I'll be back."

After he disappears in the direction of the bar, I take a deep breath and turn my attention back to the crowded room. This is the perfect chance to make my escape. Choose a broad-shouldered piece of hot and horny from the dance floor and be gone before Toni comes back. Blowing out a sigh, I finish my drink and wait.

The next body to drop down beside me turns out not to be Toni's. "Hey, Logan," a deep voice rumbles in my ear.

I force a smile at the familiar face. "Hey, Terry. How's things?"

"Can't complain, especially now I've found you." His hand descends on my leg, but it's nothing like the friendly gesture of comfort offered by my first companion. This touch lands higher up, obvious in its intent, with fingers that curve all the way around to my inner thigh.

"You did me a favour a while ago, and I remember owing you one," he murmurs with a suggestive grin. "Maybe it's time I paid up."

I smirk in remembrance. The favour he's referring to involved a lot of lube and a long length of anal beads. We had a lot of fun, and I do remember extracting a promise from him to return the favour before I left in the early hours of the morning. But... "That happened six months ago." Before Patrick kissed me. Before he proposed the experiment that's consumed my life ever since.

"I'm know, I'm terribly late." He waggles his eyebrows at me. "I'm willing to pay interest."

"Excuse me, Terry," a loud, sharp voice interrupts. "You're in my seat."

Terry and I look up. Toni is standing in front of us, two beer bottles dangling from one hand and a bright, blue cocktail in the other. He glares at Terry with raised eyebrows. "Kindly move your arse, so I can sit back down."

"Babycakes," Terry purrs, "we're negotiating here. Can't you find somewhere else to sit?"

"No, I cannot, and do I need to remind you what happened last time you called me that name?" Toni's voice takes on a hardened quality and his eyes flash with unexpected fire. "You couldn't sit for a week."

The hand on my thigh flexes hard as Terry lets out a quiet whimper. He tries to cover it by clearing his throat as he turns back to me. "It's time for me to head off, anyway," he says, roughly. "You coming?"

This is exactly what I came here for, to find someone willing to use me, and be used by me. I know for a fact, Terry is a sure bet. He's hot, eager, and uncomplicated. He's even blond. If I leave with him now, I might manage to wipe my mind clean of all things blue-eyed and exasperating for a while.

At this stage, an equal exchange of physical satisfaction seems to be the most I can hope for. No matter how many progressive life steps I've taken lately, I'm not sure I'll ever be the kind of man others choose for a meaningful commitment. I get chosen for the one-night stand, or the experiment, or the stand-in. But when it comes to something real, something lasting, I always end up alone.

I'm opening my mouth to accept Terry's offer when my gaze lifts to Toni. His face is blank as he watches me. He knows what I'm about to do. His hand lowers and the beer bottles he's holding clink together. They're the same brand I was drinking when he joined me—an accompaniment to the supportive ear he's already offered.

In that moment, I realise I'm the one who's making the choice here. It's not about what other people want from me, or how they see me. This is about how I see myself.

Swallowing past the lump in my throat, I turn back to Terry and shake my head. "Thanks for the offer, but I'm good here. You take care, though."

Jaw clenching, Terry gives a curt nod. "You, too." Rising from the couch, he storms off into the crowd without a backward glance.

Snorting in surprised amusement, Toni sits down and offers me the two beers.

"Thank you," I say, grinning at him as I accept. "I appreciate it."

"You're welcome." He smiles, and it's the first time I've ever seen him smile like that—as if he means it.

Suddenly, I'm glad I ran into Toni. I may have come here thinking I needed a good, hard lay to make me feel better. But hanging out with Toni will be fun, and the best part is, I don't have to wonder if I'll feel like shit about it tomorrow.

I lift an eyebrow as I watch him sip his blue cocktail. "So, you spanked the crap out of Terry, huh?"

"Just because I'm smaller than the average man doesn't mean I can't take charge," he tells me with a hint of petulance. "Some boys need a good spanking."

His lips curve, bringing those dimples out full force. "And some boys enjoy getting it."

Relaxing back against the cushions, I laugh my head off.

PATRICK

I get in my car on Saturday morning and drive down the coast to visit my father. If I stay in Brisbane one more hour, I'm going to end up on Logan's doorstep. While seeing him, even for a few minutes, might help relieve the near-constant ache in my chest, it wouldn't be fair to him. Or me, for that matter.

The quick text I sent Dad early this morning to let him know I'd be coming has gone unanswered, but I'm not worried. I have a key to his house. If he's not home, I'll be able to let myself in, as I've done dozens of times before when I needed to get out of the city.

A thousand memories of childhood greet me as I park in the driveway. Days spent building sandcastles on the beach and body boarding in the ocean. Fresh salad sandwiches for lunch and lazy afternoons. I've always loved coming here.

Dad lucked into this place. My great-grandparents bought the sizable block back in the days when beachfront property was still relatively cheap. It's worth millions now, and most of the properties along this stretch of sand have long since been sold, the old ramshackle houses knocked down to make way for architecturally designed replacements. Dad inherited the place when my grandmother died, not long after I was born. He and Mum renovated the house rather than rebuilding. It does a poor job of keeping up with its neighbours, but it's a good size, and it's comfortable, homey. Our family had been happy here—before everything went to hell.

The door opens as I approach. "Patrick," Dad says, with a smile. "I only saw your message a few minutes ago. It's good to see you." He pulls me in for a quick hug, but when he moves to let go, I hang on, needing the extra few seconds.

"Hey, kiddo," he murmurs, his voice laced with concern. "What's going on?"

I've been a little off kilter ever since I yelled at Logan about how my father ruined my family, disturbed by the idea I'm harbouring unresolved anger towards him. I had been angry, in those first few years after my parents separated, and I'd kept that anger on full display. I blamed him for the disintegration of our family and, for a long time, that was all I could see when I looked at him. Over the years, I thought I'd gotten over it, but apparently not. It's yet another issue to add to the growing list of shit I had no idea festered inside me.

Sighing, I give his back a good-natured thump before letting go. "I needed to get out of the city for the day. I hope you don't mind me showing up like this," I add as we make our way into the house.

"Of course not." Dad's still smiling, though his gaze darts towards the back of the house as we enter the open plan living area. "Any day I see one of my boys is a good day."

I tilt my head to one side, narrowing my eyes at him. "It's my turn to ask, what's going on with you?" Now I'm looking closer, I see the subtle signs of forced cheerfulness. Oh crap. "Do you have company? Because I can skedaddle."

He dismisses the suggestion with a wave of his hand. "Don't be silly." Going into the kitchen, he grabs three glasses from the cupboard. "Your mother's here. She came down to... um... visit a client." He's a terrible liar. "She wanted somewhere to freshen up before her meeting."

My mother chooses that instant to swan out of the corridor in casual pants and a loose cable-knit sweater, the kind she's always worn during Winter visits to the beach. Her makeup is light, not at all like she wears when she's working, and her long hair is loose around her shoulders.

"Patrick, darling," she comes forward for a hug of her own, wrapping me up in her slender arms. "How lovely to see you." She presses her cheek to mine with a kissing sound, so as not to mess up her freshly applied lipstick. "What a coincidence we're both here at the same time," she says with a quick laugh. As liars go, she's not much better than Dad.

"Isn't it just," I drawl, my gaze shifting between the two of them. "What are you doing down here?"

"I've taken the day off work to visit an old friend," she says, before my father can jump in. "She's not free until after lunch so..."

"That's funny," I tell her, casting a sidelong glance at my father. "Dad said you were down to visit a client." The chagrined expressions on their faces have me snorting in amusement. "If you're going to lie, you should at least take the time to get your stories straight. Any good solicitor knows that."

Rolling her eyes, Mum waves her hands in a dismissive gesture. "Fine. I came down to spend a couple of days at the beach. Sue me."

Dad passes us fresh glasses of iced tea. "Why don't you two go sit out on the deck while I make us a something to eat."

"It is the least you can do," Mum says with a haughty air, a secretive smile tugging at the corners of her lips, "since I've been so amiable."

With a grin, Dad winks at her before turning to open the fridge.

My brain deftly avoids any and all attempts to interpret that comment as I follow my mother out onto the large back deck. The ocean opens up before us and I breathe the sea air deep into my lungs, even as I cross my arms against the chill. Logan would love this place. My eyes close at the thought, regret stabbing at my chest. Turning away from the view, I take a seat at the old wooden table.

"So, you've been down here for a few days," I begin. "Just you and Dad?"

"Yes," she says without hesitation. "And yes, to spare us both the pain of your inquisitiveness, we have enjoyed each other's company," she raises an eyebrow at me, "in all the ways that implies."

"Okay, okay, I get it." I grimace, hoping to stop her before she feels the need to indulge me with further details. "How often do you visit?"

She gives a small shrug. "Whenever I feel the urge."

My eyes widen and I try not to gag.

"I don't know why you're so surprised, Patrick," she says, laughing. "We're both single adults, and we share two beautiful children. If we want to spend time together upon occasion, we have every right to do so and it's not anybody else's business." She points a finger at me. "Not even yours."

I hold up my hands. "Agreed. I don't want to know about your urges. But most of the time you two have trouble being in the same room together. How does this even happen?"

Her gaze drops as she contemplates my words. "Maybe because most of the time we only see each other at Christmas and birthdays. I start to remember how things used to be and then I get nostalgic and then..." She pauses, exhaling a deep sigh. "I don't know, I rage against the dying of the light, I suppose."

I nod my head towards the glass door, where we can see Dad moving about in the kitchen. "What about times like this?"

"The older we get the more glimpses I see of old Keith. The more I learn about new Keith." She makes a sound of reluctant surrender. "New Keith is not totally devoid of charm."

We share a smile, enjoying the scenery and this unexpected moment together.

"I've always loved this place," she says a few minutes later. "There's something about the fresh ocean air. Walks along the beach at dusk."

"How long are you here?" I ask.

"I'm driving back to Brisbane tomorrow afternoon. I have to be in court on Monday," she says, a heaviness pervading her tone. "I don't enjoy the work the way I used to. Perhaps it's because I'm getting older, but I don't feel the same energy and purpose I once had when I walked through those doors." She sighs, running her hands through her hair. She looks so much younger here than when I saw her on the night of Charlie's birthday. So much more relaxed. "Sometimes I wish I could give it all away and move down here to the ocean."

"Why don't you?" I ask. "You'd be closer to Dad." She gives me a pointed look. "Hey, none of that. I know what you two have been up to now." Logan will totally get a kick out of the fact he was right about them—if I ever get the chance to tell him. "Have you fallen back in love with Dad?"

Her frown melts away, to be replaced with a kind of sadness. "I'm not sure I ever truly stopped, though it took me years to realise it. Our lives are so different now, though. Every time I turn around, he has some new hobby or he's travelling to some new place. All the chopping and changing, that's not me."

"You don't have to do the same things he's doing," I point out. "You've always followed your own interests, even before the accident." Seeing them here together, after all these years, I can almost imagine them the way they used to be. "I remember, when I was a kid, the two of you talking about retiring down here. Maybe you still could."

"You mean, uproot my life for a man who's one new-aged epiphany away from leaving me behind for some new adventure? I don't think so."

Standing, she crosses her arms as she walks over to the edge of the deck. When she turns, I see the mother I've come to know over the past decade, instead of the carefree creature of a few minutes ago.

"I am who I am, Patrick. Take it or leave it, I'm not going to change now," she says, sternly. "You of all people should understand."

She's right. I should understand. It's what I've always said, after all. Know who you are, live your truth, and you'll be happy. Except I'm not happy. And neither is she.

After lunch, Mum curls up in a chair on the patio with a blanket and a thick hardcover.

Dad suggests we take a walk. Nodding, I take off my shoes and follow him down to the beach. Countless broken shells litter the sand, their fragments a stark reminder each was once the happy home of some sea creature. Until it was outgrown and discarded. Or until its inhabitant died. Either option sounds depressing for the shell.

"You and Logan," Dad begins as he picks up a handful of shells and lobs one into the ocean. "How's that going?"

I don't talk for a long time, keeping my gaze on the distant horizon. "We broke up."

He gives a slow nod. "That's your doing I take it?"

"What makes you assume it's my fault?" I ask indignantly.

"Son, that man looks at you like every word out of your mouth is his new favourite." Another shell hits the water with a splash. "He's in love with you."

I bite down on my bottom lip, welcoming the pain. "He is." Logan has loved me harder, and with more care, than I ever thought possible. I have no idea how I ever would have gotten through these last few crazy months without him by my side.

"And you?" Dad picks up another shell, despite the handful he's still carrying. This one is whole, and he dusts the wet sand off it before putting it in his pocket. "Are you in love with him?"

"Yep." Tucking my hands into my pockets, I wish I'd brought a hat with me. The temperature may be on the low side, but the sun is fierce overhead. I don't want to burn.

"So, what's the problem?"

I open my mouth several times to answer him. I could talk about how it's too soon for me to love anyone. Or how appalled I am I didn't even know I could fall in love with a man. I could tell him I don't have a clue who I am anymore and how can I expect

Logan to love me if I don't know who *me* is? But I've been thinking a lot about my discussion with Prof Mitchell, and I'm beginning to wonder if any of it even matters.

"I don't know if I'm ready." The words are simple but, in a lot of ways, they cover every one of the thoughts tangling together inside my brain.

Dad laughs out loud, clapping me on the shoulder. "You're not ready," he says. "None of us are. I'm fifty years old and I still feel like I'm trying to figure life out. Although, I do know this, if you sit around waiting for the perfect moment to do something, you'll miss out altogether—because there isn't one."

I smile in agreement. I think I'm finally beginning to realise that.

We walk in silence for a few more minutes before I ask, "Do you think you and Mum will ever get back together?"

"I'd like to think it could happen," he admits, "but your mother is so stuck in her ways. I think I'd need a crowbar the size of this beach to pry her out of the city."

"I'm not sure that's true anymore." Not the way she talked earlier.

"Trust me, son. I've known your mother for almost thirty years, and I've loved her that long, too." His expression is sad, but certain. "She left me because she wanted me to be the man she married. She still does," he adds with a sigh, "and I can't be that man for her."

"The man you are now isn't devoid of charm," I murmur.

Dad laughs heartily. "Thank you for noticing," he says with a mock bow. "You should let your mother in on the secret. Maybe I'd be in with a chance, hey?"

I come to a halt, right there on the sand, and stare at him, dumbfounded. "What the hell is wrong with you two?" I cry out loud. "She loves you. You love her. Why aren't you talking to each other about this shit?"

Dad stares at me in shock. Which is understandable, given I don't normally make a habit of yelling at him, but what the ever-living hell?

"What do you mean?" he snaps, putting his hands on his hips. "We *are* talking."

"Booty calls don't count."

"Patrick!"

"You need to tell her what you want." I'm gesturing wildly now, as I start walking back towards Dad's house, leaving him little choice but to follow. "You need to ask her what she wants, and you need to listen to the answer."

Is this the real reason my parents broke up all those years ago? Did they simply stop listening to each other?

Thinking back on it now, I remember the months after Dad's accident. How excited he'd been by the new lease he'd found on life, and how my mother dismissed every fantastical idea with an air of fearful impatience. I remember Mum trying to remind him of how happy they'd been before the accident, and how he'd constantly rejected her overtures.

Their early arguments had covered the big issues. How Dad's view of the world had changed and what those changes meant, not only for his life but for all of us. After a while, those issues seemed to get pushed aside in favour of pettiness and one-upmanship. Did they run out of energy to deal with what was really going on? Perhaps their conflicts simply fell to a level that made it easier to go into battle, even if it hurt more.

They still argue over little things, never touching on the issues that continue to lurk beneath the surface. And damn it, how many times have I complained to Charlie that Mum and Dad talk at each other, but neither of them is ever actually listening?

Dad and I are making our way back up the beach to the house before I finally stumble upon the truth that has eluded me all these years. It wasn't the change in Dad's identity that destroyed my parents' marriage. It was fear. Her fear of losing what she had. His fear of missing out on what he wanted. When they stopped talking to each other, stopped listening to what the other had to say, that's when they lost their sense of who they were as a couple.

All these years, I've been working to avoid their mistake, only to realise I've been avoiding entirely the wrong thing. I don't need to stop growing to keep Logan's love. He's already been confronted with multiple versions of me and he's loved all of them because... I was open with him. I told him who I thought I was, who I wanted to be, what confused me, and how wanting him changed me. I involved him utterly in the process, and he stood by me every step of the way.

"Did you have a nice walk?" Mum asks as we climb the wide steps leading to the patio.

"Patrick yelled at me," Dad announces with a frown.

Mum pulls a face, before asking, "Did you deserve it?"

"I don't bloody know." He throws his hands in the air before pointing at Mum. "Brace yourself, I think he might yell at you, too."

Her sunglasses come down as one eyebrow goes up. "My sons do not yell at their mother." She favours me with a wide smile. "Isn't that right, darling?"

Right now, I'd happily tear strips off both of them if it would get me out of here faster. Instead, I settle for a hurried lecture while I shove sandy feet back into my shoes. "I love you both, but you need to sit down and talk to each other. That includes listening as well. Okay?"

"Talk about what?" Mum asks, looking confused.

"Everything," I reply with exaggerated feeling. "Open the freaking lines of communication."

"You see what I mean? The boy's lost the plot." Dad drops into a patio chair at Mum's side. "Boyfriend trouble," he adds, to which Mum gives a knowing, "Oh."

They both turn to stare at me like I've gone crazy. They wouldn't be too far wrong.

"Whatever," I say, shaking my head at them. "I'm leaving. I have to go figure out how to fix things with

Logan, but I want results from you two. Do you understand?" I storm off without waiting for an answer, but then pause long enough to add, "Results, not details. Just results."

Grabbing my stuff from the kitchen counter, I rush out the front door. I need time to figure out how I'm going to get Logan back. He's already proved he can love all the versions of me I can ever hope to be. Now, I need to prove that—if he can forgive me for being a total arse—I will spend a lifetime returning the favour.

CONCLUSION

LOGAN

A young woman gasps in relief as she spots me on her way through the library entrance. "Excuse me," she says in a hushed tone, "can you tell me where the toilet is?"

Smothering a grin, I gesture to my right with one hand. "Go that way. Turn right at the end. The Ladies' Room will be on your left."

With a quick word of thanks, she rushes off again.

A light giggle sounds behind me. "Are you sure you won't miss being a walking, talking map?" Naomi asks.

"Pretty sure," I reply with a nod. "But hey, there'll be plenty of people at my new office. I can randomly direct my fellow entrepreneurs to the bathroom as they pass by my desk."

She laughs. "You might want to hold some of your crazy back until you've made some new friends there."

"Maybe," I reply with a shrug.

Once I made the decision to take the plunge back into full-time self-employment, I concluded the best way to avoid becoming a recluse in my own home is to *not* work there. A quick Internet search turned up a heap of coworking spaces where I could lease a desk, a studio, whatever I need. I chose one that's close to home and housed in an old factory. It's huge, with plenty of light and a variety of usable spaces. It's already home to over a dozen small businesses and sole traders, like me. It's still early days, and I'm not positive the arrangement will work for me yet, but the lease on my space is month-by-month, so I can take a shot and see how it goes. Now I've figured out what I want, I'm willing to keep trying new options until I find one that works for me.

"You're going to miss me, though. Right?" Naomi asks a few minutes later.

I shake my head. "I won't have a chance to miss you, Na. Because we'll still see each other—often."

Her eyes narrow. "You promise?"

"Promise." I bump my shoulder against hers and she grins up at me. "Of course, I may have to beg you to make time for me. What with that gorgeous girlfriend of yours taking up so much of your time."

"My girlfriend *is* gorgeous, I agree. However," she grabs on to the front of my shirt, "I will always have time for you."

Smiling, I wrap her up in a big hug. "That's because you're a sucker for a sob story."

I get a poke to the gut for that one, which only makes me hold on tighter.

"What about Patrick?" she asks when we finally let go. "Do you think you two will ever be friends again?"

"I don't know." It's something I've been thinking about a lot. We were good for each other, even before we started to get involved on a physical level. I miss my lover, but I miss my friend even more. "It's going to take some time," I tell her honestly. "I don't want to lose him entirely, but I need to take care of myself first."

She smiles in understanding. "I reckon you're gonna be okay this time. You've changed."

"Yeah, I have." The sadness is still there, a gnawing ache inside me, but there's hope too, for a better future. "The weirdest part is, Patrick is the one who helped me do that."

The sun is setting by the time I finish my shift and walk out through the big, glass doors for the last time. A part of me is sorry to be saying goodbye. This place, and the people in it, have been good to me. But I know now, I need to keep moving forward, and this time I'm not going to let anything stop me—not even a broken heart.

"Logan."

My steps falter at the sound of his voice. Gripping tight to the bag I have slung over my shoulder, I turn around.

Patrick comes to a stop a few metres away, out of breath from running to catch up to me. "Hey."

I acknowledge him with a small up-nod, not trusting myself to speak. My heart is already leaping out of my chest in an attempt to get to him. My arms ache with the need to pull him against me. I hold back. I'm not that man anymore. If he wants me, he'll have to come to me.

"I'm glad I caught up to you," he says with a tentative smile. His gaze moves over my face quickly, as if he's drinking in the sight of me. One hand lifts to the back of his neck, but he curls his fingers into a fist and brings it back to his side.

"It was your last chance," I tell him, glancing at the building that, up until ten minutes ago, provided my most secure form of employment. "I don't work here anymore. Today was my last day."

"Really?" His eyebrows lift in surprise. "You decided to go back to working for yourself?"

"Yes."

His smile widens and he nods. "Good for you."

"Thank you." I wasn't sure if he'd approve. "I needed a change." I don't mean to sound petty when I say the words, but I think they might come across that way.

Patrick doesn't seem to notice. "I hear they're as good as a holiday," he says, taking a step closer.

My leg moves to do the same, but I plant it right back on the ground. I am not giving an inch—not this time. "Why did you want to see me?"

He hesitates, licking his lips. And, holy fuck, my mouth opens all on its own at the brief glimpse of tongue. A deep and desperate want stirs low in my gut, but it's overridden by the disappointment slamming at my chest. If this is what it feels like to be around Patrick, there's little hope we can one day be friends again.

"I, um…" He sucks in a breath, takes another step closer, tries again. "I've been thinking a lot about our experiment over the last few weeks. About what I was trying to achieve and what it all means. I've finished drawing my conclusions and I'd like the opportunity to share them with you."

I have no idea what to say, or where he's going with this. But I'm willing to listen. "Okay, what did you conclude?"

"Not here." He shakes his head. "I was hoping I could take you out to dinner. We could discuss it then."

"Dinner."

"Yes."

I pause to consider the implications. "As in a *two old friends getting together* kind of dinner?" I ask, gesturing between us.

"Nope." One more step and he's right in front of me. "I'm asking you out on a date, Logan. No experiments, no rules, and no bullshit."

His mouth is right there and he's asking me out and I have to pull my lips between my teeth to stop from closing the distance between us. "I don't know if that's a good idea." I'm supposed to be putting myself first here, not rolling over and offering my dick the instant he shows up and licks his lips at me.

"Please, sweetheart." His voice is low and rough. It tingles over my skin and makes every hair stand on end. "Give me one last chance to prove how much I love you."

Aaand I'm done.

I don't know if it's right or if I'm putting myself back on his rollercoaster, but there's no way I can turn him down.

Taking a step forward, I willingly put myself inside his personal space. "Will there be a PowerPoint presentation?"

He huffs out a laugh, running his hands through his hair as the tension leaves his body. "I wasn't planning on it, but I can make one if you want."

Grinning, I shake my head. "Just checking."

PATRICK

H e's fifteen minutes late.

Not that I mind. I'll wait all night if I have to. It's just… what if he's not coming?

It's been less than three hours since he said yes. We parted shortly after, without so much as a handshake. I managed to get reservations for a restaurant he once mentioned as having lamb shanks so tender, they could make baby angels cry. I texted him the details and he sent a thumbs up emoji in reply. That should mean he's coming. Right?

I check my phone again. Twenty minutes late. No messages.

My fingers drum against the white linen tablecloth as I take deep breaths. This is no time to panic. Even if he doesn't show up tonight, I can always try again. He may not be working at the library anymore, but I know where he lives. I can be standing at his front door in less than half an hour. Once I have him alone, I know I can convince him to give me another chance. I don't care how determined he is to resist, even Logan will have trouble rejecting me if I have his cock in my mouth.

"You really need to stop frowning. You know what it does to me."

My gaze snaps up to meet his and a smile leaps onto my face. "You're here." I stand to greet him. My arms start to reach out, but I hold back. "I wasn't sure…"

"Neither was I for a while there," he admits, remaining in place behind his chair. "It took me ten minutes to walk through the front door of the restaurant."

"Oh." Damn it. If I'd known he was out there, I would have gone out and dragged him inside myself.

"Yeah," he murmurs. "But after everything we've done in the name of the experiment, I have to know how it all turned out. So, if you want to share your conclusions with me, I'm willing to listen."

"Thank you," I tell him, my heart squeezing so hard it hurts. "That's all I ask." For now, anyway.

He nods and gestures at the dining table between us. "Shall we?"

We take our seats and order in record time. As lush as the surroundings are, neither of us is here for the food.

"Okay, so here's the thing," I begin, "the best research always begins by asking the right question. My question has always been the same: Who am I?" Logan nods, familiar with this part, so I continue. "I've always seen myself as some kind of puzzle that needed to be solved, one piece at a time. I thought, with every experiment I conducted, I was collecting more of the pieces, and eventually I would get to see the complete picture and then, I'd finally have my answer."

"Is that what's happened?" he asks with a deep frown. "Do you feel like you have your answer?"

"No," I tell him, reaching a hand across the table. "Instead, I've come to realise there is no answer. In fact, I haven't even been asking the right question."

He looks down at my hand, but doesn't reach for it. "What's the right question?"

"I'll get to that." I did not spend all weekend going over and over this crap in my head, only to have him skip the best parts. "I've tossed out the whole puzzle analogy and chosen a new one."

Logan's eyebrows lift in surprise. "Do I even dare ask?"

"You just did." A grin tugs at my lips as I lift my hands, eager to share my new epiphany. "Paint by numbers."

He rolls his eyes and his head drops to his hands. "Patrick, mate, you're starting to take this whole overthinking thing to a new level of weird."

"I know, but I've figured it out this time!" I'm forced to wait as our meals are delivered but, the second we're alone again, I push my plate away. "You eat," I say, gesturing to his meal, "I'll talk."

"You usually do," Logan grumbles, picking up his cutlery.

Ignoring his sarcasm, I shift on my chair, ready to wow him with metaphorical goodness. "With paint by numbers, we start with the completed picture, right? All the broad strokes are already in place. Those are our genetic predispositions, the foundations of our personality. It's us at our most basic. It's not until we start to live and have experiences that we start adding paint to the picture. Some experiences are big and important, adding bold colours. Some are more subtle and only add a bit of shading. Overall though, we end up with a whole mess of colours. Bright, happy yellows, sombre shades of grey, romantic reds and contented blues."

"I get it," Logan says between bites, waving his knife around. "Keep going."

"The point is, the picture is never finished, Logan." I pause for dramatic effect. This *is* dramatic. Or, at least it was for me when the new analogy first started to take shape. I'd been cooking dinner at the time and ended up burning my onions. "What I mean is, the basic foundation of who we are will always be there, but every experience we have changes us, teaches us something new about ourselves, and about who we could be." My smile grows wider as I reach the end of my speech. "Which brings me to the new question, the one I want to start asking from now on."

"Which is?" he asks.

"Who would I choose to be, if I wasn't afraid?"

Logan stares at me, his knife and fork held frozen in his hands. "That is a better question than the old one," he says finally.

I smile, nodding at him. "I think so, too."

Dropping his gaze, he places his cutlery on either side of his plate. "So, who do you choose to be, Patrick?"

"I'm not entirely sure yet," I tell him. "But, for the first time in my life, I don't feel like there's any rush to figure it out.

"Although, I do know a few things," I add. "I know being your friend changed me. Being your lover changed me even more, and falling in love with you..." I shrug, with a new air of nonchalance. "I'm not even close to being the man I was when the experiment started, and I have no idea who I'll be next month or next year. But I'm not afraid anymore. I trust you to love me, the way I love you." I swallow hard, my stomach churning and hope hammering at my chest. "Right now, all I want is for us to keep growing and changing together. I do want to be open with you. I want to be yours, Logan."

His jaw clenches, causing the muscles there to move. "Mine," he growls in a quiet voice and my libido goes into overdrive at the fierce thread of possession in his tone.

"Completely." I manage to hold his gaze, but staying in my chair is harder and, damn it, he really is always this sexy. "Take me back," I demand, managing to get a little growly myself. "I will love the hell out of you. I will stay by your side through any change you want to make. And, holy crap, given half a chance I will ride your dick like you're a thoroughbred and I'm the man from Snowy-fucking-River."

Logan groans, his eyes sliding closed as he curses under his breath. "Focus, Patrick."

Blinking, I drag my attention out of my arse and back to the semi-crowded restaurant. "Sorry," I mutter, grinning as I clear my throat. "I may have missed you a little bit."

His smile, when it finally shows up, is big and broad and full of unrestrained pleasure. "Patrick, my love, I missed you, too."

LOGAN

O ur meals are lukewarm by the time we get around to eating, but neither of us minds. We talk for hours, opting to follow dinner with lavish desserts and lingering over the last of the wine.

I tell Patrick about my plans for my business and about the unexpected friendship that's sprung up between me and Toni, who may or may not give him a verbal lashing next time they meet. Patrick laughs and promises to win him over by complimenting his dimples.

He talks about the ways he's expanding his research theory. He's already planning the research he wants to do after his PhD is over, to further develop his program for helping adolescents form their identity—with more emphasis on the process this time, and less on the outcome. It all assumes he can get his hands on enough grant money to fund the research, but I have no doubt he will succeed in anything he sets his mind to. He's persistent like that.

I'm not at all surprised to hear Patrick's parents have been getting it on behind everyone's backs and I glory in my chance to say, "I told you so." He doesn't know what will happen there, but I know he's rooting for them.

Eventually, the restaurant empties around us and it's time to leave. I slide my hand into his as he walks me back to my car. "My place or yours?" I ask with a leering grin.

"Yours." His hands settle on my waist and he walks me backward until I'm pressed up against the driver's side door. "I want to sleep in your bed," he says as he fits his hips to mine and drops brief, tender kisses to the corners of my mouth. "I want the scent of you surrounding me and the feel of your cock filling me."

"Fuck, yes." We're both hard now and the urge to grind our erections together is almost overwhelming. With enormous effort, I manage to push him far enough away to separate our bodies. "We will get there, baby," I tell him. "But we're going to need privacy for the things I want to do to you."

Patrick nods in agreement, his tongue reaching out to swipe at my bottom lip. "Can't wait," he says with a breathy laugh. "As in, seriously, this fucking hurts."

Pressing our foreheads together, I smile at him. "How far away is your car?"

Without taking his gaze off me, he lifts an arm to point to the right. "About fifty metres that way." Sucking in a breath, he backs up. "Okay, I'm going. See you in about... twenty-five minutes?"

"Let's try for twenty," I say, my voice rough with desire.

He grins. "Done." He takes off at a run and I can't help but laugh out loud as he disappears up the street.

I force myself not to break any road rules on the way home. Getting pulled over by the cops would only slow me down. Not to mention, the hard-on I can't get rid of would be awkward to explain.

Patrick is already waiting at the front door of my apartment when I arrive. "About bloody time," he mutters as he grabs hold of me and covers my mouth with his. Our tongues meet and tangle at last. My back slams against the wall as we drink each other in with unrestrained passion.

Fumbling with my keys, I somehow manage to get the door open between kisses. We stumble inside and I kick it closed behind us.

We make our way to the bedroom, shedding clothes on the way. Patrick's kisses taste different tonight. Something about him is wholly changed from who he used to be. There's a freedom to the way he moves, like he's finally comfortable in his own skin, and I want to get to know him all over again. The new him. Even though I've loved him in all his forms, from confident to chaotic and back again, I want to taste this new version and savour its unique flavours.

Once we're naked, I fall back onto the bed, pulling him down on top of me. My hands and mouth are everywhere, relearning his body, his responses, the way he likes to be touched. He is willing and eager for my fingers when I find his entrance. I open him up, preparing him for my aching cock.

When, at last, I thrust inside him, he stiffens, his body gripping me tight, head thrown back and mouth open in a silent cry. Blunt fingernails dig into my shoulders, claiming me as his.

"Fuck." The word comes out in a harsh whisper as he shudders and convulses above me. "That's it. Right there."

"Right here?" My hips push upward, and I smile when he grinds himself down further, greedy for more.

"Yes." His eyes are closed, his breathing shallow. "Need you. Love you. Please."

I take hold of his hips, encouraging him to move with me. "Come on, baby," I drawl, "ride me hard now."

His eyes snap open and he looks down at me. "Yes." Licking his lips, he smiles and starts to move.

We spend hours making love, over and over again. Skin sliding against skin. With whispered words and occasional laughter. By the time we're done, we're both a mess of sweat and come. It's a familiar feeling, but at the same time there's something new between us now. An understanding. A new promise.

This isn't an experiment anymore.

This is us.

And this will last a lifetime.

IMPLICATIONS FOR
FUTURE RESEARCH

PATRICK

Two years later

"I think I'm dying." Logan lies flat out on his back on the golden sand. His face is red, and he looks exhausted. But the wild laughter following his mournful wail has me rolling my eyes at him.

"You know, if you do die, I'll follow you into the hereafter and drag your arse right back to this beach. There is no way I'll get through another two hours of this without you." I drop the stupid, piece of shit surfboard onto the sand before joining him, every muscle screaming in protest as I lower myself to the sand.

Lifting himself up onto his elbows, he grins at me. "Who would have guessed it would be so hard to stand up on a board while hurtling along a wave."

Giggling, I lean over to drop a quick kiss on his lips. "I know, right? I expected to be an expert by the third hour."

Our instructor for the day trudges over to smile down at us. "How's it goin' boys? You almost ready for another go?"

Logan and I glance at each other, before staring up at him. Logan speaks for the both of us. "I think we're gonna need a couple more minutes."

"No problem." Our instructor isn't laughing at us out loud, but the amusement is there, behind his perfect teeth. "You let me know when you're ready."

We watch him walk away, all tanned skin and mess of sun-bleached hair. "Holy hell, that man is superb," I say with a long sigh.

Logan nods, laughing. "Look at that arse, it's ripe like a freaking peach." Turning back to me, he narrows his eyes in mock suspicion. "Don't tell me you finally found a man you're attracted to, who isn't me?"

"Are you kidding? After what he's put us through today?" My gaze returns to the perfectly sculpted vee of the instructor's back. "I hate every bone in his perfect body."

Throwing his head back, Logan laughs out loud. "Me, too." Sitting up, he turns to kneel in front of me, his knees tucked between my feet. "I'll bet his dick tastes like sunscreen."

"Probably." I move closer, so I can cup the face of the man I've spent the last two years adoring. "Logan, love of my life, I have to tell you something."

He chuckles. "This should be good. What is it?"

"After being out there on the water with you today, riding the waves and feeling the sun on our faces, I've learned something about myself I didn't know before."

"You hate surfing," he says, with a crooked grin.

"Fucking hate it." My voice is ripe with feeling and I close my eyes to add extra emphasis. "I never want to do this again."

"I'm with you on this one," he laughs with a nod. "Never again." We seal the deal with a salty kiss.

"This is good," he says as he stands. "I feel we've grown as people today." He puts a hand out and I take hold so he can pull my tired body upright. "I'm feeling supremely self-aware."

I snort at the familiar dig. I already know I'll never live down my former obsession with *knowing myself*. Not that I've stopped learning or being curious about what makes me tick, but I'm more relaxed about it now. I know there's no rush, no deadline I have to meet. Plus, I have someone to do it with me, which makes it way more fun.

Logan and I have tried so many new things over the past two years—usually together, but not always. Sometimes we find things we both love, sometimes one of us discovers we enjoy something the other isn't keen on. Which is how Logan discovered his new infatuation with baking bread. He's become obsessed with the different types of bread, and how they're made, and weird shit about gluten content and the size of the holes it creates inside the different loaves. Honestly, it's bread, I don't get what the big deal is, but I can say I've enjoyed the outcome of his many and varied wheat-based experiments. My stomach wholeheartedly supports his interest, as he's supported all of mine.

I'm glad we're both coming down on the side of no for surfing, though.

"What do you say we ditch the rest of the lesson," I suggest, tugging him against me. The layers of wetsuit between us feel strange, which only makes me more eager to get out of them. "We could go back to our hotel room, take a hot shower, see where that leads."

He gives a low hum of appreciation for my idea. "It's going to lead to my dick in your arse."

"That's where I'm going with this, yes."

His hands clench tighter around the sides of my waist and he nods. "Sounds like a great idea."

Before long we've ditched the rented boards, the wetsuits, and the instructor, who waves us off with a knowing grin. We hold hands as we walk along the beach on the way back to our hotel.

My dad offered us the use of his house, since he and Mum are off enjoying the wilds of New Zealand together for a few weeks. But in the end, we opted to splurge on a suite.

As we walk, I marvel at how much our lives have changed in the past couple of years. I graduated my PhD program and started working full-time as a researcher for the expanded *Outside and In* program. The results so far have shown great promise and several journal articles have already been accepted for publication. My ambition to get Logan to call me Professor as often as possible is on track.

Logan's business has gone from strength to strength. He ditched his original desk space last year, instead renting a larger studio in the same building to accommodate himself and Toni, who turned out to be a graphic designer sent from heaven to make his life easier. Toni with an I may be a drama queen with dimples for days, but the man has a knack for designing websites that are a developer's dream, as well as pleasing to the client's eye.

Though I know Logan was initially sad to leave the safety of the library behind, he's found a renewed enjoyment in working for himself—especially now he's figured out how to avoid the isolation traps of his last attempt. Plus, he always insists he took the best of the library with him, in the form of Naomi. She and Stacey are still two of our closest friends. The four of us hang out together often enough, Penny has started to complain the two women are eating into her and Charlie's rightful double dating time.

It's a full life we live, and I'm so grateful we're living it together.

Arriving back at our hotel room, we ignore the large balcony and its view of the ocean, instead opting to get wet all over again. This time the water is hot and the sand in uncomfortable places has been replaced with soap. My hands are flat against the tiled wall of the shower as I thrust back onto Logan's cock. He moves slowly, his hips rocking up into me. A harsh moan leaves my throat with every thrust. I love the way he moves, the way he claims me as his, always his. I love the feel of his bare skin against mine, having long since done away with the need for barriers between us.

My skin zings as his hands wander over me in long stroking motions, as if he can't get enough of touching me. I don't want him to ever get enough. I want to be his forever. No matter what happens, or how we change.

Leaning my head back, I take his mouth in a deep, thorough kiss. Fucking his mouth with my tongue as he fucks me in the arse.

"I love you." I breathe the words into him, wanting them to fill him up, so he feels the truth of them.

One of his arms tightens around my torso, while the other strokes my hard length. "Love you," he growls before latching on to my neck, sucking hard.

His hand jacks me faster and he increases the pace of his thrusts to match. My body shudders as I start to come, and I feel him stiffen as he joins me. Our cries mingle under the stream of water and everything about us feels right. We are a perfect fit.

Later that afternoon, Logan suggests we head out for an early dinner.

A grin tugs at my mouth and I try not to launch out of my own skin. "Actually, I've got dinner covered," I say as I slip on a pair of sandals. Picking up my phone, I check the time. "I'm waiting for a delivery, and then we can head out."

Logan's brows draw together, and he gazes at me suspiciously. "What did you do?"

I shrug. "I guess you'll have to wait and see."

It's not long before there's a knock on the door and I open it to accept the pre-packed picnic basket I asked the hotel staff to make up for me. Logan smiles in delight when he sees it. "A picnic? That's awesome."

He tries to sneak a peek inside, but I smack his hand away. "Where are we going?" he asks.

"I happen to know of a small beach that's usually empty. The perfect hiding place."

And it is perfect. This section of beach is tiny, but the Pacific Ocean is spread out before us in an endless stretch of blue. We open a blanket on the sand in front of a huge black rock, which hides us from the occasional person walking on the footpath above.

I unpack the picnic basket, revealing a feast of Logan's favourite picnic-friendly foods, including gourmet sourdough bread rolls filled with roast chicken and salad, generous servings of tiramisu with whipped cream for dessert, and a bottle of white wine. We all but fall on the food, both of us famished after the long day of exercise.

The sun is hanging low in the sky by the time we polish off the dessert and pour out the last of the wine. My back is resting against the rock. Logan sits between my parted thighs, his back to my front and his head resting against my chest.

"Well, this is pretty goddamned perfect," he murmurs, tilting his head slightly so he can look up at me. "Thank you for organising it."

I lean down to kiss him. His mouth is soft and giving as it moves languidly against mine. "It's hard to believe it's been two years since I lost our bet... and all because I fumbled one shot," I add with a soft laugh. "Best thing I ever did, losing that game."

"Worked out pretty well for me." Logan raises a hand, curving it around the back of my neck, then he frowns, turning his ear towards my chest. "Are you okay? Your heart is pounding like a jackhammer."

He wasn't supposed to notice, but yeah, I'm kind of freaking out here. "I'm fine," I say as he sits up, turning to face me. "I, um…" This is way harder to get out than I thought it would be. "I want you to know these last two years have been the best of my life. You've taught me so much about myself. Shit I never would have been able to figure out on my own. You've taught me I can keep learning and changing, and you won't stop loving me."

Smiling, he shakes his head. "Never gonna happen."

"I know that now," I say taking his hands in mine. "You allow me to be any version of me I want to be, and you love all of them. The same way every version of me loves every version of you. It's taken some time, but I trust in that, in us." I swallow hard before continuing, "I want us to conduct one more experiment."

The flash of surprise in his eyes makes sense. We've run so many experiments over the past two years, we stopped bothering to refer to them as experiments ages ago. But this one is big, it's huge, and I decided it deserves the title. An experiment is how we got here, and it's how I want us to move forward.

"I love you, Logan—more than I thought possible. Being your husband would be the greatest experiment I could ever undertake, and I want it to last for the rest of our lives."

He's staring at me, his mouth open. The sheen to his hazel eyes makes them shine brighter than ever before.

"Marry me?" I ask, my voice shaking so much the words sound garbled.

"Yes." There is no hesitation or doubt in him. He laughs out loud before yelling, "Fucking hell, yes." Then he drags me to my feet and wraps his arms around me. "I love you so much."

I laugh as I bury my face in his neck, hiding my own tears of happiness. Kissing Logan all those many nights ago was the best, craziest, most unexpected experiment I could ever have conducted. And it led me right here, to this place where I get to spend the rest of my life loving my best friend.

Author's Note

Thank you for reading *The Experiment*. I hope you enjoyed it!

If you enjoyed this book, please consider leaving a review on Amazon.

Reviews help readers find books they love. They also help authors spread the word about their work. Please consider taking a few minutes to let others know about your reading experience.

I love to hear from readers, and you can find me in the following ways:

Email: rebecca@rebeccaraine.com
Website: www.rebeccaraine.com
Instagram: www.instagram.com/rebeccarainewriter
Facebook: www.facebook.com/rebeccaraineauthor/
Pinterest: www.pinterest.com/rainewriter
Goodreads: www.goodreads.com/rainewriter

To receive the latest information regarding my books, please visit my website and sign up for my newsletter.

Also by Rebecca Raine

About the Author

Rebecca is a long-time lover of all things romance. Whether it's a book, movie, or real life, she will always have more fun if there's a love interest thrown into the mix. She lives in Queensland, Australia with her very own hero husband, two quirky kids and one big, black dog. Other than reading and writing books, her favourite things include loud music, enjoying a glass of wine on the patio, organising everything in existence, and spending too much time on the Internet.

Acknowledgements

I could never do any of this without the love and support of my best friend and husband, David. Thank you for bringing me so many cups of tea and listening to me complain about my boys. A big thanks also has to go to my children, who put up with Mum's crazy and her soundtracks.

Thank you to Sylvia Marson, for your feedback on the book and your awesome editing skills. Also, to Georgia Henry, thank you for helping me work out the kinks. I'm so lucky to have both of you in my life.

Finally, thank you to everyone who has purchased a copy of this book. I really do appreciate your support. And for those who go the extra step and leave a review, you rock more than words can say.

Made in the USA
Monee, IL
12 September 2020